THE GRASSLANDS

KENNETH TAM

CAPTAIN
GEORGE
TUCKER

THE GRASSLANDS

THE **FIRST** NOVEL OF ADVENTURE SET UPON
HIS MAJESTY'S NEW WORLD

KENNETH TAM

ICEBERG

Published in Canada by Iceberg Publishing, Waterloo

Library and Archives Canada Cataloguing in Publication
Tam, Kenneth, 1984-
      The grasslands : the first novel of adventure set upon
His Majesty's New World / Kenneth Tam.
ISBN 978-1-926817-02-6
      I. Title.
PS8589.A7676G73 2010   C813'.6   C2010-901996-2

Iceberg Publishing
55 Northfield Drive East, Suite 171
Waterloo ON N2K 3T6
contact@icebergpublishing.com
www.icebergpublishing.com

First paperback printing: April 2008
Special international edition: April 2010

Photos: Men of the Princess Patricia's Canadian Light Infantry Living History
Unit, Canadian Military Heritage Society. Photographed by Kenneth Tam,
Peter Tam, and Mikael Christensen.
Additional stock images by istockphoto.com.
Cover Design: Kenneth Tam

For
Richard Joseph Barron,
my grandfather.

Rest Well.

And for
all the men who
fought with the RNR.

We won't forget.

ACKNOWLEDGMENTS

Welcome to a new series, and one that's been a pleasure to write! This alternate history involving a new world is something of a departure from the future-based science fiction I've written in the past, but it's just as much fun... well I think so anyway. Though I suppose I am slightly biased... In any case, I need to thank many people for this book, and those to come.

First, I want to offer a big thank you to the men of the Princess Patricia's Canadian Light Infantry Living History Unit. This organization, part of the Canadian Military Heritage Society, is preserving the memory of Canada's soldiers in the First World War. When we found that there were no First World War re-enactors for the Royal Newfoundland Regiment, these men agreed to step in and play the RNR in the photos you see on the cover. Their care for historical accuracy is unmatched, and it's a real privilege for us to have their involvement with this series. For more information about the PPCLI unit, visit www.newworldempire.com.

The ideas for this series have been developing since I first started studying history at Wilfrid Laurier University. I wouldn't have been able to put together this alternate timeline without the fine courses I was able to take at Laurier, and I want to extend thanks to all of the professors who might recognize the subject of one of their lectures wedged subtly into this book. Any historical faults, though, are mine alone!

My good friend Mikael Christensen must be thanked next, for bounding around in a grassy field with me, taking photos of the PPCLI for this book and those to come. Along with my good friends Peter Caron and Wes Prewer, Mik has offered strong support for this new adventure. I'm indebted, as always, to these excellent gentlemen.

The formidable John Fioravanti joined Iceberg's editing team for *The Grasslands*, bringing his expertise as a history teacher to the table, and helping make sure this book was the best it could be. Thanks to my good friend John for all the help and input!

Finally, of course, thanks to my partners in Iceberg Publishing — my parents, Jacqui and Peter. I need to come up with a convenient stock line to use in thanking these two, because I do it in every book — and rightly so. Best parents I could have ever asked for, best business partners, and best friends. Iceberg wouldn't exist without them.

And my old friend Atlas, who would have loved to run on the grasslands...

"This, if I understand it, is one of those golden moments of our history, one of those opportunities which may come and may go, but which rarely return."

"Remember the rights of the savage, as we call him. Remember that the happiness of his humble home, remember that the sanctity of life in the hill villages... among the winter snows, is as inviolable in the eye of Almighty God, as can be your own."

– William E. Gladstone

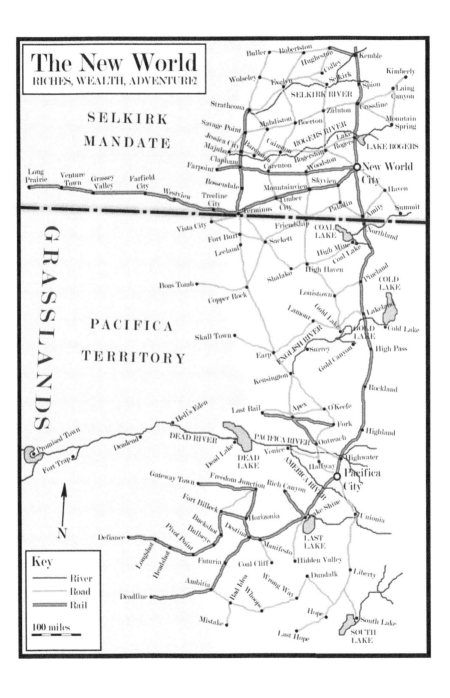

PROLOGUE

The trail unwinding before Smith was just the sort he liked. Quiet.

A crisp wind was cutting through the valley, on its way west from the mountains behind him, through the trees around him, and out to the grassy plains ahead. It was a good feeling, calming and fresh.

That was what this new planet did best: made a man feel fresh.

These valleys and the foothills and grasslands beyond were filled with men and women looking to make money. They wanted to find their gold mines, their coal deposits, anything they could take out of the land and send back to civilization to make a pretty penny.

Smith didn't want any of that. No, he was a drifter. He'd come to this world with his horse and his gun because he wanted to be left alone, like the drifters who'd gone before him. In the old days of the American west, they'd roamed the states, herded cattle, lived with the Indians.

There were no Indians out here, though, just real savages. There were no states out here, either, just open land. That was as it should have been. Smith reckoned a man like himself would lose something if he got tied down by civilization. He had no inkling of what he'd have turned into if he'd been forced to live his life in a west that had filled up, where a man couldn't just drift.

Sure it probably would have been more secure, more regular and predictable, but who wanted that? Not him. Some folk wanted that, and that was their right — he wouldn't judge them for it. But it wasn't for him, so by rights no one should judge him for his own wants.

He'd just roam out onto those plains again, see where this new trail took him.

Coming to a clearing, he slowed his horse and lifted his canteen to his lips, taking a deep swig of water before moving on. He was riding further north now than he'd ever been. The line that separated American territory from the British mandate couldn't be too far away. In all his dozen years out here, Smith had never ventured north of that line, on account of having heard that the British weren't too forgiving of men just looking to drift. The British didn't see the new world as a place to explore and be at peace, they saw it as a place to civilize, or at least organize.

The savages didn't seem much interested in civilizing. As much as some called them men, and as much as they looked like white men, those savages weren't human in any way that mattered. They weren't about to be sitting in schools and reading the Bible. No sir.

But the British could have their way. The north of this land was theirs by treaty, theirs by law, and Smith didn't see any reason to disagree with that. He didn't see much reason to disagree with anything that didn't try to stop decent people from having their rightful peace.

Sometimes a reason to disagree did find its way to him, though. Days when it did, he tended to deal directly with the problem.

Right now, in fact, he was hearing two horses riding hard down the trail, a ways behind him. He slowed his sixteen-hand tall, brown-blanketed Appaloosa and cocked his head to listen, one hand slipping the thong off the six shooter on his belt, the other sliding the Winchester out of its scabbard and laying it across his saddle. He didn't think he had trouble coming after him, but Smith was one who believed in caution. Kept him living.

Turning his horse, he edged her over to the side of the trail, finding some cover behind an outcropping of grey rocks covered in moss. He waited as the horses came closer, watching the bend in the trail behind him patiently, silently. As he sat, he thought about his last few days, coming out of the new town, Leeland. Nothing of interest had happened there, so the horses probably weren't bringing men looking for him especially... but then Smith was a man who'd made enemies over the years. It wasn't that he was a bad man, or at least he didn't reckon he was particularly off-putting.

No, he'd just found himself in certain places at certain times when doing the decent thing was bound to make an enemy of someone. And Smith tended to do the decent thing.

That was his way, so now he sat on his mare and waited for the two riders to find him.

As it turned out, they didn't even see him. Two young looking clean-cut types, neither close to Smith's six feet in height. They were fresh off the train by the look of them, with the fancy new Colt magazine pistols — the 1911 guns — in their hands, and were riding quite carelessly.

The first rider looked to be the leader, and he was spending too much time looking over his shoulder. He could ride his horse, but he looked to be one of the old world types, trained in it as a sport, not as a way of living.

As he came along, Smith decided to announce himself, "You boys running from trouble or looking to make it?"

Smith was a direct man. The question surprised both the boys, and they reined in their horses, the second one nearly being thrown when he did. They were on a steep slope, and it took a sure hand and some skill to handle the horse on it. Both boys froze at the sight of the wiry drifter. Smith was whipcord lean and clean shaven, but he had the weathered, steady appearance of a man who'd been through trouble enough times to know how to get out of it again. He still wasn't sure if the boys were going to point those fancy new guns at him, but if they did, he'd have to make use of his rifle.

"Sir, you better move — we have savages after us!"

The lead boy was panicked, and not without cause. He was definitely from the old planet, based on his way of talking, so being chased would be new to him. And when the savages decided they wanted you, nothing stopped them coming for you. They weren't men, they were animals that happened to look like men. And while Smith had heard that said of many men just because their skin color wasn't white, it wasn't the case on this new planet. Savages weren't the Indians of Earth's plains — they didn't reason or have honor. As much as some folk said the Indians didn't have honor, Smith had known some, friends of his father, who'd had plenty. No, savages looked like white men, like naked Americans or British, and they didn't think.

They were vicious, too. They hadn't gotten the name savage because some old worlder with a large self opinion and a poor understanding had decided they weren't as good as him. They'd earned it by killing people, including the eastern scientists who came out to Pacifica to study them, certain that because they looked like white men, they could be civilized. The scientists had stopped coming after the savages ate the first few expeditions.

If these boys had come across a band of savages, they'd been found by trouble.

"How many savages is it?" Smith asked, pulling his Winchester off his saddle.

The lead boy, not really a man at this stage, was waving his fancy pistol up the trail as his horse sidestepped dangerously, "I counted at least five! Six maybe!"

Now Smith decided it wasn't so much trouble after all, "Did you already shoot some?"

"No sir," the second boy was looking at him now, and his panic was pretty obvious. "We kept missing."

That sounded about right to Smith — these boys obviously hadn't been out here long, and they hadn't seen the savages move. Even if they were crack shots on horseback at home, and he reckoned by the look of them that they weren't, they'd need some time to get used to shooting at savages, even with those new guns.

"Alright, they aren't smart, those savages. They just come for you, see, so they'll be down the trail. You come on down here past me, stay on your horses, but get set to shoot."

The boys obeyed, not seeing much choice.

Trying to calm their horses, they came down to the rocks Smith was using for cover. Meantime, Smith steadied his trusty mare, who he'd chosen long ago for her calmness especially around savages, and lined up his Winchester, pressing the butt to his shoulder.

Six savages wasn't many. On some bad days out here, he'd seen hundreds ravaging towns. Six was just a small band, probably lost from the group and looking for food. Savages loved eating.

And here they came. The boys behind him started to get twitchy, and Smith realized putting twitchy boys with shiny new guns behind his back wasn't so smart.

"You boys get into the middle of the trail, I don't want anyone accidentally shooting me in the back."

"Yes sir."

Well, they were obedient enough, and soon their horses were sitting abreast of his and they were waiting with guns outstretched.

The savages didn't make much noise, but Smith had been out here long enough to recognize what sounds they did make. His trusty mare, who knew the sounds of savages but never seemed spooked by them, stood her ground attentively. He had taken the slack off his trigger, so when the first monster came around the bend, he waited just a second, lined it up and squeezed.

As the first savage dropped, Smith was already levering the Winchester. It was his new gun, his 1892, and he was a better shot with it than with his father's old '73, which was still on his saddle as backup.

He shot twice more, fast, and the next two savages went down in a heap atop their leader. The boys were firing now, peppering the trail with .45 caliber lead, and not hitting much other than dirt. The last three savages came, and with one shot each Smith added them to the pile.

Now, the boys had said six, but he wasn't so confident they'd seen all the savages, so he waited with rifle at his shoulder, eyes peeled. He didn't hear anything. His mare relaxed too, and that was as good as proof that no more were coming. It was done. Just six, odd as that was.

"Alright boys, we're all clear. You reload those fancy guns, don't ever forget to reload out here. If it ain't savages, it'll be bandits," Smith laid his Winchester across his lap, then pulled six rounds out of his belt and slid them into it.

The boys were still too fearful to be thinking clearly, but they did as they were told, and installed fresh magazines into their guns.

"Now, whereabouts are you boys going? It's not all that friendly out here," Smith slid the Winchester back into its sheath.

The boys looked at each other, holstering their pistols, the leader swallowing and getting his voice back, "We're supposed to be prospecting. At the bottom of this trail is some land my father is investing in. We're looking for gold."

"I reckon there's gold all around. Well I'm headed that way, I'll ride with you that far if you like," Smith offered. He wasn't a man who sought much company, but he wasn't going to abandon these boys without telling them some of the more important facts of life on this world.

"We'd certainly appreciate that, sir," the second boy nodded. "We haven't been out here long."

"I could tell, no offense," Smith nodded. "Come on, let's ride down."

They headed down the trail, and left the six savages behind them. The beasts always ate their own dead, better not to be around for that.

CHAPTER I

The train was moving quite well, and as he strode back to his seat in the private car, Major Tom Waller watched the mountains going by outside with interest. He was a British North American, and yet for all his travels with the Imperial Army, and for all the service he'd seen abroad, he'd never actually come west into Canada — never been through some of the most spectacular mountains of the country his regiment was now closely tied to.

Indeed, if the confederationists had their way, his home country — a fine island known as Newfoundland — might someday join Canada. Quite a day that would be.

But of course that was no matter. The Royal Newfoundland Regiment was part of the British North America establishment of the British Army; whether Newfoundland and Canada were one country or not, his unit was part of the same command structure that protected Britain's North American holdings. The Empire needed every regiment raised on this continent to serve either here or on the other side of the tunnel; the Indian Army, as he'd recently found, was being fully utilized in the push into Siberia, and the Home Army in Britain was preoccupied with Africa, and with reminding the Germans to abide by the peace.

Such troubled times...

But North America, and the new planet, these were places away from the wars. Waller was rather pleased to be in this quiet hemisphere again — somewhere where conflict with a mechanized power was unlikely — and at last to be going to the place he'd always wanted to see.

Tom Waller's life had been an interesting one up to this day. The younger son of a Newfoundland merchant, he'd had no interest in continuing the family business, and had convinced his father to purchase him into the Newfoundland Regiment. He'd entered the regiment as a Captain in 1914, and been with it when it had been sent to Egypt during the threat of a great world war.

Of course the war had not come — not for Britain at least. Protecting Belgian neutrality, the Empire had threatened the Germans into avoiding the small country during their attack on France, and had then abandoned both France and Russia to their battle with Germany and Austria. The old European countries were of little use to the Empire, thanks to the close relationship between Britain and the United States, and to the resources of the new world.

Indeed, it had been the promise of divisions of British and American soldiers storming the Belgian coast that had convinced the Germans to avoid striking through that country. The Kaiser had no interest in clashing with the mighty armies and navies of the English-speaking powers.

Egypt had been a quiet assignment for the Newfoundlanders, many of the officers filling their time with leisure reading. There were some colonial uprisings — uprisings with which Waller couldn't help but sympathize — but as the war went on and the Russian Empire collapsed under the German onslaught, the Empire had organized a new offensive through Afghanistan and into the Urals and Siberia. The Japanese had happily aligned themselves with Britain for that venture, and in the massive buildup for it, the Newfoundland Regiment had been pulled from Egypt and placed on India's Northwest Frontier.

For a year, then, the unit had driven into Afghanistan, and those were long days. The campaign had been poorly conceived — the War Office had seemingly forgotten that, to control any part of Siberia from India would require absolute control of Afghanistan, the mountainous country which lay between.

They'd been withdrawn after a year, having been granted the 'Royal' prefix in recognition of their hard fighting. Behind them, the Amir of Afghanistan had been given independence, while a new corridor into Siberia had been obtained from the Chinese. With the fighting in Afghanistan finished, the Royal Newfoundland Regiment had been sent home, to join the British North America establishment.

And, of course, the Canadian Prime Minister in Ottawa had decided that the Newfoundlanders would be perfect for the new world, so off they went. Waller had been made a Major in Afghanistan, and now he was leading the first contingent through the tunnel.

Seating himself, he looked at the men around him in the train car. Most were staring out at the majestic Rocky Mountains rushing past, doubtless comparing them in their minds' eyes to the much less friendly mountains of Afghanistan. There were no riflemen here waiting to pick them off, which was a nice change of pace.

Checking his watch, Waller frowned, then looked back to his men, "Well b'ys, should be just another half hour until we stop at the tunnel station."

There were some murmurs of acknowledgment, and that was as much as Waller expected. He ran his outfit far more casually than the British might have liked. Perhaps that made him a poor officer, but he thought his style more appropriate for the men he commanded. Newfoundlanders were a hearty bunch, prone to speaking their minds, but willing to do the business when it was needed.

His men had distinguished themselves beside the elite of the Indian Army, beside Guardsmen and even beside some of the vaunted Japanese during that push into Afghanistan. If anyone brought Waller a complaint about the b'ys, they'd need plenty of evidence to back it up.

Letting out a long breath, Waller leaned back in his seat and watched the mountains pass.

Rogers Tunnel Station was named for the man who'd first discovered the caves that held the gateway tunnel to the new planet. Hired by the Canadian Pacific Railway to find a route for their trans-Canadian line in the 1880s, A. B. Rogers had found a pass around the tallest of the Selkirk

Mountains in 1881. Sheltering from an avalanche, Rogers had ended up in what he'd thought was a typical cave. Then he had discovered that the cave was in fact a tunnel, and that the tunnel exited onto a new planet.

It always impressed Waller — so momentous a discovery made by sheer accident. A discovery that truly had changed the course of history...

As Waller stepped out of the car onto the platform at the station, he breathed in the crisp mountain air, and then repelled a shiver as a cold wind snapped at him. The platform around them was, of course, quite busy, and it only became more cramped as the two companies of riflemen and support weapons unloaded from their various cars.

"Lieutenant Devlin, see to the mules, make sure they get off alright. I'll find out about our transport," Waller called to one of the other drab-green clad officers who'd stepped out of a car further down, and the man saluted loosely in reply, turning and hurrying off.

Waller looked around him. The platform was full of people in various states of dress; gentlemen in top hats and coats, probably the wealthy agents or owners of large mining operations, were keeping their distance from the black and Chinese workers who were also waiting on the platform. There was nothing quite like the arrogance of class — no matter where in the Empire Waller went, he saw it, and he was never particularly impressed.

Walking carefully through the crowds, Waller looked for the Army Office where he needed to check in — it was supposed to be on the end of the platform nearest the tunnel and the embattlements that protected the opening. Waller could see the tunnel now, and the fort that stood next to the track (insurance against any of those damned savages coming through), but not the office. He headed that way, side-stepping and avoiding those who didn't notice him, touching the brim of his cap to all those who did.

After some minutes, he arrived at the end of the platform, and the Army Office appeared, set back further than most of the station. He approached the building, and the Glengarry Rifleman on guard came to attention as he passed through the front door.

Inside, a clerk waited behind a desk, and Waller pulled off his hat and approached the harried man, "Lieutenant, I'm reporting with the Royal Newfoundland Regiment."

The clerk looked up from a paper he'd been writing on, then nodded, "Oh yes. You'll be Major Waller... your train..."

Flipping through pages on his desk, he came across the right paper, "Yes, platform behind me, sir. We have your cars ready, train departs in an hour, if that's time enough for you to move your men and equipment."

Waller frowned—this wasn't what he was expecting at all. He'd become accustomed to facing great difficulty when it came to getting anything from the Army. In India, Army transport and supply had been precarious at best, and he'd expected it only to be worse here nearer the frontier. Well, as his nan would say, there was no point looking a gift horse in the mouth.

"Thank you Lieutenant, an hour will be quite enough. Good day to you," Waller offered a smile and a nod, and the clerk nodded back.

"Good luck to you, sir. And to your brave Newfoundlanders!" the man came to his feet and saluted sharply, even though neither was wearing a hat.

Waller managed to stop his frown — was this the treatment all units going to the new world received? Much more friendly than the Newfoundlanders were accustomed to — in India, or Egypt, or even Toronto, it would be 'Oh you lot, over there. We'll squeeze you in.'

Well, the b'ys would be pleased.

Waller left the Army Office, looking for a moment at the fort below. The tunnel was like any other rail tunnel he'd seen, though wider — an absurd-seeming five tracks now ran through into the new world, trying to keep up with the vast number of shipments going to and from. The station he stood on was built higher up — the tracks running into the tunnel were in the base of the valley, the station on the slope just above, and the fort further along the slope, nearer the tunnel itself.

That fort must have been quite the posting. From his vantage point, Waller could see a half dozen Vickers machine guns lined up on the tunnel, and a half dozen 18-pounders as well. He knew little about the actual abilities of the storied savages, but he could be rather certain that if any came through the tunnel, there'd be hell to pay.

As Waller stood there and stared at the firepower in the fort, he wondered for a moment if it was such a good thing to be passing through the tunnel. If His Majesty's Government was so concerned with what could come from the other side, could it be worse than Afghanistan?

What a thought. Waller needed to stop thinking, it was only one fort.

He went to summon his officers.

CHAPTER II

In a lot of ways, the new planet was rather like the old one. Waller had been told there were two moons, but the sun was up when the train carrying the two companies of the RNR — and *only* the two companies of the RNR — arrived at the New World Station. Waller still couldn't quite understand why his men had been granted exclusive use of a train... there were more than enough seats for every man, and the stock cars were rather spacious for the mules. Usually the army liked to cram men into every available space.

Either the military operations here in the British Selkirk Mandate — it had been named after the mountains that led to it — were very, very well organized, or his Newfoundlanders had been singled out for something.

And in the Army, singling out was not often a good thing.

Stepping onto the new world's rail platform, which had been built from planks of wood harvested and cut down on this new planet, Waller looked up and around him. The landscape was much the same as on the Earth side, and the air didn't seem too different. Was this really another world — a new planet lost in the cosmos somewhere?

Well, His Majesty's government believed so, and the government of the United States of America believed so, and that was more than enough to convince a soldier that it was.

Waller directed his gaze down to the platform again, looking around to find it quite similar to the one at Rogers Pass, just ten minutes back through the tunnel. The journey through the gateway had been entirely unspectacular... just like passing through any rail tunnel.

But Waller needed to stop dwelling on these similarities. The fort on this side had its back to the mountain, with Vickers guns and artillery positioned to keep savages away from the tunnel mouth. As he began walking in that direction, Waller saw the Army Office for the New World Station was almost identical to the one on the Canadian side.

Entering the structure, he found another clerk, not dissimilar to the Lieutenant who'd been operating the other one, and with equal friendliness, the man directed him to headquarters, and advised him to keep his men on the platform. They'd be re-boarding the train and moving on from New World City soon.

Waller passed orders to Captain Tucker and Captain Kearsey, his two company commanders, to keep the men on the platform, then took Lieutenant Devlin with him down towards headquarters. The Army's chief building in the New World was close to the tunnel entrance and thus to the station.

New World City itself was in fact quite large, and had already been fitted with electric lights and plumbing systems for most buildings. From what Waller had heard, many of the settlements here were still in dire condition, not unlike the Wild West of America, but development was being driven by the presence of crisp businessmen, and some wealthy investors set to turn themselves into the next Cecil Rhodes. They were just the first of many rich men, some of whom wanted to come to see this famed new world, and all of whom would demand the comforts of home when they did.

"Jesus, sir, they'll have this place posher than St. John's before we're home again," Lieutenant Jimmy Devlin had a more pronounced Newfoundland accent than did Waller.

His observation, though, was no less apt, and Waller smiled, "Well, we're sitting on fish, these lands are full of gold. We're not as well loved by the world."

"They just don't understand the charm," Devlin shook his head, watching as gentlemen and ladies walked along the boardwalks to stay out of the dust on the street, while black and Asian workers tramped along through it, averting their eyes.

"Just as well, wouldn't really want some of these types cluttering up home, Jimmy," Waller waved at the boardwalks and said that quietly. He personally preferred walking with the workers in the street, whatever their race, and so did Devlin. These men were making a living, going about their business. It was something Newfoundlanders knew how to do all too well.

Rich men from London didn't do quite the same sort of work.

That, perhaps, was why Waller and Devlin were walking through the dirt instead of up on the boardwalks with them.

Not that it was terribly dusty here — not compared to Afghanistan, anyway. The dust in some of Afghanistan's plains had been incredibly fine, and terribly invasive. Here it was good Earthy dirt, more familiar to the Newfoundlanders even though it was in fact from another world.

"I have to wonder, sir, are all the planets of the cosmos just like Earth? Because this one is right close, ain't it?" Devlin was getting a little too lofty in his thinking for Waller to follow.

"You know Jimmy, I just hope we don't have to find out. Because you can be damned sure if there are others out there, the Empire will claim them. And then we'll be the first ones they send to meet their savages," Waller spotted the headquarters as Devlin cracked a grin at the comment.

"Yes sir," the Lieutenant nodded. "That's headquarters up there. I'll wait out front for you, if that's alright, sir."

"Perfectly fine, Jimmy. Just remember, we're moving on in a few hours, so there's no time to properly woo any ladies. If you're not here when I get back, I'll spread word that you've caught a strange exotic disease, and no lady will see you."

Devlin scoffed and folded his arms as he fell behind his Major. Clearly he wanted to wait outside to take in a view of the frontier girls — there'd been no ladies wearing such fine-fitting clothes in Afghanistan, and Jimmy Devlin did enjoy the odd soldierly tryst now and then. But not today.

Stepping up the stairs to the grand two-storey headquarters building, Waller was surprised at its stone construction. He pulled his hat off as he stepped into the lobby, and a Lieutenant sitting at a reception desk there looked up at him, frowned, then looked down at a pile of papers, flipping through them until he found one with a photograph clipped to it.

He then looked back up at Waller, standing instantly, "Major Waller, sir, the General is expecting you. If you'll follow me."

Waller again was stunned by the reception — he couldn't imagine being so well treated if he were a Colonel, let alone as a Major. Either they operated differently here in the Selkirk Mandate, or there was something serious in store for his men.

He could just guess which.

The Lieutenant led him up a staircase and around a corner to a closed door, then knocked on it. A moment later the door opened, and a Colonel stepped into view, "Yes, Simon?"

"Major Waller, sir, of the Royal Newfoundlanders."

The Colonel looked past the Lieutenant and nodded, "Very good. Come in please, Major."

Hat still tucked under his arm, Waller nodded and entered deftly, coming to attention as he did. Standing next to him the Colonel smiled and looked to the General standing behind the desk, "Indian Army trained him to be formal, sir."

"Of course they did, Bobs would have had nothing less," the General nodded. "Major Waller, at your ease. We're on a different planet from our own, man, and we tend to relax some to enjoy it."

Waller stood at ease, trying to contain his surprise.

"You'll become accustomed to it, Major," the Colonel nodded. "And not to worry, we're not lax where it counts. I'm Currie, Colonel of the Canadian Rifles."

The Colonel extended his hand, and Waller took it, "Pleased to meet you, sir."

"You'd know me, I suppose man?" the General asked, coming around his desk with a steady gait.

"General Byng, sir," Waller nodded, and then with a little surprise again found that the General was extending his hand, so he shook it.

"Good to have you here, Waller. My friends in the Indian Army have told me your Newfoundlanders are some of the best around. I was in India, you know. And Africa. I much prefer it here, and you might as well," Byng turned back to his desk. "Unfortunately, your first mission isn't going to be quiet."

Waller nodded, taking the spirit of this informal meeting to suggest that he could speak his mind, "I'd thought as much, sir. Seemed that dedicated trains to bring us out here was a little above our status."

Byng chuckled as he returned to the other side of his desk, "Well, I do like to give my lads as fine a treatment as I can, since we're sitting on such wealth. But you're right, that train you've come in was set aside for the mission. And you'll have to leave at once."

"I've told my men as much, sir," Waller said that as Currie stepped towards the General's desk. The Major followed.

"The reason I asked for your two companies to come ahead, Major, was because I need an escort for a particular dignitary, out to the prairies beyond," Byng looked up at Waller, then down again, indicating a map spread on his desk.

Waller approached and frowned as he looked down at the relatively sparse piece of paper — the surveys were still being done out here, so the maps were not as complete as many he'd seen. That said, they were far better than some of the rough sketches he'd drawn for his men in Afghanistan.

"The steppes are dangerous, to be quite honest," Currie put in, pointing his left forefinger at the open space on the map, into which a single rail line stabbed. "The rail line is reasonably secure. The savages don't seem to bother with the tracks, and my regiment has men in every town along the way. That's why we need you — my men are all out there already, and we're keeping the rest of the force here or close to here, ready to respond to heavy attacks."

Waller frowned at the map, somewhat surprised he was being told so much. The whole day was proving a surprise, and he looked up at his two senior officers, "If I might ask, then, where are we going? If there's a whole regiment strung out along this line…"

Byng looked up again, drawing Waller's attention, then indicated a point on the map beyond the last railhead, "Typical luck, the new General Staff has decided that the dignitary you'll be escorting knows about something valuable on the land out here, beyond the rail line. You're going out there to find it, and to bring it back if you can. If you can't take it, come back to Long Prairie and report to me what you've found."

Byng's finger slid along the map back to Long Prairie, the last town on the rail line.

"Captain Quinn is my man there, and he's quite reliable. If you need help, wire in the request through him. You'll find that it's good marching country out there, Waller. You'll be surprised how quickly you cover the miles… but that means you'll be getting further from help every day. If you run into trouble, I have some Voltigeurs and dragoons I can scrape together as reinforcement," Currie added.

"Obviously, you don't want to have to commit them to this operation, though, sir," Waller observed, looking at Currie. "We'll do our very best to make sure you don't have to mess about with your plans on our account."

To Waller, that sort of statement was just a bit of courtesy — Newfoundlanders didn't tend to put people out if they could avoid it.

Currie looked at Byng with a smile, "My God, sir, I think this one's going to be liked around here."

The General chuckled, "I daresay so. Fight as well as you talk, Major Waller, and you'll be promoted quickly. And I will say this, because I care to keep my men informed of their odds. This is *not* a one-way mission, not that it'd change your orders if it was. I do believe your men, as highly recommended as they come, should be equal to it. Just remember there'll be times to mass your fire. It's not Afghanistan or Africa out here. The savages aren't Pathans or Boers. They don't shoot. They're not men of any sort, even though they look it. If they come at you, you form a line and introduce them to the .303. Clear?"

"Yes sir," Waller wasn't going to turn down advice like that.

"Very good. Now, I must get off to a meeting, gold mining companies and such. Arthur will provide you with an orders packet, the clerk should be finishing up with it now. That will answer the questions you've been wise not to bother me with. And it will tell you where to find your dignitary. I'll leave that as a surprise for you," Byng smiled as he rounded the table and collected his hat from the stand next to the door. "Good day, Major. Good luck."

Waller snapped his boots together and came to attention, and Byng's smile widened, "Well done."

With that, the General left.

Currie took a couple of steps forward, then turned back to Waller, "He's General and Governor, you know, very much tied up with the constant stream of companies and prospector-types. There's word that we'll soon be producing more than all the gold and diamonds in South Africa."

"He must be in quite a bit of demand then, eh sir?" Waller smiled.

Currie nodded, "Most certainly. And that also means we're called on to protect many rich people. Avoid annoying them, Major. They believe they can end you, and they might well try."

Waller frowned at the warning but nodded, "I will, sir."

"Excellent. Alright, let's find your orders."

The two soldiers left Byng's office.

CHAPTER III

"Whatever's in the water here, sir, they breed 'em some pretty," Devlin was grinning all the way from headquarters into the nearby neighborhoods of pressboard houses, lifting his hat to every pretty lady who walked by.

"So if you marry one, what will you do, Jimmy? Think she'll leave a place like this to go home with you, to fog, rain and fish?" Waller was containing a smile at his younger subordinate's enthusiasm.

Devlin shrugged, "Well sir, she might be convinced. Or I could stay here... I'd manage, I suppose."

"If you became rich, you could move home and she might come with you, if you treated her right," Waller offered.

"Rich, eh? Yes, sure I could do that," Devlin nodded, still grinning. "Right after I become a Field Marshal I'll become rich. How's that, sir?"

"Depressing," Waller chuckled. "I think this is it."

He came to a stop, indicating the house that stood on his right. It looked just like all the others on this dusty street, but it had a Voltigeur light infantryman standing guard in front.

"Number twenty-six," Waller checked against the piece of paper Colonel Currie had given him, then nodded. "This is it."

Waller and Devlin ascended the stairs to the porch, and the Voltigeur came to attention, "Corporal, we're here to collect the dignitary."

The soldier nodded, "*Oui*, sir."

The mix of French and English indicated the man was a Quebecker — no surprise there, being that he was a Royal Canadian Voltigeur.

Devlin, closer to the door, knocked on it, and after a moment's pause a young maid answered, "Yes?"

Waller and Devlin both removed their hats, the former introducing them both, "Major Waller and Lieutenant Devlin, we have orders to collect a dignitary from this house for a mission."

The maid looked them both over somewhat anxiously and then nodded, opening the door all the way to let them in. They stepped in quietly, and the young girl disappeared into the other room for a moment, then returned, looking slightly flustered, "Sorry we have no niceties here, sir. We're not accustomed to company."

"I don't know, I think you've been right nice, if I may say, Miss," Devlin smiled and made use of some of his Newfoundland charm. "Can't ask for more than that."

Taken off guard, the maid smiled, "I'll call on her Ladyship."

Waller was already looking at Devlin as she hurried off, "A pretty young maid, Jimmy? I'm..."

He was about to say 'surprised' — the word was to be his motto for this day — but he stopped as his mind registered what he'd heard, and his head turned quickly back around.

"Jimmy, did she say *Ladyship*?"

Devlin had been grinning, but as he too thought it over, his smile faded, "Jesus, sir, I think she did."

Waller's smile disappeared. Byng was sending him and 400 of his men out to the prairie because of a Lady? Not a woman, but a *Lady*.

What could a peer want in the middle of the grasslands?

He'd prepared himself to handle a Lord, perhaps — a pompous man, a would-be Cecil Rhodes, out to find gold and riches at all costs. Or a man on a real mission. He had not thought of a woman. The complications could be great — what would she think of his 400 Newfoundlanders? Would she be offended by his own lack of graces?

Currie had warned him not to cross the wealthy people out here...

He stopped his thoughts as the sound of shoes on the clapboards upstairs drew his eyes upward and he stiffened slightly, his cap becoming fully wedged under his left arm as he straightened to nearly full attention.

The maid returned, standing aside as a pretty woman, twenty-five at most and wearing an unusual black cape, appeared at the top of the stairs. Behind her came an older woman, herself quite attractive and perhaps five years older, in a similar black cape.

Waller could almost hear Devlin's mouth drying. Poor boy. But if that was his reaction, Waller might have to hog-tie some of the men. They would never, of course, do any manner of harm to the Lady or her young companion, but her Ladyship might be too haughty to appreciate the charms of the average Newfoundland soldier. And even Waller would be hard-pressed to keep the b'ys from showering these ladies with extra care and attention.

The caped women descended the stairs with remarkable elegance. Waller had not seen such long attire since the robes of the Muslim women in Afghanistan, but with their pretty faces bare, and an unusual air about them, these two women made a different impression.

As they reached the bottom of the stairs, Waller and Devlin nodded to them both, "Major Waller and Lieutenant Devlin, of the Royal Newfoundland Regiment, at your service."

"I am Emma Lee, and this is Kara Lynne," the younger woman addressed him without expression, but in a cordial tone. "As soon as our maid is prepared, we'll all accompany you to the train. Colonel Currie said you would have one waiting?"

Waller nodded at the younger woman, trying not to actually look at her too closely. He was not so immune to beautiful women as he might like at the moment, "We do, Miss. James, why don't you assist the maid with luggage."

"We have little, just one case each," Emma Lee was the younger of the two women — the one standing before Waller.

He frowned, but then realized that was impolite and forced the frown away, "Even so, Miss. Jimmy, hop to it."

He'd not wanted to reveal quite how informal his relationship with his officers was, but as Jimmy bounded off — quite happy to be assisting the young maid — Waller realized he'd slipped. Her Ladyship, standing quietly behind Miss Emma, would realize all too quickly that the RNR didn't put much stock in overt formality.

Something else then occurred to Waller, "I'm afraid we have no carriage or car to take you to the station Miss, Your Ladyship. I wasn't informed we'd need one…"

Emma Lee began to redden, and she glanced back at the Lady. Dammit, Waller had already damaged this situation beyond all repair.

The younger girl looked back, having exchanged a pleasant glance with Kara Lynne, "Major, we're quite content to walk. We prefer it really. And I should say that it is I who has lately become the holder of the title. Kara is my dear friend."

Waller locked his jaw for a moment and cursed his foolishness, "My apologies, M'Lady. I presumed too much."

Lady Emma shook her head, "No, I rather would prefer if you wouldn't address me by my title. It's not something I wanted."

"Emma," Kara Lynne's tone carried a note of warning, and Waller decided that, perhaps not surprisingly, there was something odd about those two.

But he would deal with that later, "Should 'Miss Emma' be sufficient?"

"Emma would do, and Kara as well for my dear friend. Isn't that right, Kara?" Emma glanced back, but her companion's expression had become rather stony.

Waller decided to stay on the polite side, "Very well. Emma. As soon as Lieutenant Devlin returns, we'll be off."

As if summoned by a shout, Devlin appeared at the top of the staircase with two small suitcases, and the maid came behind him with her own, "Really sir, I can take those…"

"Now what sort of gentleman would I be, letting a lovely young lady like yourself do all that lifting?"

Waller contained a smile as Devlin returned to his place beside his Major, "All set, sir."

"Well done, Jimmy. And gallant too," Waller smiled, for some reason allowing himself to become more casual in that moment. It was hardly appropriate, of course, but neither was addressing a Lady as just 'Emma'.

This was turning into such an unusual, surprising day. Soon his head would hurt.

"We should go then, I think, Emma, Kara," Waller took a step back and pivoted, opening the door. The ladies filed out, and looking at each other with a raised eyebrows, Waller and Devlin followed.

CHAPTER IV

The women truly hadn't minded the walk, and Waller and Devlin had contained their surprise at the brisk pace Emma and Kara were setting as they moved — floated, it almost seemed — over the dusty ground. Within a quarter hour they'd returned to the station, and Emma and Kara were first onto the platform.

Waller found the sight he came upon as he followed them to be rather comical. The men of his companies had been standing and sitting about, chatting amongst themselves and paying only limited attention to passers by, but as the two women appeared on the platform, they fell completely silent.

Indeed, the strange air these women carried about themselves was affecting.

As they noticed Waller and Devlin behind the ladies — the Lieutenant carrying luggage — the sharp men of the RNR realized these women were their charge. Waller had never seen his men come to attention, shoulders back and chests puffed, with such speed.

The officers — Captains Tucker and Kearsey, the Lieutenants, and the Second Lieutenants — materialized before the ladies immediately.

"Gentlemen," Waller moved quickly to intercede, "we're to continue down these tracks in this train to the very end. We will then assist these ladies in locating something beyond the tracks. All men re-board the train, a platoon to each car."

Waller gave those orders smoothly, then watched as the men paid him only half attention.

He gave them a moment, then reinforced his words, "Alright, gentlemen... *move!*"

"You heard the Wall, move your arses b'ys!" the Sergeants began barking, instantly forgetting their company and referring to Waller by his hard-earned nickname. Waller turned round to the ladies.

"My apologies. You'll have a private car, of course. The third," he nodded to both Emma and Kara, and Emma smiled.

"Thank you, Major. I expect we will have to meet as well, perhaps for dinner?"

Waller could have sworn he heard curses from the officers standing behind him — muttered, 'lucky bastard' sorts of curses. He ignored them, and focused himself on the awkward feeling that suddenly settled over him, "Miss Emma. Of course. It would be my pleasure."

Emma smiled sweetly, then went to her car, trailed by her maid. Still wearing a stony expression, Kara went as well, followed by Devlin with the bags.

Waller stood aloof for a moment, then turned on his officers, ready to release some thunderous and disapproving words.

They'd all gone. Leave it to the Newfoundlanders to realize the storm was coming — and to get out of the way.

He boarded the train shortly after.

Waller was traveling in the second car, again with some of the men and with Lieutenant Devlin. Devlin, of course, was regaling his Second Lieutenants and his men with the stories about he and the lovely young maid — the maid they'd all seen and approved of — and they listened with duly rapt attention.

Though amusing Devlin might be, Waller was obliged to ignore the stories, and instead he sat at a table, laying out his orders and examining the few documents provided. A map similar to the one on General Byng's desk lay before him, yielding only a little more detail than Byng's had — this one was not just of the Selkirk Mandate, it showed some of the American Pacifica Territory as well. The border, at least, was clearly marked.

Written orders to the effect of those he'd received verbally were included too, with authorization to requisition additional transport and supplies at Long Prairie. There was no explanation, though, of Lady Emma Lee, or Miss Kara Lynne. Both were simply referred to, quite astonishingly, as 'the dignitary' — as if there was only one of them.

There certainly were two. Men in both companies were by now pairing off to try their luck together, Waller was sure of it. Poor devils.

But they were being sent out to the grasslands, and even in Afghanistan, Waller had heard of those plains. In many ways they were like the Canadian prairies, but they were supposedly full of springs, and were the grassy steppes in which the savages most liked to roam.

This train would take a day to cross the 700 miles from New World City to Long Prairie, and then it would be a march. That was another thing Waller did not understand: why infantry, why not horsemen? A cavalry regiment such as the Canadian Dragoons, already here in Selkirk, could have covered fifty miles a day out in the grasslands — if the conditions were as good as Currie had said. His Newfoundlanders were good on the march, a skill Afghanistan's passes had taught them, but they were still rated at only twenty-five miles under the best of conditions. They would be much slower than cavalry, so why were they being sent into the steppe?

Just another question, Waller supposed — one more that he had no business asking. Perhaps had Lieutenant Colonel Tobin, the head of the RNR, been present, he would have asked. But Tobin had been wrapped up in too much politics in Newfoundland, so he quite possibly was still in St. John's with the other half of the battalion. They would follow on, eventually.

For now, this mission into the grass was strictly Waller's and he would have to make certain all was prepared for it.

"Jimmy, when you have a moment, could you call the Captains in please?" Waller called back over his shoulder, and Lieutenant Devlin held up a hand to the men listening to his tale.

"Sorry b'ys, duty calls. Finish it later," he smiled and stood up. "Have to go back through the ladies' car to get George and Fred."

Waller smiled as he pulled the map closer to him. Looking at the straight-line border that divided the Selkirk Mandate from the Pacifica

Territory, he found that the railway on which he now rode came out into the grasslands only ten miles north of the American border, then ran essentially parallel to it. The company building the British New World Line (the NWL) had probably hoped that Americans seeking access to the northern reaches of their own territory would prefer to come through Selkirk (and spend their dollars at British businesses) to get closer to their objectives. The US rail lines were far to the south, and didn't extend nearly so far. That left a long walk for Americans heading west.

But then, perhaps not so long as the walk the RNR would be making.

It took a few minutes for the Captains to return with Devlin. Each of Waller's two companies had its own Captain — George Tucker had 'C' Company, Fred Kearsey had 'D' Company. Each company was roughly 200 men strong, having lost some thirty of their number in Afghanistan, and having found no replacements upon their return to St. John's. Both Captains should by rights have had another Captain serving as the second in command of their companies, but one of those men had been badly wounded and the other moved to command 'B' Company, still back in Newfoundland.

Waller's half of the battalion was thus more fragmented than he'd have liked.

George Tucker and Fred Kearsey both removed their hats as Waller greeted them, "Gentlemen, take a seat."

Waller waved them to the chairs on the opposite side of the table, then nodded again to Devlin, "Back to your story now, Jimmy."

With a smile, Devlin tossed a salute and went back to the men, "So the maid was happy to see me right then. I've got her, b'ys!"

"Gentlemen," Waller ignored his Lieutenant again, "it's about time you find out what I know, though I have to say I don't know much. Not that that's unusual for us."

The Captains each smiled — the British Imperial Army, as a rule, didn't confide in the lowly battalion officers. Horatio Nelson had been dead for over 100 years, and with him the belief that every officer should know the plan. In the twentieth century, men were obliged to do their jobs, and not to ask too much while they did them.

"We're escorting those ladies, as you well know, but to where I don't know. Out beyond the tracks, though. The General doesn't seem to have any idea of how far, but I have authorizations here for us to draw stores for up to a month in the field."

Tucker whistled, "A month? Expecting much shooting? Ammo's what I'd think we need the most."

"Couldn't agree more," Kearsey nodded. "This is why they had us bring our own mules from home?"

Waller nodded, "Must be. We'll need more than twenty mules, though, by the look of that. I understand there's water out on the steppes, but no one seems to have a map with the springs on it. I'll want a wagon with water in it, and one with more ammunition. If we run into savages, I imagine 150 rounds a man will run down quite quickly."

"We could leave behind the mountain guns, don't see much point to them if we're not after camps of any sort. Free up the mules to carry more ammo," Tucker suggested, frowning down at the map again.

Doing the sums in his head, Waller paused for a moment. A mule could walk all day with 300 pounds on its back, and a case of 1,000 .303 rounds would weigh around sixty pounds. This he'd learned quickly in Afghanistan. Twenty mules that had previously been carrying two 3.7 inch mountain guns... that would be 100,000 rounds of ammunition.

"That's what we should do, then. And if we can find a cart to take more, then we certainly will," Waller nodded.

The Short, Magazine, Lee-Enfield rifle carried by the men of the RNR was perhaps the best service rifle in the history of the British Empire — it was accurate beyond 300 yards, and it could fire quickly. His men had become quite handy with it in Afghanistan, where tribesmen could hide in hills and sharpshooting was essential, but the use of ammunition could be prodigious. Each man was carrying with him 150 rounds of .303 caliber ammunition, but at rapid fire that could evaporate in less than ten minutes.

And distributed between 400 men, 100,000 rounds, would amount to only another 250 rounds each. And those figures didn't even factor in their Lewis guns — the hasty replacements for the Vickers machine gun they'd lost at Jalalabad — which also fired the .303.

According to British regulations, he was required to have 550 rounds per man and thousands more for the machine guns, though that requirement was supposed to be supported by an Army baggage train, that he wouldn't have access to. They'd been sent out here with only their mules, none of their wagons, and with virtually none of their logistical support. Colonel Tobin had been certain that most of these things would be provided to Waller's men here in the new world... so they would have to be requisitioned.

It was perhaps pessimistic to assume they'd run into so many savages that such a load of ammunition could be exhausted, but Waller was hardly inclined to find out the hard way that he'd underestimated the beasts.

"And we'll need two wagons beyond that," Waller nodded to his officers, "one for water, and one for the ladies."

The Captains nodded, George Tucker taking on the job, "Very good, sir. I'll see to it when we're there."

"Now do you figure they'll have the kind of ammo we need at that post there?" Kearsey pointed to Long Prairie. "Doesn't look like much of a spot on the map."

Waller glanced at the orders he'd read again, "The note from Colonel Currie here says there's an arsenal at Long Prairie. It's probably a point of rearmament for patrols and cavalry in the area, I imagine they'll have what we need."

Hopefully that was not assuming too much.

The Major and his Captains continued to plan, and the train rode west.

CHAPTER V

Smith decided that his day was not going to be quiet. Wasn't much that could be done about that now — he'd helped the boys because that'd been the decent thing to do, and he'd even taken them down to that patch of land they were prospecting… but trouble was coming.

There were some days when Smith could hear the trouble coming, some days when it made itself louder than others.

Today it was coming as the thunder of hundreds of hooves about a half mile back, riding down a cross-cutting trail, probably from Fort Burt. Smith had been by that post now and then, and to the town that'd grown up outside the walls to meet the needs of the men there. He usually left the United States Cavalry alone, though. He'd never been a man who figured himself for the army. They ordered a man to do things, and Smith valued his ability to drift too much to join them.

But the cavalry still seemed to like him. He would tell them the truth when they asked for word on things, and he'd even help them in a scrape. Cavalrymen often found themselves in scrapes, too.

Smith had seen it many times, out here. There were different kinds of cavalrymen, some of them doing their jobs as best they could, which Smith had no grudge with, and some who believed Custer had been on the path to the presidency, just died because of bad luck on the way. It was those Custer-loving types who could get their men killed. Smith reckoned that any man trying to be like Custer all these years later was fixing to end himself like Custer.

As the horses of the troop pounded down the cross-cutting trail, Smith sat steady in his saddle, hands away from his guns, waiting for the khakis to appear.

The boys he'd brought down here had ridden on into the woods off the trail, and being as unfamiliar with this world as they were, they probably didn't even pay attention to the cavalry approaching. Smith was content to just wait, he wasn't on any clock.

After a minute or two, the first riders came rushing out of the cross-cutting trail, then turned and rode hard on down the trail Smith himself had been following. These troopers were heading for the grasslands, and they were in a mighty hurry. Must have been a cable about savages, Smith guessed. There were many little towns far from the tracks out here, most of them connected by trail and coach to the rail line, some with their own telegraph cables. The men and women who set up these towns were either brave or foolish. Some of them survived, many of them didn't.

Problem as Smith saw it was simple: the savages were just irregular. They didn't always jump you, they came and went as if guided by the roll of the dice. He'd known towns on the grasslands, sitting on rivers and deposits of gold, that had gone for ten years without being attacked. People living in those towns reckoned they had the savages figured out — that one magic chant or fence or bribe had somehow bought them their peace. Maybe it had, but if peace is what they bought, it came with an expiry date. Those towns were eventually wrecked, just the same.

Only towns with good walls all the way around, with telegraph wires, and with every man and woman good with a rifle, stayed alive out there.

The cavalry usually got called to help towns like those, not that the cavalry was immune to the savages. Not by a long shot.

As the column of troopers in khaki continued to ride down the trail, an officer slowed his horse at the intersection and looked around him, pausing as he noticed Smith. Friendly was the best way to handle the cavalry, so Smith raised his hand and waved, "Hello, sir."

The officer rode his horse up towards Smith, and neither man recognized the other. Smith decided from the young officer's face that he, like the boys, was new out here, but he didn't seem to have the determined look of a Custer type. He sat easy on his horse, short, stout and unimposing.

Touching the brim of his wide hat, the cavalryman stopped short of Smith, "You might want to head back the way you came, sir. We've had word there's a horde coming, thousands strong. Heading for Vista City, just out into the grasslands."

Smith frowned and looked past the officer, "Vista's another three hours down that way, at the speed your boys are riding."

"Yes it is, but we should have five hours or so, sir. We received the warning from Copper Rock, before it was overrun. Big horde out there, and it's been moving north, towards the border."

Listening to the young Captain talk, Smith decided he approved of the man. He was speaking plainly and firmly, but didn't sound too eager to start tangling with the savages. That was good.

"Well, I was riding on down towards Vista as it was, I could lend you an extra gun."

When hordes of savages got together, it was a good idea for folk to cooperate. Bandits, cavalry, drifters — the savages would eat one just the same as the other. Eat them alive. Better to work together, stave off the attack. Smith could probably turn around and escape, but it wasn't his way. Wouldn't be the decent thing.

"We'd be obliged for any help," the officer touched his hat again. "I've pulled all the men I can afford to out of Fort Burt, right down to some of the clerks."

"Then I'll be along," Smith nodded. "You reckon they'll sweep up this far? I was just riding with two boys who're in them woods prospecting."

The officer shook his head, "I doubt it, they're cutting across the grasslands so they can move fast. Up here they can't run as well."

Smith knew that of course, but he hadn't heard the reports from the cavalryman's sources, so he'd thought it better to ask. The boys should be alright. He'd explained some things to them, even shown them how to shoot a bit better.

"Well, we better ride," Smith nodded to the officer. "Name's Smith."

"Captain Donahue," the officer nodded. "You're the drifter, Smith? I believe one of my superior officers knows you. Major Kendrick."

As Smith eased his mare down the trail and Donahue turned his horse to ride along with him, the drifter nodded, "I know Kendrick. Good man."

"Rare to find good men anywhere, these days," Donahue agreed. "I'm even more grateful for you riding with us, Smith. Kendrick says he's begged you to join as a scout."

Smith nodded, "Just not the life for me. I get by on my own, doing odd jobs and the like. But when there's honest folk in trouble, I won't ride away."

"Good man," Donahue eased the pace of his stallion up a bit, and Smith followed. The cavalry troopers had all passed through the intersection, so Smith and Donahue followed them down, kicking their horses up to a gallop.

They'd be at Vista City in a few hours, and the savages wouldn't be far behind.

CHAPTER VI

Waller was getting hungry, which made him think it must be time for dinner. His watch, which he had not reset since his men had left Calgary, read 7:00, but in fact it was only midday on this world. The days here were supposed to be the same length as on Earth, but of course the planet was in a different time zone than western Canada.

So perhaps it was a bit early for dinner; lunch, however, could be justified. The train did have a food car, and he sent Devlin to collect some for him while he sat and continued to look over the maps at his table.

Hearing the car door open a few moments later, he simply called back to Devlin, "If you wouldn't mind bringing it over, Jimmy."

He didn't notice that the men, who'd been chatting boisterously about the new planet, and the new women, had fallen silent. His mind was too busy dissecting the map, deciding on the directions he thought Lady Emma would most likely want to take, and which ones he'd prefer. Knowing food was coming, though, he slid some of the piles of letters and orders on the table aside, to make room for a plate.

A shadow appeared next to his table, and he continued to frown at the map, until it registered that no plate was forthcoming. Then something told him the shadow that had appeared was not Jimmy Devlin at all, and he looked up.

Indeed, it was Kara Lynne, wearing her stony expression.

"I'm afraid Mister Devlin was detained by our maid's need for assistance in reshuffling baggage. Emma would dearly like to lunch with you, though, in our car."

Waller had to take a few seconds to digest the words, and he nodded, slowly standing up, "I'd be delighted, of course."

"Good," Kara Lynne said in a clipped tone, and Waller followed her back to the car door.

This woman was most curious. She moved with graceful assuredness, and she allowed her maid to fraternize with a Lieutenant while coming to call on a Major for a friend who was indeed a peer, but who denied her title... much was curious about this whole affair.

Passing silently between the cars, Waller emerged into the train's third carriage and realized he was smiling as Emma stood up behind a table just like his own, two plates of food already set on it, "I took it upon myself to presume."

"I'm glad you did," Waller nodded, and as she gestured him to do so, he sat opposite her.

They began to eat, making small talk as they did. The weather, the landscape, the quality of the train cars, and then some on the Newfound-landers, and how they'd come to the Selkirk Mandate. Stories of Afghan-istan, properly romanticized to avoid shocking the young Lady, drew wide eyes of excitement — stories of climbing rocky hillsides, hiding behind mud walls, firing at shadows and so forth all seemed to be interesting to her.

It appeared, for a while at least, that Lady Emma could be entertained as many other young wealthy and titled women could — with exotic stories of gallantry and adventure.

But after telling her about the march to Jalalabad, and explaining to her the Newfoundlanders' part, she asked a question that was unusual, "So your men are skilled at irregular fighting — a single shot for a single kill, even in difficult situations?"

That question stopped Waller for a moment, because it was rather specific, and not the sort of 'it sounds terribly dangerous' question he'd been asked often when talking to other women. Nodding slowly, then, he answered her, "We are well experienced in that, I'd say. It's a requirement in Afghanistan, because they can spring up from anywhere, any time. You seem to be quite interested in that specific ability, if it's not too impertinent for me to say."

Emma's smile faded, "I am… not. Just making conversation, of course."

Waller's eyes may have narrowed slightly, but he let her flimsy explanation pass without comment. Interested to learn more of his charges, he instead turned the conversation in a different direction, "So, Emma, if I may ask, are you British born?"

"Oh no, I was born out here…" Emma waved her fork at the windows going past, and then Kara Lynne nearly hissed an interruption.

"I fear, Major Waller, that we are not at liberty to speak of ourselves too much. At least not until we are safely away from walls with ears."

Waller frowned, looking around the train car for a moment. There was no one here save for himself, the three ladies and Lieutenant Devlin, who was taking a remarkably long time helping Annie sort out the luggage. Three small bags evidently required a great deal of effort to move around.

"I can't say I've seen any walls with ears here," he smiled.

Emma smiled too, approving of the humor, but Kara Lynne did not, "We will not speak of it. Not yet, anyway."

Marvelous, there were to be more secrets.

At that very moment, with some seemingly dramatic flare, Waller felt the train begin to brake. He frowned instantly, then his eyes darted to Devlin, "We shouldn't have to stop yet, we should have miles to go before we need more water."

The Lieutenant nodded, "If you'll pardon me, Annie, I'm going to see the engineer!"

He rushed out of the car, and after quickly finishing the last couple of bites of lunch, Waller stood, "I'm afraid we'll have to continue this later. And depending on what's afoot, I may have to send men here to guard your car. Please stay here until I send word."

Looking from Emma's pleasant, smiling face, to Kara Lynne's stony eyes, Waller turned on his heel and left. He was not fond of secrets… particularly those in the care of beautiful women.

But the train was slowing, and that was a more immediate problem.

***

Devlin came back into the second car just as Waller arrived. Having bounded forward to the locomotive quite quickly, he was huffing as he reported, "Big horde's coming up from the south, the Yanks are trying to stop it with a troop of cavalry, but they wired saying it's thousands strong. We're ordered to wait up here at Treeline City, fort up with the Canadian Rifles."

Waller nodded, "Alright, we're close to the city?"

"Engineer says it's about five minutes away, just out into the prairie."

Being on the tracks, even doing thirty miles an hour, would not be a good thing if thousands of savages were going to come across them. If the beasts somehow derailed the train, the RNR would be in very poor shape to resist. Better to stop.

"Go find George and Fred, get the men on their feet and prepared to deploy," Waller nodded, and with an ironic smile, Devlin caught the last of his breath, just in time to bound away and lose it all over again.

The Sergeant commanding the men in the compartment with Waller barked them to their feet, and they assembled their kit and checked their weapons.

Evidently they would be meeting these savages before they marched off the rails.

Waller stepped onto the platform and put his hat on. The station was not as crowded as the one in New World City, but the men and a few ladies who were there were hurrying around. A few soldiers of the Canadian Rifles were rushing by as well, and didn't see Waller as they hastened to what he assumed was a machine gun post up on the station's roof.

He watched a Vickers setting up in that post, facing south, and nodded to himself. The Captain here was certainly preparing.

The men started coming off the train behind him, waiting for orders from him to move. The platform would be quite crowded for the moment. Taking a few steps forward, Waller surveyed the town. Treeline City would not qualify as a city in the old world — it was just five or six dirt streets across, with no electric fittings that he could see, and clapboard buildings. A palisade of logs surrounded the town, and to the west he could see a large gate that had already been closed, with men in the drab green of Imperial soldiers standing in towers on either side of it.

There should be 200 men of the Canadian Rifles here, and given the small size of this place, 200 would probably be enough, particularly with the help of their heavy Vickers machine guns.

As Waller thought that, an officer hurried up a set of stairs on the western end of the platform, then immediately noticed the Major and approached him. Coming to a halt he saluted quickly, and Waller returned it, "Major Waller, Royal Newfoundlanders."

"Lieutenant James, sir, 'C' Company of the Canadian Rifles. Captain Benton is overseeing the defensive arrangements from the hotel down there," James turned and pointed to a large two-storey building in the middle of town. A Vickers gun was being installed on the roof as Waller watched.

"Has the Captain got a particular idea of where he wants my men?" Waller asked curtly, and the Lieutenant shook his head.

"Nothing particular, sir. You can't see it from here, but the wall is lower over there, by the houses down that way. He figures that'll be the weakest point, sir."

Waller narrowed his eyes and looked down the wall, not seeing what the Lieutenant was referring to, but trusting that he spoke the truth, "Very well, I'll deploy my men and then join the Captain in that building. Lieutenant, can you wait a moment to lead one of my companies down to the vulnerable area?"

The man nodded, "Of course, sir."

Waller nodded and turned away, "Captain Kearsey, your b'ys will go to the west end of town, apparently the wall is lower down that way. Two platoons up front and two flying, Fred."

The Captain saluted, "Yes sir! Lieutenant Hickey, Lieutenant Sullivan, your platoons to the wall. Form up now!"

As the men of 'D' Company formed a marching column and followed the Canadian Lieutenant off the platform, Waller waved Captain Tucker to his side, "George, I need you to hold the station."

The two men looked around them for a moment: the palisade walls came all the way up to the platform, but stood just inside the tracks — the train was not protected by the wall.

"I'll put a platoon on the roof of the train, one on the roof of the station up with that Vickers, leave one on the platform... bayonets fixed for all of them. You'll want Jimmy's platoon with you?" Tucker was thinking as he spoke, and Waller smiled thinly at the last remark.

"At least one section. I don't know what sort of reserve Captain... whatever the man's name is, I've forgotten... I don't know what his reserve will be like, but I want to have some options," Waller tended to explain himself to his Captains, even though many of his rank might not agree with the concept.

Tucker nodded, "You always do like your options, sir."

The Captain then moved away, barking orders to his men, splitting the platoons appropriately and getting them in position. They would have to use the train as a part of the wall, to try to block the station. Waller frowned as he looked over the arrangements here again — there was little provision for guarding the platform. It was probably assumed that the natural height of the position would make it more defensible, and that was perhaps true. A weaker point, nonetheless.

But with the Vickers gun up high, they should be well protected.

"Here we are, as usual, sir," Lieutenant Devlin and his platoon arrived near Waller, and Devlin saluted.

All through Afghanistan, Waller had found he'd needed a platoon near him to get things accomplished. Majors were, in theory, supposed to have a more administrative role — more distant from the fighting. In Afghanistan, distance was illusory, and Waller had found a need to keep at least one body of men with him at all times. He expected it to be no different here.

"Jimmy, good. We need to evacuate the ladies from the train. The command post is in that hotel," Waller pointed down to the building in question, a few hundred yards away in the middle of town. "We'll take them there, and I'll meet with the Captain as well. Should be the safest thing."

Devlin smiled and nodded, "I'll go and collect them. Thank you, sir!"

That young man could not be dissuaded, Waller decided with a small smile of his own.

A moment later, Devlin was emerging from the train with the three ladies in tow. Both Emma Lee and Kara Lynne still wore their black robes, concealing themselves completely. Indeed, Waller just now realized that Emma Lee had somehow eaten without pushing the cloak too far aside. Remarkably graceful, those women. Emma particularly so.

The ladies hurried up to Waller, and he touched the brim of his hat to them, "I'm afraid for the moment we'll have to withdraw you to the field headquarters here — that hotel."

As he pointed, the ladies nodded, and without words they started off for the building.

While Lieutenant Devlin formed his platoon in the street outside the hotel to wait, Waller led the ladies inside, removing his hat as he did. The desk was unattended, and there was no sign of anyone around.

Frowning, he turned back to the women, "If you'd wait here a moment, please."

Emma Lee nodded pleasantly, and Waller tucked his hat under his arm and climbed the stairs to the second floor. At the top of the stairs he looked to his left and saw one Canadian Rifleman, who came to attention. He went that way, and at the end of the corridor, he turned again to his left and through an open door saw two officers standing in a guest room, looking southwest with field glasses through the window.

"Captain, I'm Major Waller, Royal Newfoundlanders," Waller strode in, coming to a stop next to the man whose name he'd forgotten.

The Captain did not stop looking out with the field glasses, "Benton,

'D' Company of the Canadian Rifles. Come to enjoy the party?"

Waller didn't often get irritated by the informal treatment of rank, but then he only usually saw it among his own Newfoundlanders, and they had proven their loyalty and respect. He wasn't sure what to make of Benton, but the first impression wasn't stunningly good.

"Captain, what's your deployment?"

Benton didn't answer for a moment, but seemed to get his wits about him after that pause and lowered the glasses, "I have three platoons along the palisade side, there, on roofs and in second floor windows of houses. The defensive arrangements are long standing. Last platoon is divided by sections and is looking after my two Vickers, one on the roof here and one at the rail station."

"You've put precious few men on the platform, and to the left," Waller observed, "I've placed my companies on both those flanks, save for a platoon that's standing outside. I also have three ladies downstairs, they'll need to stay in here for the battle."

The Captain glanced at the Lieutenant who was with him, then looked back at Waller, "Sir, there's not going to be a battle here, I'm sure. If a few of the savages come up we'll shoot them down, but I don't care what the Yanks say, the savages don't like coming to this part of the plains. I've been posted to Selkirk for six years, this place has never been struck."

Waller was not impressed by the claim, "Well that may be true, but I still want the ladies up here, and since your men are spoken for, I'll assign a section to see to them. You're going to join your men on the roof?"

"I was going to stay right here and—"

"You're going to join your men on the roof, Captain. Direct the fire from the Vickers."

The Captain ground his jaw, then snapped his heels together, "Sir."

Those two left, and Waller looked south. He'd foolishly left his own field glasses on the train — he'd have to go back and collect them — but he could already get a sense for the defensive arrangements. To the west he could see Captain Kearsey's men moving wagons and crates to form a firing step behind the low palisade, and over on the train platform Captain Tucker's b'ys were setting themselves up.

It would be quite an event here, if the savages did arrive. But although Captain Benton hadn't made a good first impression, Waller was willing to bet the man's skepticism wasn't entirely unfounded. After all, why would the savages suddenly take an interest in this place?

CHAPTER VII

Smith had been on this frontier for many years, and he'd seen more than most men could imagine. On some occasions he'd seen hundreds of savages, and those were days when he was sure his number was up. But he had never in his life seen the number of savages that were running across an open grasslands plain before his eyes, just a mile away.

"My God," Captain Donahue reined in his horse. "Lieutenant, hold the men!"

The cavalry boys had been hoping to arrive just in time. After all, that was the cavalry way, or so Smith had heard it said. But today they weren't about to have their way, because thousands, maybe even 10,000 savages were in Vista City. It had taken only three hours' hard ride for the cavalry to get here, but the savages had come quicker.

"They shouldn't be here so soon... my God..." Donahue walked his horse forward.

The trail had just taken the riders over the last foothill, and now Donahue's Lieutenant lined all the cavalry troopers on the crest of that last hill. A hundred men. Smith reckoned by the look of them that they knew how to handle themselves better than some troopers he'd seen, but there were only 100. Down the slope, in the golden grasses around Vista City, the savages were raging. That was never a pretty thing to see — men, women and children were dragged screaming from the town, then they were torn apart by the hands of these beasts of the new world.

It was no way to die, and as Smith watched it, he regretted not being able to stop the slaughter.

But now there was nothing to be done — not against that many, not with so few guns. A hundred men at a mile's range weren't a foe for savages, they were a meal.

"Captain, I don't mean to be cold, but we need to move on. Nothing we can do for these folks now. Try anything and we'll die," Smith turned his mare and started her walking to the north. "We should get behind the trees, before they see us."

Already they might have been noticed, but Smith had to hope the savages were too focused on the town they'd overrun to care about 100 horses and riders right now.

"We can't just stand by, sir — we have to do something!" one of the cavalrymen exclaimed.

"Will we just sit here while Americans die, Captain?" one of the Lieutenants asked righteously.

Smith sensed this was going to end badly.

"No, Lieutenant, we can't. We're responsible for more lives than just theirs. We get ourselves killed, the rest of the citizens out here will be as good as dead until more troops come," Donahue's voice was sullen, though Smith figured he'd have disapproved of the man — as much as he disapproved of any man — if it had been any other way.

Unfortunately for Smith and Donahue both, one of his Lieutenants had fallen in love with the story of Custer, "Come on men! We can save a few and ride on! Are we cowards?"

"Heroes of this sort die," Smith advised as he slowed his horse. "Don't go down there. If you do, shoot your horses and yourselves, or you'll suffer."

The Lieutenant scowled, "You men going to listen to some drifter? With me, to glory!"

With that the brash Lieutenant turned his mount, charging down the hill towards the savages. Many of the troop followed him... fifty or more, by Smith's guess. He felt particularly bad for their horses. Savages ate horses and riders alike.

Donahue screamed after his men, demanding they return, and one of the other Lieutenants looked at him, "We can't let them go alone, sir."

"No, we can't," Donahue shook his head, then drew his Colt magazine pistol — like the fancy ones the boys had been carrying back on the trail.

Smith didn't want to see Donahue dead, but there was no question that any man riding down this hill wouldn't ride back up.

Donahue turned his horse towards Smith, "I can't let my men charge alone, Mister Smith. I must ask, though, take some cover, watch from the trees. If the savages drive north, go to the British, warn them. I cabled them, but I obviously underestimated the bastards' speed. Do that for me please, Mister Smith."

Smith watched the earnest face of the Captain, then nodded, "I will."

He wasn't the sort to deny a brave man's last wish, especially not when it was a very decent one.

Donahue nodded, then turned his mount and charged down the hill after his men. For just a minute Smith sat up on his mare, transfixed by the sight of the khaki cavalry riding into the golden grass. He entertained no illusions that the savages would leave any alive. Over short distances, savages could run with horses, even faster than horses. Horsemen were doomed when they were surrounded by so many.

Wasn't any way around it.

Letting go a sigh, Smith turned his Appaloosa around and walked her down the other side of the hill, then eased her up to a canter to get back into the trees. He found a notch and walked her into the woods, then turned her around and watched as the first of the Custer-lovers clashed with the savages.

The Lieutenant who'd ridden down first went in shooting, whooping in a bad imitation of an Indian, hitting two or three savages with .45 caliber Colt lead before being hauled down. After that it was a bloodbath. The savages saw the cavalrymen and piled onto them. Some of those who'd ridden down out of loyalty to their foolish friends tried to turn and run for it, but their cavalry steeds — some fast horses, Smith knew — were run down by savages on the sprint.

Captain Donahue was the last man to reach the horde, and as soon as he did he dismounted and shot his horse with his pistol. He then shot one savage, put his gun to his temple, and denied the beasts the pleasure of eating him alive.

The screams of his men crossed the plain, and Smith shook his head, turning to the north. He walked his mare just inside the tree line, then saw the first savages start to run the same way. Savages were never organized, they never moved with a strategic purpose. Somehow they all just decided they wanted to stampede and they went together, and some of them seemed to have an understanding of a mission — like the first one to move north. But there were no leaders, none who told the others what to do or when to do it. Made no sense to Smith, but then he reckoned it didn't matter if it made sense to him or not. He'd seen it often enough.

The first savages heading north began to draw the notice of the rest, and soon enough they'd all be running. Smith had to get ahead of them. He'd promised a dead man he'd warn the British.

Though he'd never been up that way, Smith knew some drifters who had. Mostly they'd gone to see what the British called Selkirk, and they came back saying that it looked the same as Pacifica, just with more rules. They had also mentioned a trail that ran north near the tree line. He'd find it, and he and his mare would ride hard to get to the British before the savages did.

CHAPTER VIII

It was late afternoon at Treeline City, and as Captain Benton had predicted, no savages had yet come into sight. Waller had looked at the original dispatch that had come down to Benton — one that had passed from US Fort Burt through Pacifica City, the town at the mouth of their tunnel to the new world, up the telegraph line to New World City, then down the rail line telegraph wires to Treeline. It had been hours old when it reached its destination, and it gave no clear indication of when to expect the attack.

That was a bit of a problem.

The men had been standing to at their defensive points for over two hours, and all they'd seen was blowing grass. There was a ridge on the south side of the town, about a mile beyond the palisades. Benton had determined that it would hide the approach of any savages, so he'd sent a half dozen scouts on horseback out to watch it, but so far they were silent.

All of this waiting could make the men careless, and soon hunger would be distracting them further.

"Jimmy, get over to the station, tell George to start rotating his platoons out for supper. Then get down to Fred and tell him the same. And find some food for yours as well. I don't want the b'ys lying there hungry and tired when the savages show up," Waller addressed Lieutenant Devlin, and the energetic young man nodded.

"Yes sir!"

He hurried from the second floor room and headed down the stairs, barking some orders to his Lance Corporals as he did.

Waller was left alone in the room with the three ladies, though he didn't really notice them as he raised his field glasses, recovered earlier from the train, and swept the horizon. Nothing at all to the south, just blue sky over the grasslands.

"Do you think we'll see them soon, Major?"

Waller looked to Emma Lee with some surprise as he heard the question — he'd truly forgotten her presence.

"I don't know, Emma. The Captain here doesn't believe we will, but I tend to be cautious about these things. Too many clear days in the Khyber Pass that ended badly."

Emma nodded, "I agree with you. They're coming, I can almost feel it!"

Waller smiled politely — the Lady's enthusiasm was rather *interesting*, to say the least.

He looked back to the horizon, "Well, I hope your feeling is wrong, Emma. I can't say I'd really like to have a big battle. But if they come, we're ready."

Devlin left a single section outside the hotel, telling the men to wait for their meals while the rest of his platoon followed him to the train station. Taking the stairs up to the platform two at a time, he found Captain Tucker and the flying platoon at ease.

Tucker frowned at his arrival, "They see something coming, Jimmy?"

The loud question drew a surge from the men, and they all turned their eyes back to the horizon, squinting against the sun. It was still crisp and cool here, thankfully — the mountains were blowing a brisk wind down onto the grasslands. Had it been too hot, the wait would have been unbearable.

Devlin shook his head, "No sir, we're to rotate the men for meals. Major doesn't want us getting hungry or sleeping, owing to the long day."

"Ah yes, we'll have a good feed. Or as good a feed as we can manage on a train platform, eh b'ys?" Tucker grinned and called that out to his men, receiving a chorus of approving grunts for his effort.

"Right, Lieutenant Kennedy, see if you can—"

"Rider to the east!"

That alert came from a sentry posted at the far end of the train, watching for savages cutting through the brush. As they heard it, both Captain Tucker and Lieutenant Devlin rushed across the platform to its eastern end — the one facing the mountains — and watched as a man, looking much like an American cowboy, kicked his mare into a run down the rail bed.

"Looks like he's running from something, sir!" a Sergeant at the end of the platform observed, and Tucker nodded.

"Let him through. Sergeant, a section up here, if you please," Tucker wasn't about to welcome a racing rider without men ready — if he were a bandit he might well try something unwise, so the RNR would be prepared.

A section of twelve men lined up behind Tucker and Devlin, standing to with rifle butts against the planking of the platform. The rider slowed his horse, a brown painted mare who clearly knew how to run, and was glistening with sweat despite the cool.

About fifty yards from the end of the train, he held up his hands in a wave, "I'm coming in friendly. Not looking for trouble with you... chaps."

"By God he's a Yank," Devlin observed rather crassly, glancing at Tucker, and the Captain smiled.

"Is that a fact, Jimmy? And here I was thinking he was a Frenchman!" Tucker was already descending the stairs to the ground east of the platform as he spoke, and as he passed between his picketing men, he held up his hand to wave back. "Come on in, friend. We hear there's loads of trouble on the way, you might like to get behind the walls before it arrives."

The rider eased up to Tucker slowly, and the Captain watched the weathered American's eyes as they took in the train, the station, and the platform. Tucker got the sense the newcomer was sizing up his preparations.

"You have a lot of men in town?" the American asked, stopping his Appaloosa next to Tucker. The Captain had never been a horseman, but he thought the animals to be quite fine, so he deftly rubbed this one's nose.

"Two companies more than were posted here, sir," Tucker looked back up at the American. "We were passing through and got a cable. Though by the look of you I'd guess you know what the contents of the cable were. Rode hard from the south?"

The rider seemed surprised that Tucker had caught on, "I did. I met the man who sent the cable, cavalry Captain named Donahue. Watched him and his men get slaughtered by 10,000 savages who're running this way."

Tucker's eyebrows shot up, "Did you say 10,000? Holy jumpin... Devlin, get this man to see the Major. Sergeant, get his horse to some safety, will you?"

The Sergeant descended the stairs behind the Captain, then waved to two Privates, "You heard him, b'ys, see to the man's horse. Do it right now!"

"If you wouldn't mind seeing our Major," Tucker turned back to the American. "He needs to hear all about what you've seen. We were about to get a feed going, are you hungry? Looks like you could use some food. If you like, we can set you up after you see the Major."

This American had the air of a man not easily surprised, so Tucker took some pleasure in getting a bewildered look from him.

"I'll meet your Major, then I'll decide," he replied after a moment.

The cowboy then dismounted, adjusted his six-shooter belt, and walked towards the stairs to the platform.

"If you'll just come along with me," Devlin pointed the way to the hotel, then looked at one of the Lieutenants standing on the platform. "Kennedy, get down to Captain Kearsey and tell him the Major says to get the men fed. Trouble's on the way!"

Smith was honestly surprised, which didn't happen to him as much as it once had. He'd ridden his mare hard and covered the thirty miles of trail in under three hours, probably a full hour ahead of the savages. Savages could run fast over short distances, but they couldn't outrun his mare over longer range. Now he was in the Selkirk Mandate, and the people here were not what he expected.

He had expected a British Captain in his drab green to be very official, and very condescending towards a drifter. That Captain wasn't. Didn't even ask questions about how Smith came by his information. He'd expected to be questioned, to be accused of being a liar or a man out for his own ends, but instead these British soldiers had taken his horse to safety, were leading him into the town, and were offering a meal.

But then, they didn't sound British. He'd heard Englishmen and Canadians talk before, and they sounded different.

This young Lieutenant leading him to the hotel seemed a pleasant sort, so Smith decided to ask. No better way to find out.

"If you don't mind me asking, what outfit are you?" his question was direct to the point.

The young man smiled as he looked back at him, "Royal Newfoundland Regiment, sir. 'C' and 'D' Companies if you want that more precise. Newfoundland's a country off the coast of Canada... further east than Nova Scotia, if that helps."

Smith slowly shook his head, "Never learned much geography of the old world."

"No shame in that, b'y, neither did I. Found out where Egypt was and where India was when I stepped off the boats. Mom'd never have thought of her little Jimmy seeing the world like that. No idea what she'd say now, seeing another one too, eh?"

The Lieutenant was very likable, and Smith immediately warmed to him.

"Been across the old world?" he asked. The prospect of new lands he'd not seen always interested him.

"We have been. Posted across the Empire, see. Fought in Afghanistan, and that's a nasty place. Yes b'y it's rough out there. Mountain passes, dust as deep as your boot and sharpshooters taking shots at you from all over. Learned a lot there."

Something about the way the Lieutenant was walking made Smith take notice. He was young and light-hearted, but he didn't have the air of being naïve. Not at all.

"Well I won't lie to you, Lieutenant, I was expecting a colder welcome. I'm glad I didn't find it."

Flashing a smile again, the young man stopped, pointing to the front door of the hotel they'd just arrived at, "Well, call me Jimmy."

"I'm Smith. And thank you."

Jimmy nodded and grinned, then bobbed his head towards the staircase, "The Major's upstairs on the left, corner room."

Smith looked up and saw the window to that room open, and a man with field glasses looking out through it. It'd be interesting to see what this Major was like.

Waller heard the clunk and chink of boots and spurs coming down the hall behind him, and he lowered his glasses. He'd learned to recognize that sound while the b'ys had been waiting in Calgary, though he hadn't heard it much here in the new world so far.

Looking down at the street, he saw that Devlin was back, and as the Lieutenant noticed that Waller had seen him, he called up, "Just had a cowboy arrive from the east, says he's seen the horde coming. He's on his way up the stairs to see you."

Waller nodded, "Thank you, Jimmy. Get that food sorted out?"

"The companies are eating, I'm about to find something for my b'ys. You want anything, sir?"

Waller smiled, "If you can find cod I'll make you a Captain. Other than that, anything edible."

Grinning, Devlin offered an easy salute, "On it, sir!"

Chuckling to himself, Waller let his glasses hang from their strap against his chest, then turned. The cowboy was standing in the doorway, looking awkwardly at the women. Waller studied the man for a second — he clearly hadn't expected to walk into the room to find three women sitting on the bed and chairs, two of them wearing black robes.

To Waller the man looked weathered. Six feet tall and lean in build, he appeared rather like one would expect a man of this new world west to look — good natured, but with an ability to take care of himself in a spot of bother. He'd probably lived all of his life on this land, and likely knew his way around it very well. The six-shooter at his hip, which Devlin evidently believed he could be trusted to keep, spoke volumes about him — it was a Colt New Service revolver, not one of the new 1911 pistols with the magazines. This was a frontier man, a real cowboy.

And an American.

Smith managed to get over his surprise at the presence of the women in the room — he hadn't seen a female in weeks, let alone three very fine women, two with mysterious dress. When he realized the Major was already looking at him, he looked back. The officer was a youngish man, perhaps twenty-five years old to Smith's thirty. Where most of the soldiers Smith had seen were five foot eight or shorter, this man was six-feet tall, with a similar build to Smith's own, though the officer had a different, more precise way of standing and carrying himself.

But like Jimmy the Lieutenant, this man had none of the arrogance Smith had been expecting, and he had the look of a man who could look after himself if the situation warranted it.

"I'm Major Waller," he extended his hand, and Smith looked at it for a second in surprise before taking it.

"Smith. I'm a drifter down south of the border, but I promised a man I'd come warn you that about 10,000 savages are running up this way," Smith got direct to the point again — no reason to waste time when that many beasts were afoot.

Waller smiled, appreciating the directness, "Mister Smith, you have no idea how happy I am to get a straight assessment of things. I've been hearing nothing but half-answers all day. How far off would you think the savages are?"

Smith turned his head a little as he looked at the Major, "About an hour, maybe two. They're fast on foot, but over distance a horse lasts longer."

"Excellent, that means there's time for the men to eat. Has someone offered you food?" Waller nodded as his mind started to unravel the tactical implications of the report.

"I've been offered, and I'd surely accept a meal. Suppose I won't be riding out for a while either," Smith nodded.

"No, probably a quick way to get eaten, from what I've heard," Waller nodded, then looked to the ladies — who all seemed to be staring at Smith. "Ladies, forgive my manners. Would you like some food? I'll have Lieutenant Devlin find a proper place for you to eat, of course."

Before any of them could respond, he looked back to Smith, "Now Mister Smith, we should talk away from the ladies, I'll need to know some more gruesome details."

Smith nodded, and the two men walked out of the room.

As they left, Emma Lee glanced at Kara Lynne, "That man's been drifting a while."

Kara Lynne was smiling, "I think you're right."

Emma Lee frowned, "And a few hours ago you were telling *me* to focus!"

CHAPTER IX

"Well, I can guarantee your safety as long as you're with us, Mister Smith," Waller said as they emerged onto the street. The Major had his hands linked behind his back, Smith's were at his sides.

"I tend to guarantee my own safety, sir," Smith said sedately, and smiling, Waller looked him over.

"Yes, I expect you do. So 10,000, that's your best estimate?"

Smith nodded, "And the cavalryman from Fort Burt who cabled the warning to you showed up at Vista City too late to reinforce them. Town was overrun, and his boys wouldn't ride away. Half of them charged in, he and the rest had to follow. Couldn't let them die alone."

Waller's smile faded as he listened, "Of course I can understand. Poor discipline among the men, though."

"Well, take this as the word of a drifter, Major, but your men don't seem too over-formal," Smith said cautiously, and Waller's smile returned.

"We're Newfoundlanders, Mister Smith. Where we come from, the land and the sea are our constant foe. We learn that you don't need to be formal to be disciplined. Or to do the right thing," Waller said quietly, coming to a stop. "In Afghanistan, we had that belief put to the test. Messy place, a lot of blood there. But we're here now, and I don't think the savages will trouble us too much today."

Smith had heard claims like that before, though he had to admit he'd never heard them from a man quite like this Major. His accent was not nearly so pronounced as Jimmy's but it was there. That was one difference. There was also a level of confidence in this soldier, not of brash glory-hunting, but of quiet certainty.

That sort of modest confidence was something Smith could relate to, if it was warranted.

"You're sure about that?"

Waller smiled again, "I'm never *sure*, Mister Smith. Any commander who meets the enemy convinced he's going to win will probably get himself killed. But we have 600 rifles, four Lewis guns and two Vickers machine guns pointing south, so I take that as some comfort."

Smith didn't know any of those guns — he knew names like Colt and Winchester, Springfield and Marlin. But it did sound impressive.

"Well, since I'm here I can make it 601 rifles," he offered.

Waller laughed out loud, "Mister Smith I like you. And I'd be quite happy if you'd stay with me and Lieutenant Devlin, then. We're the flying platoon, we'll plug the gaps if anything gets through."

Seemed fine to Smith, "Sounds like a plan to me."

"Good. Now let's find some food. And find Lieutenant Devlin. I need to make sure he waits on those ladies... not that I think he'll need coaxing."

Waller and Smith ate quickly at a small diner down the street from the hotel. It wasn't fancy, just good, plain food and Smith was satisfied with it. Waller himself barely noticed what he was chewing, but instead kept checking his watch. The savages were closing in, based on Smith's appraisal, and he had no intention of being at dinner when they arrived.

When the food was finished, Waller stood, "We should go back to that room, it's the best vantage point in town."

Smith nodded, "I'll go find my rifle, then I'll join you there."

"Very good," Waller gave another single nod, and the two men went their separate ways.

Waller headed to the hotel, noticing that the section posted on the street was quickly eating as he arrived. He entered and made his way up the stairs and back to the room, where Devlin was pouring tea for the ladies.

"Sorry again that it isn't fancier, ladies," Devlin was saying, and then as Waller walked in he nodded. "Everyone's been fed, sir. We're ready."

With a smile, Waller looked out the window, "Never doubted your ability to distribute food, Jimmy."

"That's sure enough," Devlin chuckled, making eye contact with Annie as he poured her a cup of tea.

"Are you ladies comfortable enough here? We can try to find another room for you, if you'd like some privacy," Waller was looking out at the horizon again, and Emma Lee shook her head.

"We're quite alright, Major. We'd like to be able to see what's coming, as well," she said softly, and Waller turned back and nodded.

"Of course."

They waited for long minutes, the ladies sipping their tea. Only their arms appeared from beneath their robes, offering no hint of what lay beneath, and Waller forced himself not to be distracted by that. He had no business becoming curious about what lay under ladies' cloaks... but in spite of his best efforts, his mind was still sidling back to that question...

It wasn't for him to wonder such things.

Smith hadn't returned after twenty minutes, and Waller was beginning to wonder if the drifter had decided to drift on. He didn't have a chance to think too much about that possibility, though, because the sound of rifle shots came from the ridge south of town. Waller's field glasses came up to his eyes instantly, and he swept the horizon yet again. The men on horses who'd been posted atop the ridge were riding hard down towards the town.

"Jimmy, I believe the party's about to begin."

Putting the teapot down on another small table, Lieutenant Devlin smiled at the ladies, "Pardon me, please, ladies."

He came to stand next to Waller, and as he did, a surge of movement appeared on top of the ridge. The riders wisely didn't look over their shoulders, instead making for the city gates to the west of the train station, where they could gain entry to the palisades.

"Seems Captain Benton's confidence was misplaced," Devlin observed, and lowering his glasses, Waller nodded.

"Have Private King and Private Connolly ready to run orders for me, will you Jimmy?"

Devlin nodded, then leaned out the window, "David, Ryan, you're on runner duty. David to the station, Ryan to the western wall. Clear?"

"Thanks for the exercise right after supper, sir," Private King snorted a laugh and started dropping some of his kit on the side of the road. He'd run with only rifle and ammunition — two things no man in this town should be without right now.

Waller raised his glasses to his eyes again. The estimate of 10,000 could not be far off — the savages were pouring over that ridge in numbers no Imperial officer could have seen since Omdurman.

"Why aren't the Vickers firing?" Waller asked the question quietly, and Devlin frowned as he did. Those machine guns were easily capable of firing at a mile's range.

"I'll find out, sir, just excuse me a minute," Devlin left the room, heading for the other end of the hotel, where an open window led to a second floor platform and a ladder that went to the roof.

When he neared the top, Captain Benton was standing still, looking through his glasses, the Vickers gun next to him silent.

"Wait for it…" Benton was saying.

Climbing up, Devlin crossed the roof quickly, surprising some Canadian Rifles who hadn't seen him arrive, "Begging your pardon, Captain, but Major Waller would like to know why you're not firing. Range is a mile, isn't it?"

Captain Benton lowered his glasses, "Range is a mile, but they'll be more effective at 500 yards."

"Yes, but at 500 yards the more of them there are, the worse it will be, or is Major Waller wrong to think that, sir?" Devlin's tone was bordering on insubordinate, and it drew Benton's stern gaze.

"If the Major thinks so. Open fire."

The roof above Waller rumbled as the Vickers let loose, and on that signal the Vickers on the roof of the train station cut out as well. The savages were tiny, tiny targets at this distance, but they were advancing in a dense horde, so once the machine guns found the range, the fire started to tell. Machine guns were absolutely devastating, and hundreds of the savages began to fall.

The rest of the creatures continued to charge, with startling speed.

Over short distances, Smith had told him, the savages could outrun horses. A mile perhaps qualified as a short distance, because these beasts were bolting. Evidently a day's running did not slow them down.

"Runners!" Waller looked down through the open window. "Our b'ys to open immediately!"

Privates King and Connolly raced away, and Waller felt Devlin return to his side, "Good job getting the guns going. I get the sense we're not wasting our ammunition."

"Hmm?" Emma Lee frowned and looked at him, just as Waller looked to his left, discovering that it was she, not Devlin, who'd turned up.

"Oh very sorry… I thought you were Devlin…"

She smiled, "Well, I suppose you couldn't see me with those glasses at your eyes. I won't be insulted."

"I should hope not!" Waller said quickly, then looked back out at the approaching horde. It seemed the Canadian Rifles were holding their fire, Vickers guns aside — there was no rumble of Short, Magazine, Lee-Enfield rifle fire from the houses in which they'd taken up station, behind the palisade.

The town was small enough, though, that the runners didn't need long to reach the two Newfoundland companies, and a great thunder of .303 fire began.

The savages continued to surge.

CHAPTER X

Smith had found his horse and recovered his 1892 Winchester from its scabbard when the shooting from the machine guns began. He wasn't too familiar with machine guns, so he took a moment to listen to the sawing sound of their rapid fire before climbing the stairs to the station platform.

His horse had been tied to a post behind the station, and now that the lead was flying it didn't seem right to walk away from it. To be honest, he was curious to see how these Newfoundlanders would fare. And he wasn't adverse to being near his horse in case they fared badly.

He didn't have a mind to be eaten alive, even if the folk here were friendly. He'd do his piece to help protect this town, but if it looked like his number was about to come up, he wasn't going to lie down for it. Wasn't his way.

Climbing the stairs to the platform with his Winchester in hand, Smith stopped next to the Captain who'd greeted him when he first arrived. The man glanced at him, looked away, then glanced back, "Oh. Good day again, sir. Don't believe I got your name."

"Smith."

"Captain George Tucker, this is 'C' Company. Can we do something for you?" Tucker asked pleasantly, and Smith shook his head once.

"No sir, just here to lend a hand."

Tucker smiled, looked at the Sergeant who was standing nearby, and they both shared a smirk. Smith looked them both over slowly, trying to decide if there was hostility in that, but then the Captain walked over to him and patted him on the back.

"Any man who can walk onto a platform that's defended by 150 infantry and say he's going to lend *them* a hand has the right attitude, if you ask me,"

Tucker laughed. "Call me George, by the way. You just go by Smith?"

"I do," Smith nodded.

"Good man... pardon me a minute..." Tucker looked past Smith as Private King sprinted up to the platform.

"Major orders we open fire!"

Tucker nodded, "Very good. Number one platoon, number three platoon, rapid fire! Fire at will!"

Had Tucker wished it, he could have begun volley fire by platoon, or restricted the number of rounds fired by his men — ten rounds rapid — but that would have made no sense under the circumstances. With 10,000 savages to kill, it was time for a 'mad minute' — or many such minutes — when the men just kept firing, as fast as they could.

The air was filled with rifle shots, and Smith looked up onto the roof of the station, then over to the tops of the train cars where the men lying in that position were firing, working the bolts on their snub-nosed rifles faster than he'd seen the bolts on any American rifles ever worked.

Tucker smiled at him again, "Mister Smith, we hopefully won't be needing your help, but if you'd stand by here with me and this platoon, we're the flying platoon. If the savages come over that train and push number one platoon back, we'll give them the bayonet."

Smith nodded. Seemed these Newfoundlanders were fond of their 'flying' reserves, and that implied to Smith that the concept must work. Waller had one, Tucker another.

He stood on the platform and watched the Newfoundlanders do their shooting.

"My God look at that carnage," Lieutenant Devlin said quietly, watching as waves of the savages were annihilated by the fire of the riflemen and the Vickers guns. "That's what they say it was like in France, between the Germans and the French, ain't it?"

Waller nodded, "Thousands of men charging machine guns and rifle fire, dying to a man. Rather glad the Royal Newfoundland Regiment didn't have to try it, eh Jimmy? We'd probably all have been killed."

"Yes sir. Yes indeed," Devlin shook his head slowly, then forced his thoughts around. "But today, at least, it's working for us."

"It is at that," Waller nodded, sweeping the land beyond the south palisade with his field glasses.

It had only been a couple of minutes since the savages had appeared, but they were already nearing the wall… and they were still quite numerous. Even if the rifle fire had killed half, which it soon would have, the rest were pressing forward in such a wave that the thin palisade might not hold the weight.

Dammit, why weren't the Canadian Rifles firing yet? The range was 500 yards and quickly closing. Under normal circumstances, firing over 300 yards was not terribly effective, but when there was a wall of bodies coming, it was nearly impossible to miss…

Privates King and Connolly returned to the street below the window in that moment, and leaning out, Waller bellowed, "King, get to that line of houses in front of the palisade and order the Canadian Rifles to open fire immediately. Connolly, get to Captain Kearsey and tell him to have his reserve platoons ready to fix bayonets and defend the palisade."

Both men were breathing heavily, but neither complained. They raced away again, and Waller looked at Devlin, "I wish we had the whole battalion staff here just now. This improvised communication could kill us."

Devlin smiled, "I don't think it's the absence of the Mister Sturgis and the Quartermaster that's going to kill us, sir."

As he said that, he bobbed his head out the window towards the savages, and Waller had to nod, "True enough, Jimmy. True enough."

Tucker was pacing the platform behind the train cars, listening as his Lieutenants and Sergeants barked reminders to the men: "Check your range!"

"Keep up your fire!"

"Steady b'ys!"

"Three hundred yards now!"

At 300 yards their rifles would become a good deal more devastating, and more of the savages would fall, but there were so many...

Smith had to admit he was impressed by the calm. The flying platoon, as Tucker called it, was standing stoically around him, the butts of their rifles on the platform and their eyes front. They weren't even looking around at the noise, which even Smith could not have resisted doing. That was either strong discipline, or maybe fear. He could understand fear more than discipline, but then he figured he didn't have to understand, he could just watch.

And speaking of watching, he had a feeling the savages were up to more than just the obvious. The way he'd rode in had been open enough, and if only 100 of the creatures tried to come through that wood and up that rail bed, it could be trouble.

"George," Smith approached the pacing Captain, and the man stopped to listen, "I think you should watch that left side, where I rode in. Some of them may try to enter that way, through the trees."

Tucker frowned, turned to look in that direction, and saw nothing. Smith watched him look, and figured that the man wasn't going to believe him.

"Lieutenant Quilty, two sections in line on the end of the platform, eyes skinned for those woods," the Captain barked past Smith, addressing one of the younger officers.

Orders were given, and twenty-five men clomped over to the end of the platform and formed a line two deep, the front men kneeling down.

Smith wasn't the sort to start feeling too pleased with himself, but he did appreciate that the Newfoundlanders were heeding his advice.

"Got a feeling, Smith?" Tucker asked, leaning closer, and the drifter gave a nod.

"Been out here a long time, you get to learn the ways of the savages."

Tucker nodded, "And we learned the hard way to listen to those who know the ground. Be they Indian Army officers, or drifters."

The Captain returned to his pacing, and Smith decided to walk down the platform to stand next to the line of men. As he got there, one of them, a Sergeant, gave him a solid nod, which he returned. Their young Lieutenant Quilty was on the other end of the line.

They waited while the rifle fire continued.

"There they are... looks like Freddie's leading them himself," Devlin pointed towards the closest street to the palisade, and Waller adjusted the vector of his glasses and nodded. Captain Kearsey's men were in position to watch the backs of the Canadian Rifles in the houses along the wall.

"Good man. Alright Jimmy, get down to your platoon, be ready to move if I yell, but leave me a section."

"Yes sir," Devlin nodded quickly, turned, smiled at the ladies, and then left, putting on his hat as he did so.

Waller's glasses swept the palisade now — the man-like beasts were at 300 yards and that left little more time to watch. Soon they'd be under the protection of those palisades — the defensive arrangements here left no loopholes for firing through, and had no turrets to allow defenders to fire at savages as they piled up against the base of the long, straight wall.

Tucker would have seen that too, and positioned his men accordingly... the only place along the entire line where the defenders had the angle to shoot at savages piling up under the wall was on the roof of that train...

Waller stopped thinking for a moment, because before his eyes the savages seemed to all shift left — to the right from their own perspective — and head for the station. Over 1,000 at least, all heading there. Had they seen the weak point?

Devlin had just emerged onto the street, so Waller called down to him, "They may need you at the station, Jimmy. I'll send a runner if I need you elsewhere!"

Saluting quickly, Devlin barked orders and with three of his four sections, began a run to the station.

Smith saw them coming at the same time Lieutenant Quilty did.

"Rapid fire! Fire at will!" the young officer barked immediately as the savages began breaking from the woods. "Sergeant Kinley, the rest of the platoon immediately!"

While the last two reserve sections of the platoon raced up to extend the soldiers' line, Smith raised his Winchester to his shoulder and started choosing savages. Perhaps a dozen came out first, but the fast and very good shooting of the Newfoundlanders stopped them dead. More came, though — hundreds more. It was like a wave of beasts, more than Smith had ever seen, coming straight at him.

He squeezed the trigger of his rifle, then levered the next round into the chamber and fired again, and again. The savages rushed forward, coming for the platform, seeing the stairs that would lead them up onto it.

Smith kept shooting, and in half a minute his ten rounds were gone. The savages were 200 yards away and climbing over their dead to get at him. He started pulling .45 caliber bullets out of his belt and sliding them into the loading gate of his Winchester, then turned to look for Tucker. They'd need more men in a minute. Because more savages were coming out of the trees.

As Smith turned, a man landed at his feet. He stopped and looked down in genuine surprise until he realized the man hadn't fallen, he'd dropped prone, and he had a monster of a gun in front of him on a bipod, with a round drum of bullets sitting on top. Another man carrying extra drums dropped next to him.

The soldier squeezed his trigger, and Smith backed up as the small machine gun started roaring away, spraying the horde as it came for the platform.

His rifle reloaded, he turned and started shooting again.

He decided as he shot another savage that he'd never in his life been surrounded by so much firepower.

The station was definitely receiving the worst of it. It was as though they could smell the train, smell the way in. Waller watched through his field glasses as Devlin bounded up the stairs onto the platform, revolver in hand, and waved his men towards the far end of the station, which Waller couldn't see.

They must have been coming down the rail bed too. Dammit, all his men were committed to the south side of this town, now. If the savages flanked too wide, he'd be finished.

Turning his glasses back to the south wall, he saw the first beasts climbing up onto the palisades, and being thrown off by the fire of the Canadian Rifles from the houses. Two platoons of Kearsey's company were divided into sections, and had lined up in the intersections between the houses to fill the gaps. Presumably Kearsey could quickly redeploy to the north or east if it was needed.

At least the numbers of savages seemed to be dwindling. Looking back up to the fields beyond the town, the grasslands seemed to be carpeted with bodies. They looked so very human, like white men who'd gone native and naked, and yet their speed and power made it clear they could not be of the same species as Waller and the Newfoundlanders.

The sounds of fighting from the station grew louder, and Waller turned his glasses back there. He couldn't see the far end of the platform as it was eclipsed from this angle by the station building. Devlin would see to it...

"Fix bayonets!" Devlin barked to his men as he reached the end of the platform, discovering savages just yards away from him. He shot two with his Webley revolver, and waved his men forward. "Form a secondary line ten yards back! Quilty, get ready to displace!"

Smith watched the arrival of reinforcements and backed towards them, though he didn't stop shooting until his rifle was dry again. They weren't being overrun by the savages yet, but he figured that wouldn't take long if the men he'd been standing with ran out of ammunition.

They'd only been carrying 150 rounds each, and they'd been firing hard for minutes.

"Platoon withdraw behind secondary lines! Sergeant Butler, send two men for a case of ammunition!" Quilty roared the order, and as he did, his Lewis machine gun crew got to their feet and fled back to drop next to Devlin, while the men withdrew in good order.

As Smith came to stand next to the pleasant young Jimmy, the Newfoundlander was ordering his men to form a line two deep, and for the front rank to kneel again. This worked for them, and Smith had to say the hundreds of dead savages beyond the platform proved its worth.

"Rapid fire at will!" Devlin barked, and as the first savages bounded up onto the platform, the line erupted.

This time, Smith realized, they were too close. The first savages hurled themselves at the line of men, and as they were only twenty yards away, they couldn't all be shot down.

"Hold them with bayonets!" Devlin roared, and behind him Smith heard the other Lieutenant rally his men.

"Fix bayonets! Charge bayonets!"

The Newfoundlanders began to yell and roar to get their spirit up, and then as Devlin's line collided with the savages, eighty men lunged forward with knives longer than Smith's own bowie locked onto the front of their rifles.

Smith drew his six-shooter and started blasting.

CHAPTER XI

The palisades to the south and the west were holding, with Kearsey's men shooting savages as they tried to climb over. These beasts might have unnatural speed and strength, but they were just as susceptible to a .303 as the next creature. That was somewhat comforting to Waller as he swept his glasses across the walls, then back to the station. Things seemed to be getting chaotic on the nearer side of the platform... they must have been hit hard. Men on the roof of the train were looking east and shooting...

"Sir! Sir!" the Sergeant commanding the section in the street below called up to Waller, and as he lowered his glasses and looked down, the man pointed east. "A few over the wall, sir, coming straight for us."

Waller leaned forward out the window, looked left and saw that a dozen savages had leapt over the wall and were racing past the horses and mules tied up behind the station, coming straight down the street towards the hotel.

The people of the town, boarded up in their homes, took notice; some enterprising men leaned out of their second floor windows with rifles and shotguns and fired at the creatures, and a few went down.

Another dozen leapt over the wall, and Waller silently cursed himself. He should have tried to keep more than just Devlin back here as a reserve — another platoon at least.

Waller looked down to the Sergeant, "Form a line and let them have it, I'm coming down."

The Sergeant nodded and started barking orders immediately, and the section of a dozen men lined up in a single rank across the street. Each man dropped to one knee and began rapid fire at the savages just a few hundred yards away.

Waller leaned back in, laid his field glasses on the table, and turned to the ladies, "Please stay in here, ladies. Close the door behind me and bar it with a chair."

Before Emma Lee or her companions could respond, Waller was walking quickly out of the room, closing the door and rushing down the corridor and past the stairs.

Stepping out through the window on the corridor's far end, he found the ladder to the roof and climbed up until he could see a few officers and men of the Canadian Rifles, "You men, we have savages in the street below, come lend a hand!"

He didn't wait for an answer, just jumped down to the platform and then climbed back in the window. Crossing the corridor, he quickly descended the stairs and exited onto the street as the savages got to within 100 yards.

"Dammit, fix bayonets!" he ordered, leveling his Webley revolver and firing three times. The men drew and fixed their sword bayonets with practiced ease, and then continued firing.

At least thirty of the beasts had come over the fence, and now fifteen of them were within range of a good charge. Without thinking too much about it, Waller advanced on the beast men, leveled his revolver again, and shot two with his last three bullets.

Backing away quickly, he cracked his revolver open and started sliding new rounds into the cylinder, while his men emptied their magazines. No time to reload.

"On your feet and charge them!" Waller ordered, and with the discipline that came of having faced Pathan tribesmen in the Afghan mountains, the b'ys did as they were told.

By this time, the shooting had done its work, and only eight of the creatures came close. With four bullets inserted into his revolver, Waller snapped it shut, then lined up a savage who was coming for him and shot it in the chest. It was a gruesome wound from the heavy pistol round, and a fountain of red blood spurted as the savage dropped.

With a roar, the Sergeant led the section into the charge, and though bayonets were rarely used anymore, the Newfoundlanders demonstrated that they remembered their drill.

The savages slammed into them, one getting past the bayonet stabbed in his direction and knocking its wielder flat on his back. A Lance Corporal rushed to the fallen soldier's aid, sticking the savage in the side and heaving the creature off the Private.

Sergeant Halloran, the veteran Sergeant commanding this section, lunged with proper flair, impaling a savage and recovering his bayonet in a flash. The savage staggered backward, then stumbled at him, but the big man was unworried and bashed the creature in the nose with the butt of his rifle.

Canadian Rifles began emerging from the hotel door, hurriedly fixing their bayonets. They clumped up behind Waller, their Sergeant evidently not having come with them. Waller realized they had arrived, "Get in there, men!"

That was order enough and the Canadians rushed forward, but the savages were already falling. One of the RNR Privates had a broken nose from a powerful blow that a savage had thrown, but the section had stood its ground well.

"You Canadians, get up to that palisade behind the train station, don't let any more of the bastards over!" Waller demanded. "Sergeant Halloran, see to the men, and stay here. I'm going back up."

Waller holstered his revolver and looked up the street towards the mountains again, just to be certain no more savages were over the wall. Satisfied, he hurried back inside and bounded up the stairs.

A hundred savages had to be on the platform, and Smith had emptied his Colt and quickly reloaded twice. It was getting intense, so this might be his last reload — he'd be down to just his bowie. Jimmy Devlin was standing close to him with his black revolver, which shot with a dull thud, and seemed to kill the savages as well as any Colt.

The Lieutenant caught Smith's gaze and smiled, but then the smile immediately disappeared as he bellowed at his men, "Come on b'ys, these bastards aren't so bad!"

Some of the men cheered, most simply grunted, and they fought savagely with their rifles and long, knife-like bayonets. The savages were faced by a hedge of sharp steel, and even when they leapt over it and landed on some of the Newfoundlanders, pounding away at the poor soldiers with inhuman ferocity, other Newfoundlanders shot or stuck them off.

Though Smith would never have expected it, the soldiers were pushing them back off the platform. Or, to be more accurate, the Newfoundlanders were killing them and pushing their carcasses off the platform.

Smith noticed something he reckoned was odd, though. The savages were coming only so far along the platform, and then they were stopping and attacking the train. One of the cars, the third one, seemed to have their interest. By now the ones who'd come straight across the grasslands were pounding on the sides of the train, but the men up on the train roof were firing with a fury, and the men on the roof of the station were shooting hard enough to keep the savages from getting onto the platform from that side.

But Smith couldn't figure out the interest in that third car. It was empty, were they smelling something the people riding in that car had been carrying?

There was one way Smith would be able to tell, so he moved fast behind Devlin and over to the train, shooting a savage as it tried to pry the door. He looked in the window, saw it was a fancy looking passenger cabin, but couldn't see anything but three suitcases in there. Nothing to suggest who had been in that car.

Wasn't the proper time to ask one of the Newfoundlanders that, either. They were too preoccupied — as was he.

"Drive them back, come on men!" Tucker was on the other side of the platform, and he stretched his arm out and fired his revolver.

The soldiers followed his instruction, and Smith stayed back and watched them. Emptying his last chamber, he decided he did have breathing room for another reload, so he swung out his Colt's cylinder and started sliding in fresh cartridges from his belt.

Devlin cracked his pistol open and started doing the same, but continued to advance beside his men, "Come on b'ys, we have them now!"

The men drove right to the end of the platform, stopping there and cheering as they saw no more savages coming from the woods. They were standing on a carpet of dead, though, and Smith saw the cheer wasn't too energetic on account of the smell and the sight.

"Devlin, your b'ys hold that end!" Tucker ordered quickly, reloading his own pistol. "Quilty, reform the flying platoon, quickly!"

There were still hundreds of savages on the other side of the train, and now some of them were starting to crawl under the third car, all of them in a frenzy to get in.

Smith fired twice, and two more stopped trying, but the rest kept coming. Tucker ordered the Lewis machine gun that had been firing east to shoot at these ones now, and the Newfoundlanders left standing from Quilty's platoon — about thirty-five of the fifty men — went back to standing on the platform, pushing bodies of savages out of the way to keep their ranks.

The wounded struggled off the platform and stumbled toward the hotel, or simply bandaged themselves up and came back. Smith had to give these soldiers credit: they were doing this better than any US Cavalry he'd ever seen in the new world. He wouldn't have expected they had a real chance of getting out of this, but they did.

Smith was impressed. And he was not an easy man to impress.

Eventually these men, and the Canadian Rifles who garrisoned the town, finished off the attack. The worst was over by far. Smith was left to wonder at the strange behavior of the savages, as he went to check on his horse.

CHAPTER XII

Wounded Newfoundlanders were sitting on the porch of the hotel, and Waller looked them over as he walked by. A dozen men were out here, lightly injured, and a dozen more were inside, suffering from various injuries that made the town's doctor insist he had to see them inside.

None were dead. That much was a sharp but welcome surprise to Waller. The ferocity of the attack had been great, but they'd been able to keep enough of the beasts back to avoid serious injuries among themselves and the townspeople.

It had all been very, very odd. While the savages had done great damage before, a stampede of this size had apparently not been seen in a little over twelve years. Much smaller hordes of dozens and hundreds could be dealt with, and the odd thousand-strong attack, according to the now-talkative Benton, had been known to ravage a city. But this strength was highly unusual... and yet it had fallen before half a battalion of riflemen.

Even fortified as Treeline City was, Waller had expected worse.

Though, as his nan would again remind him, he should never look a gift horse in the mouth.

And perhaps this did make some sort of sense. In the American west, settlers had circled their wagons when attacked, as the cover could be decisive. In South Africa, the Boers had done much the same, forming laagers to resist the mighty Zulu *impis*. Waller had read of these things — and read of how, at Isandlwana in 1879, 1,400 men of a British line regiment, encamped in open territory, were overrun by 20,000 Zulus, precisely because they had no such protection.

That might be it, then. And of course, if it was — if the protection of walls was what had allowed Waller's men to survive today — then his march into the grasslands looked all the more ominous.

There were no walls in those fields.

"All men accounted for, sir. Many bangs and bruises, all the broken bones are on the porch," Devlin appeared next to Waller and saluted.

Nodding, Waller waved the Lieutenant to follow him in a walk towards the train station, "How's the morale?"

"Very good, sir. As you'd expect. The b'ys are saying a march into the grass will be nothing, we saw all the buggers today and slaughtered the lot of them," Devlin smiled, but as he recognized Waller's somber expression, he let the smile fade. "I'm discouraging that kind of talk, sir."

Waller nodded, "Yes. It's going to be different out there than it was here. But you were in the thick of it more than I was, Jimmy. What do you think of these savages?"

Devlin frowned and took a deep breath, "They look like men, sir. But no man anywhere could move that fast or hit that hard. Makes them dangerous. They're built like us but they're faster, and if it's true they're cannibals, and they got no qualms with eating the women and children too, that's a scary thought."

"Yes, good job we were here to help. Meet them with lead, they aren't so powerful. But if it'd just been settlers…" Waller made that observation and then let his voice trail off.

"Makes you wonder why anyone would come out here," Devlin said. "Promise of a fortune must be pretty powerful among some people, eh?"

Waller nodded again, "Suppose so. Is that Smith up there?"

The Major had spotted the drifter sitting on a step next to his horse a few hundred yards up the street, and Devlin nodded, "It is, sir. Man's a hell of a shooter."

"I'd be surprised if he wasn't. If a man's been living on his own in this place for a decade, he'd have to be quite handy with a gun. I'll go talk to him. You check our supplies and let me know if we need anything. After this, I don't want us back on that train short of anything we could shoot or stab with."

Devlin smiled again at the last remark and saluted, "Yes sir!"

Off he ran, and Waller made his way up the dusty street, watching men from the Canadian Rifles removing savage bodies from the ground as he walked past. Smith didn't seem to notice him. Instead, the American was petting a dog, his Winchester on his lap, probably just having been cleaned.

"Major," Smith nodded in Waller's direction, still not having looked at him, and Waller smiled. Of course the drifter had seen him coming.

"Mister Smith," Waller nodded back, then came close enough to lean down and pet the dog as well.

"Your men did some fine shooting today. I have to say I didn't expect to be sitting here just now," Smith looked up.

"I'm sure you'd have escaped if things had gone bad," Waller observed, still petting the dog.

Smith nodded, "But then I wouldn't have been sitting here."

Waller laughed, "Good point. What'd you think of the savages, though, Smith? Is that what we should expect from them on the grasslands?"

Narrowing his eyes, Smith looked up at Waller, "You're going onto the grasslands?"

"Those ladies you met, our orders are to take them out there to find something. They haven't told me what, so I'm going out there essentially blind. But if you could give us a better idea of what to expect…"

"I've never been far out into the grasslands. They say around here that those who've gone out too far don't come back," Smith said quietly.

Waller's face had turned grim, "I can imagine. So what's your opinion of the savages? Was what we saw today a good indication of what you'd expect from them out there?"

It was a reasonable question, and a responsible one. Smith could read Waller well enough to see that the man was concerned about what his soldiers were going to be facing. If there were no walls, no platforms or no trains… if it were just them, some open land, and a horde, would they get by so well as they had today?

Well, he couldn't answer that. He'd never seen men like these New-foundlanders stand up to savages in open country, though he reckoned they'd handle it better than some he *had* seen. Even so, to answer the question that had been asked...

"No, no these savages seemed to have something more particular in mind than just eating, which is irregular, at least to me," Smith shook his head.

Waller frowned slightly, "Could you explain that a little more?"

Smith nodded, then reached up and rubbed his mare's nose, "Your mules and my horse were between you and those savages that came over the wall."

"And?" Waller looked from the horse to the mules, then back to Smith. "They seem fine..."

"A savage acting normally would have stopped to tear them up, not run down a street with no food on it," Smith said simply.

Waller continued to frown, looking at the wall the savages had climbed, and its proximity to the posts where the animals were tied up.

"I'm happy they didn't, don't get me wrong. But it's not usual. Same with the train. They seemed awful interested in that third car on the train. Don't know if that means anything."

It did mean something — the connection was as obvious as it was baffling.

"The ladies you met in the hotel, they rode out here in that car. And if these savages came over the fence and headed straight for the hotel..." Waller turned and looked back down the street. "That's... that's most unlikely."

"The women?" Smith stood up, looking down to the hotel as well. "Now that makes no sense. Well, unless your women are hiding something. But I don't know what could make savages that single-minded."

Waller nodded, glancing at Smith, "Well, I can try to find out, but so far whatever they're doing out here they've kept secret from me. Explicitly so, despite my questions. And I can't tell a Lady to do as I say... my orders are to take them where they want to go."

Smith nodded, "I never have gotten a woman to tell me something she didn't want to own to."

"I imagine few men have," Waller agreed. "And I doubt I'll find out more, until they decide to tell me. For now I just want to make sure my men are as well prepared as possible. I have no ambition to die out here, Mister Smith."

Smith nodded, "I can agree with that."

The two men were silent for a moment, and Waller then turned back to Smith, "Yes, you don't seem like a man to throw his life away. So I will ask this question, but I'll take no offense if you say no. Would you ride with us up to Long Prairie — to the last stop on our rail line? It's from there we're marching out. I'd be most obliged for your advice."

Smith looked at the Major, and considered the question. Waller hadn't asked him to ride into the grasslands with them, knowing that was asking too much. But if he was looking for expertise that Smith had, it wouldn't be decent to send him out west without sharing what he could.

"Got room on the train for my horse?"

Waller smiled, "Plenty. Thank you Mister Smith."

They shook hands.

CHAPTER XIII

Captain Tucker and Captain Kearsey were getting the men back on the train when Waller returned to the hotel. Night was falling and it seemed prudent to get moving before any more savages assembled to make trouble further along the rail line. The ladies, in the interim, had stayed in the hotel, away from prying eyes and any further danger. It was about time, though, that Waller renewed his questions to them. He doubted he'd get answers, but he was obliged to try.

Going up the stairs and down the corridor to the same room in which they'd spent the evening, Waller came to a stop, then knocked and leaned in, "Pardon me, ladies. We're preparing to move again. Want to take advantage of the lull."

Emma Lee was sitting on the bed next to Kara Lynne, while Annie the maid slept quietly in a chair in the corner. She awoke at the knock and looked up somewhat surprised, "Oh I'm so sorry... I shouldn't have... I..."

"No need to worry," Kara Lynne stopped her apologies. "Come along now, though, we should get walking. We'll sleep on the train."

Emma yawned as she stood up, the cape still shrouding her. Waller stepped back from the door to allow the ladies to exit, and then followed them down to the street, where they all walked together in a loose group, with Annie trailing furthest back.

"They've cleared away most of the mess," Waller observed. He walked with his hands linked behind his back, and looked at Emma, walking next to him. "Something odd, though, Emma. They seemed most interested in two things, in all of this town."

Frowning, Emma returned his gaze, "What things? I expect by you telling me, that I have something to do with them."

Waller smiled, "You may. That was going to be my next question. They desperately wanted your train car. And they ran past some perfectly good livestock to get to the hotel. So we're naturally wondering if they were here for you."

Emma's answer was a very pretty smile, which Waller expected was meant to distract him. His raised eyebrows and pleasant but firm expression made it clear to the young Lady that he wouldn't be dissuaded.

She shook her head, "I must be honest, Major Waller. I don't know. I really don't."

Waller chuckled softly, "Please, call me Tom, Emma. And please take it as no offense to your character, but I don't believe you."

"She doesn't know, I don't know," Kara Lynne cut in with a much flatter tone. She wasn't as willing as Emma to play games with Waller.

"And yet," Waller looked back at the elder lady with a smile, "you were given two companies of riflemen for protection."

Kara's expression was not forgiving, but Emma held up a finger to make her point, "Ah, but where we're going, into the grasslands, we could expect the savages to eat us, if not for a strong escort. And as you know, Tom, the savages will eat anyone."

Waller cast his gaze back to Emma and simply shook his head, still smiling, "I wish you would confide in me, Emma."

"I will, when we're out on the grasslands. But not before. Not until we're close."

"Of course," Waller chuckled. He felt in that moment that he should be much graver about this, but something in Emma's manner, something about the air around her, made him feel less concerned about it all. "Well my first priority is the wellbeing of my men. And if it comes to it, and you don't explain yourselves, I may have to abandon you to your fates, orders or no."

Annie, poor Annie, gasped at that, but Emma simply smiled and nodded, "And you would be right to. I promise, Tom, I will tell you. In due time."

"Of course," Waller repeated, and they strode on.

***

Arriving at the train, the ladies and Waller were greeted by the ever-smiling Lieutenant Devlin, "Ah just in time, sir. B'ys are all squared away, mules and Mister Smith's horse are aboard, and the conductor says he's got the steam up."

Waller nodded, "Excellent, thank you Jimmy. Perhaps you'll escort the ladies to their car?"

"Gladly," Devlin nodded, and so Waller turned and excused himself, then went to check with his officers.

Devlin opened the door to the third car — a door from which he'd made certain the savage blood had been scrubbed — and gestured the ladies in, "If you please."

Emma nodded deeply and then entered, but Kara stopped in the doorway, "You said Mister Smith's horse... he's joining us?"

"Out to Long Prairie, Miss, yes he is."

Devlin had worked hard to inspire enough twinkles in the eyes of fine women to recognize that one. The lady had an interest in the drifter, Devlin realized. Well that was duly noted — and the b'ys would be disappointed. He, of course, didn't much mind. He knew the Major liked Miss Emma, he had no chance there. But he was definitely willing to try his luck with the lovely maid.

This was firmly occupying Jimmy Devlin's thoughts — this and his duties, of course. He was young, and Annie was young and quite pretty.

Kara Lynne stepped into the train, and Annie entered next, slightly wide-eyed, whispering to Devlin, "I think this adventure's going to be more dangerous than I thought. Major Waller thinks the savages are drawn to her Ladyship!"

Devlin frowned, intrigued by the news, but slipping naturally into his charming and reassuring persona, "Well don't you worry, Annie. If it gets too grim out there, just find me. I'll see you through!"

Annie smiled — Jimmy's skill was commendable, in part because he backed it with genuine good intentions — and then she stepped past him.

He followed her in, "Now, ladies, is there anything I can get for you?"

"No," Kara Lynne was already seated.

"Of course. Well, you seem comfortable… though if you're missing any of the comforts of home, from that house in New World City, I'm sure we can find substitutes for you…" Devlin, now, was cautiously probing.

Emma Lee and Kara Lynne both saw through the question, but Annie, still glowing after Jimmy's words, turned back and shook her head, "Oh no no, Jimmy. That wasn't even our home, we only arrived a day before you! We'll be alright."

Emma and Kara looked at each other but Annie didn't notice, and Jimmy smiled and clicked his heels together, touching the brim of his hat, "In that case, I'll leave you to settle in. I'll be in the second car — if you need anything, just call!"

As they nodded to him he smiled and closed the door.

Now he knew how long they'd been there. He didn't know if that would be important, but it was more than he *had* known…

Captain Benton stepped onto the platform and saluted sharply as Waller turned to him, "Sir, came to see you off."

Waller returned the salute, "Thank you, Captain. Your men are able to handle the clean-up? That's a lot of bodies."

"It is. We're going to pile the carcasses on that ridge and douse them in petrol, then burn them. Might be diseased, we can't take the chance."

Waller's mouth was a thin line, "Very grim business."

"Very grim indeed, sir," Benton agreed with a nod. "Thank you for your assistance with the defense. I daresay without you we'd be dead now."

Waller couldn't disagree with that, though being a good Newfoundlander, he was never inclined to leave someone feeling too poorly about themselves.

"I've begun to wonder, Benton, whether somehow our presence didn't escalate things. Just seems odd to me that this attack — the first in your time here — would come when we arrived."

Benton smiled, "I appreciate the thought, sir, but you needn't try to spare me. My arrangements weren't adequate."

"Now Benton..."

The Captain shook his head, "No sir, that horde formed the day before you got here and was blazing north for quite some time. The cable from the Americans said so. You were probably still in Calgary when they started this way."

Waller nodded, "Well fair enough. Benton, good luck with the clean up here. We'll see you on our way back, I'm sure."

Benton's smile seemed to freeze, "Of course, sir. On your way *back*. Good luck."

Not the most positive send-off Waller had ever received, and so he simply nodded, saluted again, and turned for the train. The locomotive had steam and was ready to go.

The last of his men were off the platform. Moving to the door of the second car, he found Devlin there, "All set, Jimmy?"

"All aboard, sir," the Lieutenant smiled. "Always wanted to say that. Little bit of intelligence for you, sir. I heard Annie say that you were thinking the ladies might have a connection to the horde. Well I just found out that they only arrived the day before we did. How's that fit?"

Waller frowned, both at Devlin's uncanny intuition and at the timeline, "The horde... well if what Benton says is true, it formed the same day. But that would be incredible, Jimmy. They were 350 miles away from here... probably three times that distance to where the horde came together in the far south."

"Yes sir, but you're still wondering, aren't you?"

Waller smiled, "Yes Jimmy, I am."

The train pulled out of the station moments later.

CHAPTER XIV

Smith was sitting in the second car when Waller and Devlin entered, talking quietly. The train started moving out of the station, and as it did Waller sat down opposite the drifter, and invited Devlin to pull up a chair to the side of their table. Frowning, Smith looked between them, "Something up?"

Waller nodded, "Just putting together what we know about the ladies. I'd like your opinion too."

"Sounds fair."

The Newfoundlanders looked at each other and then glanced back to Smith, Waller repeating what they'd spoken of in the doorway, "Seems the women arrived on this planet the day that horde assembled. Given the behavior you've noted, that seems a rather interesting coincidence."

Smith frowned, "I reckon it is..."

Watching the drifter's face, Waller could tell he was wondering the same thing both he and Devlin were — how could there possibly be a connection between the ladies and the savages?

"They were in your capital, right up at the tunnel there?" Smith asked the direct question for clarification, and Waller and Devlin both nodded.

"At least 350 miles from here," Devlin confirmed. "And probably three times that from where the horde got together."

Smith and Waller locked eyes, both frowning and thinking the same sorts of things.

"Well, there's no way I know of that the savages could have become aware of them. I don't reckon there's any creature that can smell a lady from 1,000 miles. Though I have seen unusual things in the world," Smith said slowly, thoughtfully.

"Indeed," Waller concurred, "so if there *is* a connection, and I do still have a feeling there is, it might be more nefarious than we'd like to think."

Smith's mouth drew back to a thin line and he let out a breath, "Could be."

"Wait a moment now," Devlin leaned in and held up a hand, "I've seen a lot of women in my time. I know the ones that are nefarious — the ones with an eye for money and whatnot. These ladies... well... there's no way. No way, b'ys... sir, I mean. No sir."

Waller glanced at his trusty Lieutenant, "Yes, but Jimmy, don't you find whenever you're around them, you feel more pliable? More agreeable? It's as though they're casting some sort of spell... an essence... a thrall."

"Well they're gorgeous, of course I've noticed that, sir," Devlin protested. "Nothing I haven't seen before!"

Looking back at Smith with a frown, Waller put the question to him, "What do you think, Mister Smith?"

Smith rubbed his neck and shook his head, "Can't say. It still could be coincidence. I've seen some strange coincidences in my days. But I think you oughta keep a close eye on them. Don't let them alone, especially once they're on the grasslands."

"But how could they be nefarious?" Devlin was still grappling with that thought. "How could they form the horde... it's not as though there's a cable line from New World City direct to the minds of the savages, is there now?"

Waller leaned back in his seat and looked at Devlin, admitting to himself that the young man made a fine point, "Yes that's true. I don't know, Jimmy, but I have the feeling that the secret these women are openly hiding from us will be important. I want you and your platoon to take responsibility for them. If you see anything suspicious, let me know, and if it seems immediately dangerous, intervene."

Devlin's expression twisted into a slightly awkward one, "Intervene? There's some places I will *not* be following them, just so we're clear, sir."

Chuckling, Waller looked back, "What, Jimmy, you bashful around the ladies? When did that start?"

Devlin looked unimpressed but Waller and Smith shared a smile.

"While you're brooding," the Major continued, "get Fred and George in here. We need to review our ammunition and stores situation based on the fight."

Huffing, Devlin stood, quickly saluted, and then left the car.

As he went, Smith looked back at the Major, "Your orders allow for you to be so suspicious of those ladies?"

Waller shook his head, "I'm sure it will be frowned upon. But I don't care how pretty and compelling Lady Emma Lee is, if she's trying to get my men eaten alive, I'll shoot her myself."

Smith tilted his head, "You sound sure of that."

"Do I?" Waller frowned and shook his head. "I hope such a thing would never be necessary. But I must be suspicious. For the sake of myself and the men."

Smith was impressed by that level of devotion. He was getting to like this young Major.

"So we'll draw more ammunition to make up for our losses..." Waller was nodding at Smith, Devlin, and Captains Kearsey and Tucker.

"Yes sir. But the way that went, I'd feel better if we could have another couple of wagons of ammo. And some more Lewis guns, if we can find them," Tucker looked serious, which was rare for him. "Those Lewis guns are worth their weight in gold."

Kearsey looked at Tucker, then at Waller, shaking his head, "Problem is, out here I'm pretty sure the weight in gold is easier to find than the Lewis gun. Things are too new, don't think the Canadian Rifles even have 'em."

That was Waller's impression as well. The Lewis gun had been designed by an American, though the American Army had, to Waller's knowledge, not adopted it. Foolish rivalries between the designer and the General officer commanding or some such thing. The British Army had recognized the utility of a light machine gun that could be carried and operated by just two men... even one man in a pinch. And it fired the same ammunition as the Lee-Enfield rifle, so it was not difficult to integrate into the unit.

But there were precious few of the weapons around. The British had accepted them in 1914, in case the war in Europe drew them in, but when His Majesty's government elected to stay out of the French and German conflict, only a small number had been purchased.

The only reason the Newfoundlanders had them was luck — Colonel Tobin, being enterprising, had used the Vickers gun they'd lost to Pathans at Jalalabad as an excuse to take four of the weapons out of the Indian Army's hands.

There were none in the hands of the Canadians — at least not that Waller knew of.

"We'll have to make do without. And with an attack like that just over, I very much doubt the company at Long Prairie would let us take a Vickers with us either. We'll have to rely on our musketry," Waller said the words with finality. "So yes, George, more ammunition. Absolutely."

"If we could get enough wagons, we could have protection from an attack. A *laager*, like the Boers," Kearsey offered.

"*If* we can get enough wagons," Devlin repeated skeptically. "Problem as I see it, sir, is there won't be enough for us to circle."

The five men sat silently around the table for a moment after Devlin spoke, each preoccupied with their own unpleasant thoughts. Smith, who wasn't up on all the jargon they'd been throwing around, nevertheless understood the gist of what they were saying.

"So," he said plainly, "you won't have enough wagons to fort up behind, and you're not moving fast enough to outrun the savages. So you'll just have to shoot them down as they come."

"That's about the size of it, Mister Smith," Captain Kearsey nodded.

"Typical of our luck, I'd say," Tucker agreed. "Problem with being the best infantry around is they keep trying to get you killed. Bastards."

The Captain threw back the last of the brandy he'd been drinking and then clanked the glass on the table, "Major, I've had enough brandy to be fool enough to ask now: there's no way out of this, right?"

Waller smiled sadly and shook his head, "No. No we're explicitly ordered out. We'll have few advantages out there, but we'll have to get by."

There was another period of silence as the officers and the drifter alternated between looking out the windows at the now-darkening grasslands, the map on the table, and each other. Smith was taking a particular interest in these men. They were victim to the lives they'd chosen, and what they were saying now made him certain he'd picked the right life for himself. He wasn't the sort to agree to go and die for some other man's — or woman's — secrets. Not unless there was another good reason, or he'd given his word.

But Smith liked the Newfoundlanders. They were not arrogant or foolish. They were seeing the problems and they were coming up with solutions, even if it seemed likely they wouldn't have the chance to use the solutions. They were good, kindly folks.

Because of all this, a thought was forming in Smith's mind. It was not exactly a comfortable thought, but it was one that seemed to him to be decent. He hadn't yet decided he'd ride with them when they walked out into the grasslands, but he was considering it.

He'd have to see.

"One thing that I was thinking..." Devlin downed his own brandy. "...now I swear this isn't the brandy talking... is that we all, us officers, should get swords."

Waller's eyebrows went up, and Tucker and Kearsey both looked at the Lieutenant with surprised expressions, but Devlin pressed on as he laid his glass on the table, "Come on now, you know how long it takes to load a Webley!"

With that he pulled his revolver out of its holster and cracked it open over the table, the auto-extractor pushing the gun's six bullets out of the cylinder so they rained briefly on the table, "Now I'm fumbling with new bullets and some savage comes along and starts devouring me. On that platform, if not for all the b'ys around, I'd have been eaten. I'm sure of it.

So I think we should find some swords. They have dragoons out here, they must have swords!"

Tucker and Kearsey looked at each other and gave half-nods, acknowledging the common sense behind the thought, "That's a good point."

Smith pulled his bowie knife out and laid it on the table, "Or one of these."

The Captains leaned back in surprise as the knife flashed in the light, and Waller frowned at it, then smiled, "Well that thing's a little ambitious for me. But yes, a sword, or a sword bayonet from a SMLE, certainly. Good thinking, Jimmy."

Devlin grinned and began collecting the bullets he'd spilled on the table, "Yes you see, sirs, Mister Smith, I'm not just a pretty face!"

"That's a good thing, too," Tucker said seriously, putting a hand on Devlin's shoulder. "If you were only a pretty face, then you'd actually be nothing at all!"

Devlin laughed with everyone around the table, as the sky faded to black outside.

Sitting in the third car with her cape open, Emma Lee looked at Kara Lynne as she walked by and sat down behind her, "What do you think they're saying about us?"

Kara Lynne frowned, "I think they're suspicious. Our damned luck to get the only officers in the British Empire who can see past orders and a pretty face. They'll be watching us closely."

Emma turned around in her chair, frowning at her dearest friend, "Is that such a terrible thing?"

"I... well. It may not be. But you know what'll happen if they find out... they might abandon us out there."

The frown remained on Emma's face, and she turned away, "I still don't understand why it matters."

After a pause and a sigh, Kara Lynne shook her head, "Maybe it doesn't. Maybe it doesn't."

CHAPTER XV

The train continued along through the night, a great electric searchlight on the front of it illuminating the track ahead. Waller stood outside on the small platform at the end of his passenger car, watching the blackness all around and breathing in the air.

In his experience, it was the air of a place that revealed the most about it. Newfoundland air was, to his estimation, the cleanest and most wonderful on Earth. The island was a rock jutting out of the North Atlantic ocean; its air was pure sea air, uncontaminated by factories and unscented by human wastes. To stand next to Cabot Tower and breathe deep was to take in the most wonderful air Waller could imagine.

Here, the air was crisp, sharp, fresh and dry — like the air that came in the winds off the Rocky Mountains. He had breathed that air in Alberta, on the way here, and he was surprised at how this new world featured air much the same. Still, somehow he found it uncomfortable — air like this did not belong in a place overrun by savages.

Smith opened the car door and stepped out onto the platform, "Good evening."

"Mister Smith," Waller nodded. "Couldn't sleep?"

Shaking his head, Smith leaned on the opposite rail and looked out at the night, "No sir, I couldn't. Not accustomed to sleeping on trains."

Waller nodded, "Ah. I lack the ability to put my anxieties to rest. It's a damned curse when it comes to keeping myself alert, but I haven't figured a way to get past it."

"Means you're worried for your men; I reckon it's not the worst possible reaction," Smith glanced at the Major. "If it'll help settle your mind, I'll tell you that I've started to consider riding out with you. Don't know if I could do much, but it seems to me that riding with you would be a decent sort of thing."

Waller looked across at Smith, trying to study the man but finding the poor light filtering out of the car's windows to be insufficient for the task, "I don't know if I could advise that in good conscience, Mister Smith. There's a good chance we'll run into a lot of trouble out there."

Smith nodded slowly, "I reckon there is, and I'm not a man who often goes looking for trouble. But I also don't like the idea of good men going to die if I can do something to help."

Waller turned around so he could lean back against the railing, "I'll ask this plainly, Mister Smith, because you seem to be a man who takes things directly. Do you think you, one man, could make the difference for us out there?"

Smith turned to face Waller directly, "I don't know, Major. But I figure it might be better for me to find out, than to hear about you having never come back and wondering if I could have helped. I know this world, you don't. And if anybody's going to survive this march, it's you and your boys. Put those two together, we might just have a shot."

Waller was quiet for a moment. In Afghanistan, he'd learned the importance of listening to the locals... or perhaps he'd always known that. In Newfoundland, he'd seen many mainlanders come in and ignore the advice of the local folk, only to end up dead on the rocks or washed out to sea. He'd never turn down the sort of help Smith was offering... unless it meant extending what was beginning to feel like a death sentence to an honest man.

"I don't like asking someone not obliged to me to put his life at risk," Waller said after a moment. "But if you offer it, I'll have to say yes. Where we're going, I doubt I could find a better guide. But I leave the decision to you. If you do it, I'll put you on the roll as a scout, if you like, and make sure you're well paid. You'll be under no obligation to us, but you will be compensated."

"No compensation needed for doing the decent thing," Smith said slowly.

Waller nodded, "No, none needed. But I'm of the opinion that if you're doing the right thing, and can be fairly paid for it, there's no reason to turn down the cash."

"That is fair enough," Smith nodded. "I'll think on it some."

"Very well."

The two men stood silently on the platform for a few moments longer before Waller excused himself, "Well, I think I'll try to sleep now. Good night, Mister Smith."

"G'night," Smith nodded.

Waller returned to the train car where Devlin and his men were already asleep, sitting in chairs or laid out on the floor. There was a private cabin forward in this car for his use, though 'cabin' in this case meant a small room with a bunk too short for him. He was about to enter that area to try to sleep when his eyes drifted to the rear window, and in the glint of the light behind, he saw a cloaked figure on the platform of the third car.

Frowning, he closed the cabin door and walked quietly past the sleeping men, slid open the door at the back of the car, and stepped out onto the rear platform. The coupling that held the second and third cars together stood between him and the cloaked figure, though he could easily step across that gap...

As he slid the door to his car shut, the cloaked figure turned, and he made sure to announce himself quickly, "Good evening."

The woman who presented her face to him was none other than Emma Lee, and she smiled when she saw Waller, "Tom."

"Emma," he replied in kind. "Trouble sleeping?"

She smiled sweetly, and again Waller felt his suspicion being fogged by her warmth.

"I've seen night on the grasslands in my dreams many times, Tom," she said turning and looking back out over the moonlit terrain through which the train was passing. "It's much more beautiful than in my dreams."

Waller's suspicion seemed fogged in, but fog alone couldn't stymie a Newfoundlander, "You lived here for many years before moving back to Earth?"

She nodded, "Half my life. We left when I was thirteen, I'm twenty-six now. I remember looking up at the stars and the moons and feeling like I should just be running naked under them, rolling in the grass, basking in it all."

Waller was worldly, but not *that* worldly, "Is that so?"

Emma turned to look back at him, realizing how awkward her words had made him feel, "Not that I ever did, of course. Just a feeling, you know?"

"Not the sort we ever really got in Newfoundland, too cold and damp really," Waller was glad it was too dark for her to see the redness he could feel on his cheeks.

"Of course," she smiled, her teeth reflecting the moonlight.

They stood quietly for a moment, and then Waller tilted his head, "We think you're connected to that great horde, you know. We don't know how, but we think it."

Her smile faded slowly, "Well, we're not."

"You must appreciate our position, Emma. You and your companions are taking us on a secret mission and you won't tell us what we'll even be looking for out there. And then when you arrive, a horde of a sort not seen in a dozen years appears and comes straight for us," Waller said softly. "Those are startling coincidences."

"You can't think I'm a threat," Emma's face was more somber now. "Look at me... I'm harmless..."

Waller studied her face for a moment, "No, Emma, you're dangerous. All my officers and I agree, whenever you're around we feel different. Not so much so that we can't reason, but different all the same. I don't know what you're hiding, or what we're looking for, and I know I'm doing you a disservice, but I must be suspicious of you..."

Something occurred to him then, "You left thirteen years ago?"

"Twelve, and a few months," she corrected, then stopped herself from elaborating further.

"Coincidence again. Twelve years since the last ten thousand-strong horde."

Her eyes drifted down his chest and she looked away, "You're not supposed to figure things like that out, Tom. You're supposed to say I'm beautiful. You're supposed to stop thinking of questions whenever I smile at you. Couldn't you just... trust me?"

Waller shook his head, "No, I can't *just* trust you, Emma. I've made this clear to my men, and I will make it clear to you: if I feel that you or your companions somehow betray my men, I will personally shoot you. I would hate it — you are beautiful, and you are incredibly lovely to speak with. But I will shoot you. I therefore beg you explain this mission to me. Explain yourself."

Emma stood still for a moment and then shook her head, "Kara says we can't share any information until we get out into the grasslands. No chance of the Americans hearing about it... no chance of anyone misunderstanding us."

"I think it's evident that we're all already misunderstanding you, Emma. Is it for Kara to decide? Is she your master?" Waller's questions continued to come, sounding soft and sweet, almost like the talk of a man courting a woman.

"She is my protector," Emma turned back. "She's the one who found me out in those grasslands, Tom. If you must know, then I'll tell you part of it. I was orphaned in the grasslands. I was but three, I don't remember very much. But she was ten, and she was orphaned too. She found me and she led our escape. She got us to safety. But now we two are the only ones in the Empire who know where it was our parents were when it happened. And the Empire has deemed finding that place to be of the utmost importance."

Waller paused at the story, trying to decide in that moment how much credence to give it.

Emma sensed his skepticism, "We cannot tell that story to anyone, because it's quite possible the location is on the American side of the line. The Yanks cannot know there may be something that valuable on their side... the Empire must claim it first."

"If it's on their side of the line, they're entitled to it. The King is willing to fight a war with our closest allies over what your parents found?" Waller's tone was hardening at that thought. He had no interest at all in standing against American infantry.

"It's not like that," Emma shook her head. "We think it's something we can bring back with us. And claim we found it on our side of the line… or not even tell anyone what it is. But we must find it first. It's the key to… well to a great deal."

Waller was still looking suspiciously at Emma, and she felt the weight of his gaze on her. She offered just a little more, "It is something that is not on Earth. Something that could make the Empire more powerful than you could imagine."

"And they send two ladies and a maid to recover it?" Waller's suspicion remained.

"Because anything more than two ladies and a maid and their escort would draw a great deal of attention. For now it appears that I, a peer, have called in favors in order to go on an expedition to find a relic of my past. That is true… it was the government's object to make certain no one realized how important the relic is."

Remaining silent, Waller looked away from Emma's earnest gaze, and tried to determine how badly his judgment was being obscured by her sweet tone and her incandescent smile. He was, of course, finding it difficult to resist her plausible but somehow incomplete tale. Something significant was being left out — besides the obvious identity of the relic.

But again, he knew more now than he had before. Or at least he was being offered some sort of plausible justification.

He decided to accept Emma's words, or at least to maintain the appearance of acceptance.

"I believe you, Emma," he said after a moment.

She smiled, and then to his surprise she reached out from under her cloak and wrapped her warm hand around his cold one as it gripped the railing, "No you don't. I can't fool you, Tom… but I won't tell you more yet. Just… just trust me. I hope that when we all come back safely from this mission you and I might spend more time together. I believe you'll be willing, when you see what we find."

Waller let go a sigh and looked into Emma's eyes, trying to detect the evil that might be there. He couldn't see it, but that was no guarantee it didn't exist.

"We'll see, I suppose," he said quietly.

She nodded, "Yes, we will."

With that, she turned and went back into her train carriage. Waller stood at the railing and breathed the air again, letting his head clear of the warm fog that she'd wrapped him in. Her story was plausible, and perhaps had it been given to him by General Byng he'd have been more inclined to believe it.

But Emma had an unnatural power over men, and though Waller didn't understand it, he was wary of being manipulated by it.

He *would* shoot her, if it came to that.

Hopefully it would not.

CHAPTER XVI

Long Prairie was much like Treeline City, except it lacked the mountain view. All around the palisades were fields of grass, rising and falling. Farther out there were irregular terrain features — gullies, coulees, springs, streams. There was an oddly artificial feeling to the place, though Waller could not decide what precisely about it seemed irregular. Perhaps once he was out in the grasslands he'd better understand.

For now, his concern was unloading his men and setting up a camp for the night. They would bivouac in the parade ground just inside the palisade on the west side of town, waiting while the arsenal arranged their transport and ammunition. The march into the grass would likely begin the next day, after a full day of rest and preparation.

As the men stepped out of their cars onto the Long Prairie station platform, their officers formed them into their columns and they marched away without ceremony. Waller had delivered the orders for encamping to his Captains on the train, so he had nothing more to say as he watched them go.

Standing next to his car he waited as they moved off, then he stood aside as Sergeant Halloran led Devlin's platoon out of that car and off the platform, marching in good order for the parade ground.

Jimmy Devlin himself came out last, stopping next to Waller, "Sergeant Halloran will oversee the setup for my platoon. Thought you might need help with the ladies."

The tone of the last part of that comment was different than it would have been the day before — no longer was Devlin's outlook as opportunistic as it had been. 'Help with the ladies' had a very different meaning after the officers' conversation last night. The ladies could be a danger.

Waller nodded, "Thanks, Jimmy."

The Major had informed his senior officers of his conversation with Emma. They'd been ordered to be discreet with the news, but he wasn't about to keep his officers in the dark when he had at least some sort of insight. Devlin's suspicion had in fact grown with the new information — he knew when someone was telling him half a story, and was the sort of fellow who wondered what they were holding back.

Smith stepped out behind Devlin, "Gentlemen, I'll collect my horse."

Waller nodded, "We'll be setting up at the hotel."

"I'll see you there," Smith agreed, putting on his cowboy's hat and walking towards the rear of the train.

Devlin and Waller watched him go, the Lieutenant shaking his head, "Any chance of taking him out with us? Man looks like he knows this place."

Waller had not yet revealed Smith's thoughts to the officers — Smith was in the same car with them, and he didn't want the drifter to feel as if he was being cornered into cooperating.

"Between me and you, Jimmy, he's already considering riding with us, just because it's the decent thing. But he's deciding, so don't pressure him," Waller nodded.

Devlin managed to smile at that, "Riding with us on this mission because it's the decent thing to do? So what you're saying is that drifters are Newfoundlanders at heart?"

Smiling too, Waller put on his hat, "I imagine home has more in common with this place than we'd think. Raises the same sorts of people."

Before Devlin could comment, the door to the third car opened and both Newfoundlanders fell silent. After a moment, Emma and Kara emerged, followed by the maid Annie who was struggling with their suitcases.

"Oh let me get those for you," Devlin's smile was instant and convincing, and he rushed forward to give Annie some gentlemanly assistance.

Waller followed his Lieutenant more slowly, touching the brim of his hat as he came to a stop before the cloaked women, "Good morning ladies,

I hope you slept well."

Kara Lynne nodded with her stony expression, "We did. Did you, Major?"

Waller couldn't tell if that was a sharp lie in response to his conversation with Emma, or if she was just being typically taciturn in offering what she believed to be the truth.

"I slept quite badly, I'm afraid. Anxieties are not something a man should normally admit to, but I'll openly say that my fear for the men on this mission has been denying me comfortable rest," Waller decided he wouldn't stop pushing, though he doubted Kara Lynne would give up any information.

Before either she or Emma could respond to his words, though, a call crossed the platform, "Major Waller!"

Hearing his name, Waller turned and saw a Captain and a Lieutenant approaching. He took a few steps in their direction and then stopped, allowing the officers to come the rest of the way, and salute in greeting. He returned the gesture.

"Captain James Quinn, 'D' Company of the Canadian Rifles. Pleased to meet you, sir," as Quinn's salute came down he extended his hand towards Waller, and Waller took it. "And this is Lieutenant Michael Gallway. He was desperate to meet you, sir."

Gallway extended his hand, "I joined the Rifles before they raised the RNR, but I was proud as hell to hear what you did at Treeline City."

The accent was unmistakably that of a Newfoundlander, probably from Conception Bay, and Waller took the Lieutenant's hand, "Well we lucked into a fine spot to receive the horde. It's good to see that what they say is true, though, Michael — that we're everywhere."

Gallway grinned, "Yes it's true, two officers and nineteen men in the Canadian Rifles, sir. All of them in this company. You'll get some hospitality while you're here, and we'll sort out whatever you need... with the Captain's permission, of course."

Quinn nodded, "I won't deny you anything we have. I don't like the sounds of your mission, Major. Anything we can do to improve your chances..."

Waller nodded, "We appreciate that, Captain. Captain Kearsey of my own 'D' Company will be bringing you a proper list, but I can say right now that we'll need as much .303 ammunition as you can spare and we can carry, as many wagons as you can lend, and if you have any, some dragoon sabers for our officers."

As he heard the list, Quinn began to nod, and then he stopped with a frown at the last items mentioned. He looked at Waller with slightly narrowed eyes, considered asking just what he needed with dragoon sabers, and then elected to simply accept the order without question.

"We'll get you set up with whatever we can," Gallway kicked in. "For now, we have rooms for you and your guests. If you'll follow us, we'll take you to the hotel."

They all left the platform moments later.

"I hope this'll suit your needs," Captain Quinn stepped into the hotel room first, and the ladies and Lieutenant Devlin followed.

"Certainly, it's quite nice," Emma replied with a smile, making sure to look directly at Quinn. He seemed warmer all of a sudden, and he nodded hurriedly.

"Our pleasure. If there's anything you need while you're here, please don't hesitate to contact me or one of my officers," he bowed very slightly, then backed out of the room. Devlin watched him go, deciding that the Captain was tightly in the grip of the ladies' thrall.

He placed their suitcases on one of the beds in the room and then touched the brim of his cap, "See you later, ladies. Anything you need... apparently find Captain Quinn."

He made the last remark with a knowing smile — one that suggested he'd noticed the power of their persuasion. Both he and Waller were determined now to remind these women that their tricks and charms were being noticed, and wouldn't get them any advantages if good sense clashed with their wants.

Annie beamed at him, and Emma Lee and Kara Lynne watched him go, closing the door behind him.

"Those Newfoundlanders aren't as pliable as I'd like," Kara Lynne said shortly after he left. "If they realize... well, what will they do?"

Emma looked at Kara with a disgruntled gaze, "I suspect they'll continue on as they are. They'll just stop being suspicious of us."

"I rather doubt that," Kara shook her head. "They'll turn on us... on you especially."

"You need to stop being so paranoid, Caralynne. They're not all bad, they're not all opportunists. They won't dissect us!"

Kara Lynne scowled at the use of her old name, "No, they won't dissect *me*."

Emma let out a breath and sat on her bed. Kara caught Annie's eye, "Annie, you must keep quiet."

The maid nodded nervously.

"We have all the ammo you could dream of. I'll give you 200 cases, if you like... half you can take on your mules, right? Well that's dandy," Lieutenant Gallway led Waller and Devlin into the arsenal. Rows upon rows of SMLE rifles on racks stood before them, and towards the back there were older rifles of various types.

"That would be 200,000 rounds — more than we could have hoped for!" Devlin glanced at Waller with a smile, but the Major continued to look serious.

"I suppose you don't have any Lewis guns we could take along?" he asked as they walked down one of the aisles towards the rear of the large room full of weapons.

"No sir, afraid we were never issued any. And after that report from Treeline, there's no way we'd be allowed to remove any Vickers guns either — there'd be rioting!" Gallway said easily. "But I do have one toy back here you might be interested in. Got it off a troop of dragoons when they got fed up of hauling it around."

Waller glanced at Devlin and the Lieutenant shrugged — could be anything.

"Here she is," Gallway stopped at something covered by a canvas sheet — something that appeared to be on a large-wheeled carriage, like a field gun.

"A Maxim?" Waller asked cautiously. He'd heard that Maxim guns — the predecessors of the Vickers machine guns — were very unhandy weapons in combat, and prone to jamming. Not worth the trouble... but then, could he turn down any sort of machine gun?

"Oh Jesus, sir, I'd never hand one of those anchors to a fellow Newfoundlander. The dragoons got rid of those damned things in South Africa against the Boers, replaced them with these," Gallway took hold of the canvas and yanked if off, revealing a strange-looking tripod-mounted gun on a carriage. "This is an 1895 Colt machine gun. Only takes a single horse to move the carriage, and it's pretty damned reliable, from what I've heard. Around 400 rounds a minute, so not as snappy as a Vickers, but I figure it's better than a kick in the arse!"

"Most things are," Devlin took a step forward, looking at the weapon. "It shoots the .303?"

"God no, it's a Yank gun. It's a .30 caliber, but I have 11,000 rounds for it back here. Bought some from the Yanks in case we ever had to use it. Now that won't last you too long... but like I said, b'ys, better than a kick in the arse," Gallway looked up at the RNR officers with a smile.

Waller nodded, "We'll take it... if you can get a cart to haul the rounds. How many carts can you get for us, Mike?"

Gallway paused and scratched his chin thoughtfully, "Oh not as many as you deserve... but six. Six without a problem. Not much for circling, I know, but you know what it's better than."

"My arse is getting sore just hearing about it all," Devlin grinned. "Now, these dragoons left you a machine gun. Did they by chance leave you any swords?"

CHAPTER XVII

The Colt machine gun and the carts began arriving on the parade ground around midday, and to get the ammunition out of the arsenal, the men of the RNR formed a human chain stretching from the arsenal door to a huge stockpile next to the camp. Having that much rifle ammunition in the open — even in cases — was perhaps risky, but Waller had seen less responsible actions in Afghanistan. At least here it was all shielded from the outside by the palisade, and guards were posted all around it to keep foolish smokers away. It wasn't as though a .303 bullet was particularly volatile on its own anyway.

The carts detailed for ammunition were loaded immediately and stored near the stack of cases; the rest would be strapped to the mules the next morning.

Smith walked between the cases, somewhat impressed at the mass of boxes that had to be moved — 200 boxes of rifle ammunition made for an impressive sight. He chewed on the end of a stalk of grass as he watched, then wandered over to the Colt gun and frowned at it. This was a weapon he'd seen before — the US cavalry was fond of it, though he'd never seen it work as advertised.

"Seen one of those before, Mister Smith?" Captain Tucker appeared next to him, and Smith nodded.

"I have. The cavalry has been known to ride with them, but I've never seen them working right myself," he said plainly.

Tucker nodded, "Yeah, I'd trade my right arm for a Vickers, but the townsfolk here wouldn't let us take one away from their defense, not after hearing about Treeline. So we get this piece of vintage machinery. Damned thing's nearly as old as the Major."

Smith nodded and then looked at Tucker, "Major's that young, isn't he?"

Tucker, a middle aged man, nodded, "Merchant father, and he wanted to be out of that business. Had his commission bought. I did the same, of course, he just happened to be younger than me at the time. And proved himself to be quite a soldier in Afghanistan."

"Buying into a rank?" Smith frowned. Didn't sound quite normal.

Holding up his hands, Tucker shook his head, "It was abolished in the British Army, but when they raised us they needed a way to make money for the regiment. Ranks went to the highest bidders. Turned out well for us, we didn't get any damned fools. Could have gone badly though, no question."

"I'll bet," Smith nodded. He didn't have a reason to start doubting the Newfoundlanders now, because he'd already seen them fight. It was surprising sometimes to find out how a man came by his life, and how a man as young as Waller came by his rank so early.

Not that Smith was more than five years older, but then Smith had lived a life where there was no rank, just a trail. Years didn't matter so much to him, except when they started slowing him down.

"A lot of boxes to carry," Smith waved his hand at the growing stack of .303 cases, and Tucker snorted a laugh.

"The joys of modern warfare, my friend. Every column has a tail of wagons full of the brass and lead we shoot. I hear in France they had square miles of ammo lying around during the war with the Germans. Millions of men, thousands of bullets to a man... must have been a nightmare."

Smith nodded, "Well, you have six wagons and your mules? Should be workable. Wagon trains move well enough out there. You just have to get handy at circling them."

"Be a small circle," Tucker grinned. "And that machine gun will be a help, even if it is a damned old thing. Anyway, sorry Mister Smith, I need to make sure the b'ys stacked 'em proper. I'll talk to you later."

Each man touched the brim of his hat and then they parted ways.

Smith had to say, he'd never seen a column go anywhere on this planet with so much preparation.

"I'll have a dozen horses for you too," Gallway was leading Waller and Devlin past the stables as he said it, "for scouts and things. Now, the sabers should be in here. We left them in the stable in case a dragoon ever came looking for one in a hurry. And it's not like they could blow up, you know..."

Gallway led the officers up to the back door of the stables and then in, stopping as he spotted a barrel with saber handles sticking out of it, "There they are."

Waller and Devlin looked to each other and then followed Gallway to the barrel. There were at least forty swords wedged into it, and as they started pulling some out it became clear that a number of the steel scabbards were rusty.

"Not in the best shape, but you'll find enough good ones for your officers," Gallway said discerningly. "You figure they'll be handy? Don't often hear of men wanting to get close enough to savages to use them."

Devlin smiled, "Believe me, Mike, I got no interest in getting this close to a savage, but last time one got this close to me, I was stuck reloading my Webley. Damned if I'll be stuck without something to hit him with next time."

"Ah. Well we have a man up the road the dragoons use when they're in town, I can have him clean and sharpen these up for you," Gallway nodded.

"Please do," Waller agreed.

"Will indeed... so is that all?"

"It is, thank you Michael. If you'll see to this, I want to get to a high point and have a look at the direction we're marching."

"Very good. Best spot is the hotel, sir, right up on the roof... and you can check on your ladies. Fine ladies they seem, sir. Knew I should have waited and joined my own country's regiment, just got damned impatient,"

Gallway grinned, then began pulling swords from the barrel.

With a nod, Waller and Devlin left him to it, confident he'd choose the best of the barrel for their officers.

As they walked back past the stables, Waller found his eyes drifting up the street towards the hotel, and Devlin's gaze wandered the same way.

"Dammit I wish they'd own up to whatever it is they're at..." the Lieutenant prompted, hoping to hear the Major's thoughts.

Waller had no insights for his friend, "At least we know there's something up. Not going to be caught unawares like the fools you always hear about in the stories. But this is damned uncomfortable."

"And I won't even ask. Orders are orders," Devlin nodded.

They'd lost enough men following orders in Afghanistan, and if necessary, they would do the same here. There was no questioning that. Job had to be done, and if they didn't do it, some other poor bastards would have to. Better just to accept it and get on with it.

"Alright, Jimmy, you check in with George and Fred, make sure we haven't forgotten anything on the list. I'll get up on the roof and have a look west. Once the ammo's stacked, stand the b'ys down for the day, let them get some rest. But not too rowdy, I want them ready to march first thing."

"Yes sir," Devlin saluted easily, and then parted company.

Waller headed up to the hotel.

Standing on the roof of the building, Waller looked west through his field glasses. The ground was undulating and covered in grass, with intermittent rises and drops, a few terrain scars and a gulch — at least as far as he could see. But on the march they would cover that ground in short order, and what lay beyond the horizon, no one knew.

"Kara says this is the town she came upon with me."

Waller lowered his field glasses and turned to see Emma crossing the roof behind him.

"She doesn't remember how long she and I were walking to get here, but it felt to her like weeks. I doubt that, though... I don't remember us stopping to drink water more than once or twice..." she stopped herself as she realized what she'd said, and Waller turned to look at her.

"You *remember*? I thought you were just three at the time. I'd be quite impressed if you could remember it at all."

Emma let out a short, displeased breath, "How do you make me admit so much, even when I've no wish to? Tom, you have an effect on me..."

"Don't try to deflect the question, please, Emma. Precisely what do you remember?"

Coming to stand next to Waller near the edge of the roof, she shook her head, "Not much, but more than I have any right to. I remember... I remember walking and walking, and not being able to say anything to Kara. I remember stopping at springs twice, and sleeping in the grass... it's all a jumble. And... and..."

Her voice started to trail off, but she glanced at Waller and saw his frown deepening at the promise of more information being withheld.

"I remember savages. I remember seeing thousands of them, women and men, all around me. I see it in my dreams sometimes... I'm there and they're not taking any particular notice of me... those are terrifying dreams. I don't understand why they don't attack me, they just stare at me. Eat people in front of me. It's terrible. But I *remember* it, I think."

Waller examined the pain on Emma's face as she revealed her memories, and then he looked west again, his mind less fogged in now than it might have been, "Well, hopefully we killed the thousands back at Treeline. If not, you're going to see people eaten in front of you again, Emma. Unless you have the power to stop it."

Emma's head turned sharply to him, "What do you mean by that?"

Pleased that he'd gotten a reaction, Waller smiled, "I can't say. But your reaction suggests that perhaps I've struck a nerve. Want to tell me a little more?"

"No," Emma's face fell. "Stop playing games with me, Tom, please. I don't deserve it."

"Emma, nothing would please me more than to stop, but until you tell me — until I *trust* you — I must not stop. I will do everything I can to help my men survive this, and until you prove to me that you deserve my loyalty as they do, I won't stop."

"Then I cannot spend time with you. I can't, I'm sorry," Emma turned and began to walk away, but Waller gently laid a land on her shoulder.

She slid out from under it effortlessly and left the roof. Waller watched her go, shaking his head. There was something altogether wrong about the events that were engulfing him. And tomorrow they'd be in the grasslands...

CHAPTER XVIII

Night had fallen, and Devlin was enjoying a quiet walk behind the palisade. The men were already sleeping in their tents, having been well fed and mildly exhausted by the moving of munitions. The horses detailed to the column had been brought out and were tied to posts around the encampment, and the ammunition was stacked in a very large pile. All was ready for the march out.

Devlin arrived at the gate that faced west, and a Private on guard duty came to attention as he passed it. The gate was not a locked one — people could come and go through it as they pleased all night. Had it been a closed position, the Private would have challenged Devlin with the classic 'who goes there'. Instead, in the lamp-lit courtyard before the rough-hewn gate, the Private simply came to attention.

Stopping, Devlin nodded to the man, "Stand at ease, stand at ease. Cool night."

"About typical for out here, sir," the Private nodded.

"Been out to the west, Private? Seen any of what's out there?"

The man shook his head, "No sir. At least not out of sight of the town. I've heard rumors like everyone else... about cities of savages with pyramids and headdresses and all the rest, but personally I take that all to be a load of... soldier's talk. Don't think them savages could build a pyramid, or a hat, sir."

Devlin nodded, "From what I've seen, I'd be quite surprised as well. Don't expect to see us come back, do you?"

The Private looked uncomfortable, "From what I hear, only people that's gone out there are wagon trains. They don't come back. I mean, we hear about the odd survivor running back and usually gone mad, but mostly they just die. No matter how prepared they are. But that said, a wagon train with women and children and forty men ain't the same as two companies of infantry. I hope we'll see you back, sir."

The Private, Devlin was pleased to find, was talkative — more willing than many to share his thoughts with an officer. Often private soldiers weren't prone to speaking so sensibly with superiors.

"Well, I look forward to coming back, Private," Devlin nodded, then looked past the man out through one of the slats in the gate. "So, anyone ever actually go out at night?"

"Um. Sir."

That was a different sort of answer, and Devlin frowned, "Don't think 'um' is much of an answer, Private. What's that mean?"

"I ain't supposed to say, sir," the Private gulped.

Devlin's friendly demeanor evaporated with some frustration, "Now don't even think of lying to an officer, Private. What man is out there? Is he drinking or gambling?"

The Private swallowed again, "Ain't a man, sir. Just one lady..."

Freezing in place for a moment, everything Devlin had been speaking about with Waller slipped into place in his mind, and he knew just who was outside.

"How long has she been out?" he asked, drawing his revolver and moving toward the gate.

"About a half hour, sir. Said she used to live around here... said she knew... I mean, I couldn't tell her no, sir, it's not a barred gate..."

Devlin held up a hand, "Which way? Left, straight, right?"

"Right. Towards the stand of trees that way..." the Private nodded in the direction.

"Good. Wait here."

Devlin rushed to the tents nearest him, then walked along the line until he stopped at one he'd watched set up, "Sergeant Halloran. Your section, rifles and ammunition. Quietly now."

The Sergeant, a very light sleeper after Afghanistan, was coming out of his tent and buttoning up his tunic in seconds — with the unnatural and somehow inexplicable speed that the best Sergeants possessed. Just moments later, he had silently woken his section and had them out of their tents with tunics on and Lee-Enfields in hand. Moving quite quietly, Devlin led them towards the gate.

Passing the Private again, the Lieutenant pointed towards the right, and the man nodded.

"Should we wake the Major, sir, if it's the Lady?" Halloran asked in a whisper, but Devlin shook his head.

"No time. We get out after her and report later. Quick and quiet, b'ys. Sergeant, take half the section out into the open field to the west, then cut to the right, across towards the trees. I'll take the other half up the right side of the palisade and then I'll cut left to the trees. We'll come at her from two sides. Stay close together in case there are savages."

The Private on guard was confused by the orders — the tone didn't fit with what he'd expect of men going to a woman's rescue. But he was a private soldier from a different unit. He just assumed the Newfoundlanders had their own way of soldiering — as they seemed to with everything else.

"Open up," Devlin waved the Private to action, and as the wooden gate creaked apart, Devlin and Halloran led the men out.

The trees the Private had indicated were about 200 yards away from the gate, on a forty-five degree angle to the right. Silently, Devlin led his five men down the side of the palisade, keeping his eyes on those trees. Despite being hastily woken, the men were accustomed to moving quietly in the dark, yet another legacy of nights spent in the Afghan mountains.

Sergeant Halloran's men were crouch-walking across the grassy field, keeping their eyes moving in all directions. If savages were about, his half of the section would be the most obvious target, so they'd have to be at the ready to receive from all sides. They were also being noisier, not because they were careless but because, if the woman — who Devlin had decided must be Emma — was paying any attention at all, she'd see them.

And if she tried to evade the Sergeant, her natural route of escape would be down to the side of the palisade, into the shadows near that wall — right into the path of Devlin and his men. He planned to squeeze her, and find out just what she was up to.

Revolver drawn, Devlin walked quickly. In half a minute, the men were near enough to see the starlight under the branches of the small stand of trees, and there was no sign of a Lady. Silently, Devlin waved the men on, and then he looked out to see where the crouched figures of Halloran's men were in the field. They were backlit by the stars, easy enough to see if you knew to look for them.

As Devlin watched, Halloran turned his men and began edging them towards the trees. That was the cue, and Devlin stepped away from the shade of the palisade, waving the men to follow him, extending them into a long, open line as they crept forward.

Still, there was no sign of a woman standing under the trees... she could be behind one of the trunks, perhaps. Or she could be beyond the trees, speaking to savages... but even if she was, the trees would be a good place for his men to take cover.

It didn't take long to close the distance, with the men creeping and watching in all directions, rifles ready...

But when they got to the trees, there was no woman in sight. Devlin waved the reunited section to the ground, then whispered, "Easy, b'ys. Lie still while I have a look."

He crept around the trees with revolver leading the way, and as he got through the stand the rolling grasslands, clumps of trees, and gulches to the north unrolled before him. Dammit, the woman could be hiding anywhere nearby — presuming, of course, she hadn't simply left for good.

As he thought of these possibilities, Devlin made a critical mistake: he stepped down on a dried branch.

The crack was a sharp one, and he winced and froze, holding up his revolver and looking out at the fields to the north. For a split second there was nothing, and then two dozen yards from the stand, a figure leapt up out of the grass. Devlin leveled his pistol, "Who goes there?"

Whirling against the backlighting of one of the moons, the figure revealed itself to be female, and for a moment Devlin almost thought it was unclothed. Then a cape swung around it with great flourish, and the woman called back softly, "Is that you, Jimmy?"

"Lady Lee, it is Lieutenant Devlin. Please come here to the stand of trees. Sergeant, move the men up."

Emma's cloaked shape approached the trees just as the silhouettes of the section of Newfoundlanders appeared amongst the trunks. Devlin straightened up and lowered his revolver as Emma's face at last came into view under the dim moonlight, "M'Lady, it's quite dangerous out here. You shouldn't have come alone."

"I was safe, Jimmy," Emma insisted, almost pleadingly. "Can't you just leave me out here? It's been so long since I've been home... to lie in the grass and look up at the stars. Do you know what it's like to miss the place you're from?"

Devlin looked at Emma seriously for a moment, "We're all Newfoundlanders, M'Lady. We all only have one home, and the sea is in our blood. We miss it everyday we're away from it. But that doesn't mean when we get there we go for a swim so we can freeze to death."

His surprisingly earnest words reflected both how much he missed his home island and the tension of the moment.

"I won't freeze, I promise," Emma's voice continued to sound pleading, but Devlin shook his head.

"You cannot stay out alone. If you must insist on staying out here, my section will remain with you."

Emma let out a long, sad sigh and turned to look north again, "Look at it, Jimmy. It's an ocean of grass, islands of trees... have you ever seen anything more beautiful?"

"I'm partial to salt water in my seas, but I understand how it could be in your blood. M'Lady, I don't think Major Waller has made it any secret that we aren't certain about you. I cannot trust you out here on your own. We can't allow you to be hurt, and we can't allow you to communicate with the savages, so you're coming in or we're staying out. That simple."

Devlin's flat tone hit Emma hard, and her chin sank, her gaze falling to her feet, "I am your prisoner."

"It does me no pleasure to say so, but more or less, yes. Until you tell us what's going on. Until you give us a reason to trust you."

Emma nodded once slowly, "Let's go back."

She turned for the gate and began moving sullenly, but surprisingly quickly for one in a morose frame of mind. The men had to step lightly to keep up with her, and Jimmy Devlin let them get a head start before quietly shuffling the twenty yards to where Emma had appeared. Kneeling, he found the grass had been flattened, presumably by her as she'd lain there stargazing... or whatever she'd really been doing.

Devlin stood slowly and backed away from the patch, not turning his back in case there were savages around.

Lady Emma Lee was proving quite a handful — quite a cryptic handful.

"Wait until the Major hears about this," Devlin said to himself quietly. When he reached the trees, he turned and jogged after Sergeant Halloran's party.

CHAPTER XIX

"Lying in the grass?" Waller had finished packing up his kit and was now putting his hat on his head. The Newfoundlanders were marching out in an hour, the men already loading the mules with ammunition down on the parade ground. Waller had just needed to finish packing up, and Devlin had returned with him to the hotel to report.

The strange incident had Waller's mind turning again, "There were no sightings of savages from the guards?"

Devlin shook his head, "Checked with Captain Quinn personally, only unusual activity was us."

Waller sighed, recalling the embarrassing conversation of that previous night on the train, "Well, there is a possibility that she truly just wanted to be out there alone. On the train, night before last, she mentioned feeling a need to run... ahem... naked, in the grass. To roll around in it."

Of course, being a gentleman, Waller hadn't repeated that to his officers — partially, it had to be said, because he was certain he'd turn red when he said it. Devlin's eyes widened slightly, "My God, that woman's irregular."

"Jimmy, you have a gift for the understatement," Waller picked up his kit. "So, was she naked?"

He managed to ask the question frankly, and Devlin reddened, "She might have been when I startled her, but I was twenty yards away. She wrapped up in the cloak as soon as I challenged her."

He made sure to add that last part hurriedly, and Waller nodded, "So it could have been... *innocent*..."

"Well, if that's what it was, we better be damned sure the men don't hear about it. My God, sir, you think she's always... you know... only wearing the cloak..." Devlin's eyes were starting to glaze very slightly, and smiling, Waller patted him on the shoulder.

"I very much doubt it. There are too many strong winds in the world. But you're right, the men can't know she has an adventurous side. I need every man watching her for her behavior, not for her body. She might have intentionally revealed herself to you, Jimmy. Hoped to deflect attention," Waller didn't like being so suspicious, but there was little choice.

Devlin blinked away his imagined images and nodded, "Of course, sir. Absolutely."

"Good. Now let's check on them."

Nodding, the Lieutenant followed Waller from the room, closing the door behind him.

A few minutes later, Waller and Devlin were escorting the ladies down the street towards the parade ground. Though cordial in greeting, Emma was now silent; between being caught out at night and what she'd revealed on the roof the day prior, the young Lady had seemingly determined that silence was her best defense.

Waller watched her quietly, and then elected not to pressure her any further for the moment. She and Kara had professed that they would elaborate more on their mission once in the grasslands, so very soon they'd have no more excuse for silence.

"Morning," Smith was on horseback as he came up alongside the walking party, and he touched the brim of his hat at the ladies.

"Mister Smith, good morning," Waller nodded with a friendly smile, determined not to pressure the man to ride out with the RNR column.

"Been thinking, Major, I believe I'd like to ride west with you, if that's alright. Always wondered what's out that way, never been a safer chance," Smith said plainly, and Waller nodded.

"We'd be pleased to have you along, Mister Smith."

"Yes, we'd be grateful too," Kara Lynne added with a smile, and Smith looked to the woman with some surprise.

Women had taken an interest in Smith off and on over the years, but he'd never been too keen or able to take advantage of their affections. Even so, he recognized the interest when he saw it, and in this particular case, it surprised him. Kara seemed a stony sort of woman, not too afflicted with feelings of romance. He'd seen the sort before, raised on the new world frontier and tough as leather, even if they didn't look it.

But Kara seemed to have taken a liking to him. That or she was nervous at the prospect of having a local drifter around to advise the Major. Smith might be able to see through her plans, so she could be trying to get inside his guard.

He couldn't say, though, so he decided to remain polite, touching the brim of his hat again, "My pleasure, Miss."

Without further event, they reached the parade ground, and by the time they arrived the men had all fallen in. The six wagons were drawn up, three containing ammunition, one with casks of water and food rations, another with the Colt machine gun's ammunition and the gun itself towed behind, and the last — the only covered wagon — being reserved for the ladies.

As the men stood in clean lines, Captain Kearsey approached the arriving party, "Major, we're all set. The wagon is prepared for you ladies. We've even gotten our hands on some cushions and things to make it a little more comfortable for you."

Emma nodded with a tight smile, "Thank you, Captain. If you'll excuse us."

Walking past Waller and Kearsey without so much as looking back, Emma headed for the covered wagon, and Kara followed. Appearing somewhat surprised, Annie looked from officer to officer with a smile, "I... um... thank you very much!"

The poor maid didn't seem to be in on their scheme, and was just following loyally. Devlin walked after them with their small suitcases, and as soon as he deposited them in the back of the wagon, the canvas flaps were closed, blocking him out.

"Well, they're a bit miffed," Kearsey said quietly, and Waller nodded.

"We're either getting close to discovering their plan and they're nervous, or we're treating them very poorly," the Major agreed. "But until they tell us what the hell we're doing out there, Fred, I'm not going to enjoy Miss Emma's smile."

Kearsey nodded, "Yes sir. The men appreciate your concern, by the way. Not that we've been saying anything particular, but you know how rumor spreads. They're thinking the ladies are trying to use their charms to lead us into a trap, and they're saying the Wall ain't falling for it."

Waller's eyebrows went up as he heard his nickname. Somehow it only seemed to get back to him on dangerous days.

"Well, I'm glad they approve," he said. "Let's prepare to march. Get George over here. I want to confirm column order."

As Kearsey left, Devlin returned, "So my platoon's set up to handle the wagons and mules."

"Yes, you're officially only looking after the baggage and livestock, but it's you, Jimmy, because I want you close to the ladies. Keep an eye on them, and if savages attack, it's up to your men to defend them. Circle the wagons, get the Colt going... all of that."

Devlin nodded, "Yes sir. And we get to ride on the wagons, right?"

"You certainly do," Waller smiled.

Tucker and Kearsey returned a moment later, and Waller nodded to them both, "I want twenty-five miles today, and every day until we can't do it anymore, gentlemen. I want to get out there as fast as we can."

Marching twenty-five miles in a day was something the Newfound-landers had learned to do in the much harsher conditions of Afghanistan, where lorries had been as scarce as they seemed to be out here in the new world. Many units couldn't match the Newfoundlanders' pace, and even in this pleasant cool, the RNR itself couldn't keep up that speed of march for more than four or five days before the attrition wore them down. But the less time spent in the grasslands, the better. There'd be no grumbling about hurrying out and back, and both Tucker and Kearsey simply nodded.

Waller went on, "George, Jimmy's going to look after the wagons and the mules... and the ladies. Rest of your company will march up front. Fred, your b'ys are rearguard, but I want you to have one platoon out as skirmishers and flankers."

"We have those horses, a dozen of them. We giving them to the officers or to some skirmishers?" Tucker frowned, waving his hand towards the line of horses that Lieutenant Gallway had obtained for them.

Waller wasn't a horse rider — it was never a skill he'd picked up. He could probably learn quickly enough, but if the men were marching, he was inclined to stay on his own two feet as well.

"Up to you two if you want them, I'm young and foolish enough to say I'll walk," Waller gazed at the horses for a moment, then looked back. "But whatever horses don't have riders, get men on them. Men who know how to ride, preferably. We must have at least ten."

Kearsey nodded, "We can find some b'ys."

Something then occurred to Waller, and he turned to see where Smith had gone. The drifter was watering his horse across the street from the parade ground, so Waller called to him, "Mister Smith, could we borrow you for a minute?"

The drifter looked up and rubbed his mare's neck, "Be right back."

Coming over, he nodded to the Captains.

"Mister Smith would like to ride with us," Waller said, looking to Kearsey and Tucker.

Both Captains grinned, and Tucker spoke first, "Well Jesus, we might actually come back then."

"Well said," Kearsey agreed, extending his hand to Smith. "Thanks for coming along, Mister Smith."

Smith shook Kearsey's hand, then Tucker's, before looking at Waller, "Just announcing it?"

Waller shook his head, "No that's not why I needed you. We have a dozen horses, and we're going to put a section of men who know how to ride on them, probably with a Sergeant. A mounted scouting force. Would you mind riding with them during the days — you'd certainly know what to look for better than we would."

Smith nodded, "Sounds right to me."

"Excellent," Waller nodded his approval. "Alright, gentlemen. Find me those horsemen, and we'll march."

The Captains saluted and turned back to their companies, and then Devlin came around and saluted as well, "I'll get my b'ys together with the wagons."

Waller returned the salute and then Devlin was off, leaving just him and Smith.

"I have Jimmy watching the women. You heard about Emma running out in the fields by herself last night?"

Smith shook his head, so Waller quickly explained, and as the drifter listened, a frown deepened on his brow.

"That lady is hard to pin down. Good thing you've got Jimmy on her."

Waller nodded, "My thoughts exactly. Listen, Smith, thank you again for riding with us."

Smith looked at the Major, then at the covered wagon, "It's the decent thing to do."

"Yes, but outside of Newfoundland, I find the decent thing is rarely the common thing — at least not without coercion," Waller replied evenly.

Nodding slowly, Smith started to turn back to his mare, "Sounds like this Newfoundland would be a place I'd like."

Waller laughed shortly, "Rain, drizzle, fog and the ocean, Mister Smith. Climate might disagree with you, but the company's good."

Smith tipped his head, "Well company's the most important part, Major. I'll see you out there."

With that, the two men parted ways. Half an hour later, the Newfoundlanders, their ladies, and the drifter marched out of Long Prairie, heading west.

CHAPTER XX

The grasslands were quite beautiful. Waller had seen all sorts of terrain over the past five years of soldiering, but few compared to the fresh and energetic landscape that surrounded him here on the new world. No place, of course, would ever compare to Newfoundland — every Newfoundlander was doggedly loyal to home — but this place was still incredible.

As the first day of marching wore on, he found the refreshing breeze coming off the mountains kept the men cool, and the low humidity made the air feel light and easy to pass through. There was no trail, but Smith and the horsemen were riding out ahead, making certain their direction wasn't blocked by any landforms.

Waller stayed close to Devlin and the wagons, letting Tucker be the officer at the column's front.

He took the time to breathe the air.

Over the course of hours of walking, Long Prairie shrank slowly in the distance, and eventually it was swallowed under a ridge with a line of trees atop it. The way forward took the men past springs, gullies, streams that seemed to come and go to and from unknown locations, and more stands of trees.

The horsemen rode ahead and checked each of these hiding places for savages long before the column got near them, but the skirmishers and flankers still had to be alert. Those men, from one of Kearsey's platoons, walked around the outside of the column, Lee-Enfields in hand, ready to alert the men marching if any savages appeared — and to delay those savages until the men were ready to receive.

So far, though, things had been quiet. The morning had passed without incident, and the column had stopped briefly at a spring to lunch. Now, in mid-afternoon, the men were marching again, and the fresh breeze was making it quite pleasant.

"We'll cover about twenty-five miles today, I'd say," Devlin appeared next to Waller, hat off and his hair blowing in the breeze. "I thought the wagons would slow us down more, but there's nothing out here to stop them..."

"Jimmy, knock wood when you say things like that," Waller said quietly, and the Lieutenant put his hat back on and nodded.

Dropping back to one of the ammunition carts, he knocked on it, and then walked back up to Waller's side, "So far, though, I don't think we've got too much to complain about."

"Stop saying things like that, Jimmy," Waller fixed the Lieutenant with a stern gaze. "We're not even a day from Long Prairie yet. When we get out further, that's when I'm concerned."

Devlin nodded, "Yes, that's true enough. Emma said she didn't know how far out?"

"No, they can't recall. I'm going to guess at least three days, but even when we get out that far, we may be in the wrong direction. I hope Kara Lynne remembers some land features... I don't like the idea of combing back and forth out here looking for a faded memory," Waller kept his voice low as he spoke — the covered wagon wasn't too far behind.

As Devlin opened his mouth to respond, a rifle shot cracked out to the left, followed quickly by another.

The horsemen were far forward, so that had to be the flankers.

Captain Kearsey and two of his Lieutenants rushed out to the right of the column. This area was rolling grasslands, without a spring or a gulch nearby. The flankers were about fifty yards out, and now two of them were running towards the column, waving their arms.

"A party of savages coming this way! About twenty!"

Captain Kearsey slowed, looking at one of his officers, "First platoon if you please."

The column came to a stop at the rifle shots, and Tucker was already heading towards Waller when 'D' Company's first platoon dashed out of marching column and, under the barked orders of Sergeants, drew up in an open order line of two ranks in the grassy field to the right of the column.

"All men stand ready," Waller barked. "Jimmy, get to the Colt. Be ready to unlimber it if there are more."

"Yes sir," Devlin snapped a quick salute and trotted back to the machine gun cart, waving some of his men to join him.

If this was just twenty savages, there was no need to disrupt the entire column by deploying all the men into line. It would be overkill, and it would take longer to get back on march. But the men had to be ready in case there were more than twenty.

Taking a few steps towards Kearsey, Waller winced against the bright light of the day and finally saw the movement of the savages. The flankers had all fallen back parallel to Kearsey's firing line, and were standing ready to add their rifles to the volley.

"Get rid of them, Captain Kearsey," Waller called across the short distance between himself and 'D' Company's Captain.

"Yes sir!" Kearsey replied with gusto.

The savages were still about 300 yards out, but they were coming up over an undulating roll in the grassy plain, and were thus plainly visible to the Newfoundlanders. Dammit all they were moving quickly.

"First platoon... at 300 yards... ten rounds rapid...*fire!*"

As the fifty men of the platoon unleashed their .303 rounds at the approaching savages, the dozen men who'd been posted as flankers on that side joined in, and the quality of their shooting told instantly. In Afghanistan, these men had been asked to shoot against tribesmen and snipers hidden all over the highlands: twenty beast men moving in an open field were simply not a challenge.

Waller watched as the last of the savages fell 200 yards short of the column, and as the rifle fire stopped, a long silence dominated. Eyes were cast in all directions, as the officers and men of the Royal Newfoundland Regiment expected another shoe to drop. They waited, and Waller walked back to the other side of the column to check the left. The flankers were still out there, and they saw nothing.

Devlin and his machine gun party stood ready to unlimber the Colt, but there was no indication that there was more to shoot at.

"Any sign of activity on the left?" Waller called to the flankers, and one of the Sergeants out there yelled back with an all clear.

"Nothing up front, sir," Tucker then declared at the head of the column, and one of the Lieutenants with the rearguard barked the same.

Waller waited another minute, and then as the silence endured, he nodded, "Thank you, Captain Kearsey. Let's get back on the march!"

One of Kearsey's Sergeants barked at his first platoon to order arms, and shortly the men were returned to their place in line, patting each other on the back for doing the business.

The column began moving again, and Devlin caught up with Waller, "Well, a little excitement."

"Indeed. Let's hope that's as exciting as it gets out here."

Devlin nodded at Waller's words, but as the Major was looking at the Lieutenant, he noticed out of the corner of his eye that the canvas flaps on the front of the covered wagon had opened slightly. As soon as he looked all the way back, the flaps shut.

"What?" Devlin looked back too. "They were watching?"

Waller turned his eyes front again, "They were. I suppose that's understandable."

"Doesn't mean a thing, of course, sir," Devlin agreed. "They could just have wanted to see what we were up against."

"Indeed," Waller concurred.

"Or to see how many savages they'd need to call to finish us..." Devlin said that almost under his breath, and Waller smiled.

"More than twenty, apparently."

Devlin snorted a laugh, "Yes sir, more than twenty."

CHAPTER XXI

Establishing a camp that evening was not a simple matter. The twenty-five mile march had certainly tired the men, but none were inclined to rest until they had a sturdy position built for repelling savages, if the beasts came in the night. Thankfully, the good fortune of two moons on this world, and the lack of clouds overhead, meant that night here was always at least as bright as it would be with a clear sky and a full moon in Canada.

Even so, as Smith walked his mare into the camp that evening, he was impressed by what he saw. Leading the troop of mounted scouts for the day, he'd found this good location for a camp; it sat on top of a high ridge with a spring running down the middle, and trees scattered across it. The slopes on all sides were shallow and open, so there was no room for the savages to creep up to the perimeter, and thanks to the two moons, there would be no long shadows where the beasts could hide.

Because there were only six wagons with the column, the Newfoundlanders couldn't simply circle them and sleep on the inside, so instead the wagons were squared — with large spaces between them — and all the horses and mules were tied up within. The perimeter was being dug out as a trench that ringed the encampment, and Smith was impressed by the speed with which these 400 men dug that ring. In just an hour, a three-foot-deep trench had been carved out, and the dirt piled up to create a parapet.

They were only staying a night here, but the place was ready to receive an onslaught.

As Smith walked his horse carefully over a flatter section in the trench — one left for him and the other mounted scouts — he swung out of the saddle and took his mare's bridle, walking her to the wagon square to tie her up.

The sun was going down and men had set up their tents all along the ridge, and were now starting up fires so they could make the most of their tinned rations. Smith heard a few surprisingly good-natured grumbles about the lack of a beer ration, but dismissed them. From what he'd been seeing, these Newfoundlanders knew how to do without.

Tying up his mare and rubbing her nose easily, Smith heard someone approach behind him. He had long ago gotten used to identifying people by their footsteps, but this person was too quiet, sounded like someone who'd learned to move silently across the grasslands.

"Miss Lynne, what can I do for you?"

Smith guessed who it was based on the stealth of the approach and the interest that particular lady had shown earlier, and his guess was a good one.

"You're quite a man, aren't you? Tell by the footsteps who's coming — even me?" she asked in a sharp but friendly tone, and Smith turned away from his Appaloosa.

"I don't call myself 'quite' much of anything, Miss. But if you're wondering, I figured it was you because you were too quiet. No man from this regiment would know how to move that silent over the grass. Have to have years out here to know that," Smith said it plainly, and Kara Lynne smiled.

"The men from the regiment don't like me like... they like Emma," she said, sizing up Smith with her eyes. "She was a young Lady in their Empire, she's refined and such. I put on the show, but I grew up here, playing in this grass."

"You did more than play out here, Miss. Way it's been told to me, you lost your family out here, and got away with Miss Emma."

Kara Lynne's friendly expression faded, "So Waller didn't keep that to himself."

Smith waved a hand towards the trench line, "Let's have a walk and we can talk about it."

For a moment Kara paused, her eyes studying Smith's face for any sign of deception, but she decided he was being genuine. They walked out of the squared wagons and crossed the trench line, moving down the slope of the ridge.

Waller was coming out of his tent when Devlin slid to a halt next to it, "Sir, Smith and Miss Kara are down on the north slope, looks like they're walking."

Devlin pointed, and Waller frowned as he followed the finger.

"He may have better luck than we've been having getting them to talk. Keep Halloran's section on standby in case, but don't move out. I trust Smith," Waller spoke quickly, then looked back at Devlin. "Where's Emma? Actually, take me to her, I'll need you to occupy the maid."

"Forgive me, Smith, but I can't tell you more. I don't trust these people. None of the folk we met in London were trustworthy. They all found out about Emma and just wanted a piece of her, to take advantage of her," Kara Lynne sounded earnest, but Smith had heard earnest-sounding people enough times to know they could easily be lying.

"Well, I don't presume to tell anybody who they can trust," Smith said simply.

Kara looked at him, "That's why I like you. You're a man from this world. You're not a politician or a bureaucrat. You don't just see me and Emma as toys. I'm glad you came out here."

"I don't believe any man out here sees you or Emma as toys, Miss," Smith returned the gaze. "They see you as threats, which you've been asking for with your secrets."

Kara let out a sigh and shook her head, "You don't understand. If we aren't quiet about it..."

"Maybe in their Empire that's a problem. But, Miss, I'll be honest, I don't trust you. Maybe you feel you need to be secretive because if we find out what you're after we'll think you're... toys. But maybe you're being secretive because what you're hiding could get us killed," Smith was speaking plainly again, and Kara shook her head.

"No, we're not trying to get you in trouble..."

"But Miss, from our perspective, what could you possibly be hiding that warrants this much secrecy unless it's bad for us? Men get to imagining things when the truth is kept from them. And these men from Newfoundland, they've seen enough hard fighting to imagine some really bad things," Smith stopped now, as they were about fifty yards down the slope from the trench line.

"We'll tell them in time. But when they find out... things will get so complicated. They won't look at us the same way."

Smith looked out at the setting sun, "Miss, look at that. We're out here looking at something no man or woman has probably ever lived to see — sun setting on this particular horizon. There are savages out here that either you're controlling, or that want you or Miss Emma something fierce. We're looking at you and Miss Emma like the enemy, so you *don't want us* to keep looking at you in the same way."

Kara shook her head and let out a breath, "I thought you'd understand."

"I might, if you'd actually tell me something," Smith was direct, and maybe that wasn't the best way.

"Well then I'm sorry to have troubled you," Kara Lynne turned and headed back for the trenches.

Emma was sitting on a log next to her fire when Waller found her, and as he approached with Devlin he was none too subtle.

"We're in the grasslands, Emma. I believe you promised to tell me something about our mission."

Looking up over the fire, Emma stared at Waller for a moment, "No, not yet. I don't want to talk about it yet. Tomorrow we just march straight west. Keep going west..."

Waller felt his jaw beginning to clench in frustration, "Emma, you either have something ghastly to hide, namely the fact that you're working with the savages somehow, or you're going to tell me now what we're doing out here."

Emma shook her head, "Not tonight. Tomorrow maybe, but not tonight. So unless you plan on *shooting* me like you said you would, you can have your answers another day."

"Why not, M'Lady? I mean, if there's no harm in what you haven't told us, now's as good a time as any," Devlin tried a more cordial approach.

"Don't try to play nice, Jimmy. I know you don't trust me any more than Tom does. You think I'm calling the savages. You think I'm responsible for that horde. Well how can I be? Can't you see me? I'm just an innocent young Lady, who's been sent out here to find something of great import to the Empire because I might remember where it is."

Waller and Devlin traded glances, neither with any particular idea of how to get more from Emma. It was incredibly frustrating.

"Leave her alone. Your orders say you're here to serve us, so get away!" Kara Lynne barked the command as she passed Waller and Devlin, and sat herself down on the log next to Emma. "Has anything befallen you intrepid soldiers? Hmm? Twenty savages today. If we were evil, wouldn't we call more? Just leave us alone."

Smith, who'd followed Kara over to the fire, arrived next to Waller shaking his head, "No one's feeling talkative."

Waller let out a long sigh and then nodded, "Very well then. My orders are my orders. You'll have your escort, but I'd recommend you decide to become more forthcoming quickly. In the meantime, if either of you plans to go rolling in the grass tonight, you'll have Sergeant Halloran at your side. Mister Devlin, be so good, would you?"

Devlin nodded, "Sergeant Halloran, your section if you please!"

The men who'd joined Devlin in the expedition to chase Emma the night prior quick-stepped into position behind Waller and Smith.

"Sergeant, these ladies are to have protection at all hours," Devlin turned to the NCO, and he nodded.

"Yes sir."

"Good evening, ladies," Waller snapped his heels together and saluted.

Devlin did the same, and watching them go, Smith shook his head.

"You're forcing the man into a corner," the drifter said. "Responsible for all these lives, man can't just trust a pretty face. Evenin', ladies."

Touching the brim of his hat, he too left the scene. After they went, Sergeant Halloran's men surrounded the fire and watched the ladies suspiciously.

The Newfoundlanders would not be caught off guard.

CHAPTER XXII

Waller did not sleep well that night, constantly wondering if the women would attempt an escape. Nothing about this mission made sense to him — why did the women want to come out here? If they worked for the savages, why would they go to the effort of having such a large escort? If they didn't work for the savages, what could be so horrible about the mission that they wouldn't reveal it? Did they think that, if it was a one-way mission, the men would abandon? And if it was one-way, why were they on it themselves?

Nothing fit together properly, and so Waller slept poorly as his mind tried to comprehend it all.

Through the night a strong watch was kept up, but no savages came. This was a part of the country where men and animals seldom ventured, so there was no food, and the savages, like any predatory animals, probably spent little time here.

But how long would that good fortune last... and how far would they have to go before the ladies found what they were looking for?

As Waller left his tent at sunrise the next morning, buttoning up the flaps of his tunic against the chill, he looked west. By the end of this day, they'd be fifty miles from Long Prairie. A horse could cover that in a day quite handily, but how long would it take a ten-year-old girl carrying a three-year-old in her arms? If Emma's story was true, that was the only gauge on actual distance Waller had.

There was no way to be certain.

"Morning, Major," Smith was up with a cup of coffee in his hand.

"Mister Smith," Waller nodded. "Someone set you up?"

Smith nodded, "Captain Kearsey did. Good coffee."

Waller smiled, "Never really taken to the stuff, myself, but I slept so badly I might indulge. Emma says we're to march straight west today. How much further out that way did you manage to get yesterday?"

Smith looked west and frowned, "I'd say about another two or three miles. But from the top of that ridge there, you can see everything. Opens up into a broad prairie, no trees and no springs that I could see. Goes on for at least another horizon."

"Open ground... nothing to slow them down," Waller said in a low tone.

"And nothing to keep you from shooting them down," Smith observed, sipping his coffee.

Waller nodded, "True. We may need to keep you closer when we get onto it, though, Mister Smith. Have you riding a perimeter around us, give us more warning if a horde finds us."

"You expecting a horde?" Smith asked, then emptied his tin mug.

Waller looked from the western horizon to the drifter, "I'm expecting the worst. Hopefully I'm wrong."

Smith nodded, "Hopefully you are, Major."

The men were rallied to march two hours later, with the wagons and mules reloaded and the casks of water and every man's canteen filled to the brim from the spring. There was no evidence of a water source ahead, so it was best to maximize what was carried, even if the extra weight might not be appreciated on the march.

Smith rode out ahead of the column on his own, leaving the other horsemen as flankers, ready to watch for savages on all sides. It worked fine for Smith, he was accustomed to riding on his own.

After an hour he was out into the prairie, and his horse trotted onto the great plain of grass, he realized it wasn't so ideal for Waller's needs as he'd hoped. The ground was low and rolling, so while it looked flat, there were dips and clefts all through it where savages could hide and spring up. Easing his way forward, Smith explored a couple of these dips before deciding it was a bad idea to try it on his own.

Smith was a fast draw and, more importantly, a good shot with both his Colt pistol and his Winchester, but if a dozen savages jumped out at him from twenty yards away, he'd be dead. Any man would be. It'd take all the horsemen to sweep the way ahead.

Turning his mare, Smith rode back towards the column.

It took three hours for the column to reach the edge of the prairie, Waller walking near the wagons for the entire time. Sergeant Halloran's men walked alongside the covered wagon, six on each side of it, and the ladies remained sequestered inside, feeling uncivil. Waller could understand their dislike of his treatment of them, but he still lacked any sympathy.

He also had a feeling he'd see their true colors today.

The column stopped at prairie's edge, near the last stand of trees, to have an early lunch in the cool late-morning air before moving on. Smith requested the help of the rest of the horses to sweep the prairie ahead, and since it was Smith asking, Waller agreed without question. If the drifter said he needed more bodies to do the job, Waller had no doubt that more bodies were indeed required.

Lunch was an hour-long stop, and then the column marched out onto the prairie, and Waller felt the hair on the back of his neck begin to rise. He did not like this land.

He walked with his left hand closed around the handle of the sword he'd clipped to his belt, the grip so tight his knuckles were reddening. His eyes dashed from side to side, looking at the northern horizon to the right, and then at the southern horizon to the left. It felt as though they were being watched... that someone was waiting for them to go just far enough into the prairie to be beyond any sort of terrain protection.

The first hour passed without incident, but Waller remained anxious.

Far out ahead, Smith and the mounted Newfoundlanders rode through dips in the ground with weapons handy. No savages were found in the dead ground of these dips, so the horsemen rode on.

A tension seemed to be settling over the ranks. As Waller walked past the men in the column, he noticed that they too were looking to both flanks, wondering where the hammer was going to come from. This prairie felt like a place where death would try to close in... but death had come for this regiment many times. The Newfoundlanders had staved off defeat on each of those occasions, though it always cost them good men to do so.

But things out here could be different, no matter how good the Newfoundlanders were. If a horde of thousands appeared, death might finally carry the day...

Devlin appeared next to Waller as the second hour of prairie marching ended, and the Major nodded in greeting to his friend, "Jimmy, how're your b'ys?"

"Tense. This field feels deadly. Like men have died out here before. It's the perfect spot for an ambush by the savages," Devlin's tone was uneasy.

The day wore on, and the prairie did as well. They reached the horizon they'd seen at the edge of the prairie, and then the horizon they'd seen from that horizon, and then another, and then more. The steppes spread out into a broader ocean of uninterrupted golden grass. Waller and Devlin walked together through the afternoon, and every man in the regiment spent plenty of time with both hands on his rifle, expecting that at any moment, the savages would attack.

After almost fifteen miles of this, Smith rode up to the column, and then down its side to find Waller.

"This is a bloody cursed place," was Devlin's sharp greeting.

"Find a spot for us to camp?" Waller asked more pertinently, and Smith pulled off his hat and wiped his brow on his sleeve as he nodded.

"A big hollow with steep sides, you can put the wagons across the low side and dig firing steps the whole way along the rim."

Waller nodded, "Good. How far?"

"Another two miles or so," Smith returned his hat to his head.

"That'll give us another twenty-five miles today," Devlin said more calmly. "A long way from help again."

"Should be the regimental slogan," Waller agreed. "Thank you, Mister

Smith. We'll see you up there."

Smith nodded and turned his mare away, and Devlin and Waller watched him go.

The first Newfoundlanders arrived at their next camp half an hour later.

As night fell, Waller walked the perimeter of the new camp, looking north and south again as he wondered where the savages were. Had they all been killed in the big push they'd made at Treeline City? Had his column somehow slipped behind the lines of beasts, into an un-roamed rear area? What was going on?

He stood at the highest point on the rim of the depression the men were camped in and looked down on them for a moment. The cooking fires had been lit, but the men were by no means relaxed. Their rifles were always close at hand — that was the soldier's way — but now the men seemed to be more conscious of their positions, and were always looking up at the rim of this depression, wondering if the site was safe.

It was probably not so safe, but it was better than parking up in open country.

Waller's eyes drifted slowly over the camp, stopping at the covered wagon. The ladies were staying in their wheeled home for the night, it seemed, unwilling to give up more information about the mission, and not wishing to be further interrogated.

"I thought they'd come today."

Waller nearly jumped in surprise as Smith appeared behind him, "This place is perfect for attacking... but they didn't come. Maybe we got past them all."

Smith didn't sound convinced, and Waller looked back at him, "Or maybe we'll see them tomorrow."

The drifter nodded in agreement, and both men looked south again for a moment.

"Well, we've done fifty miles. How fast does a wagon train move?" Waller glanced back at Smith, and the American gave a thoughtful look.

"I'd say about ten miles in a day. Your men march fast, and wagon trains don't spend as much of the day moving."

"Ah, well we can't keep this up forever," Waller released a breath. "But by wagon train standards, we're five days from Long Prairie. Hopefully we're already close to whatever Kara's family died discovering."

Smith nodded, "I hope you're right, Major. Odd as this'll sound from me, I'm inclined to get back to a town. This ain't a trail I'd be eager to explore."

"Meaningful words, coming from a man such as yourself," Waller said quietly.

"They are," Smith agreed.

CHAPTER XXIII

The men broke camp without incident the next morning, though everybody still felt uneasy. Smith rode out ahead with two of the riders alongside him, the other ten mounted scouts being left with the column to serve as flankers and skirmishers. The feeling of death had intensified over this beautiful prairie.

"First thing Major Waller said to look for is a water source," Lieutenant Kennedy was one of the two riders with Smith this morning, and the young man repeated Waller's command.

Smith nodded. The men had emptied their canteens and the casks were draining quickly. Replenishment needed to be found soon, or these Newfoundlanders were going to face a grim march back to a known source of water.

But finding water was not Smith's biggest worry. He was waiting for the attack to come.

With his two companions, he rode on, warily checking each hollow they passed with his Colt pistol drawn. Kennedy, as an officer, had a Webley revolver, and he refused to let the black gun out of his hand through the entire morning.

They rode up shallow rises with baited breath, wondering what would be on the other side… and they would always find nothing, just more prairie stretching out ahead of them. This unending ocean of grass.

"Like being at sea," the Corporal on the third horse grumbled at one point. "Never thought I'd be lost in a sea of grass."

Smith looked at the man, "Best hope you never are."

The Corporal grinned, "Yeah, let's hope."

They rode on through lunch, while in the distance behind them they saw the column stop to cautiously feed itself. The horses were working, but Smith was being sure to keep that work to a minimum. He didn't want to ride his mare into the ground on just another patrol, and if savages turned up, he'd need her to have some speed left in her legs.

It was sometime in the early afternoon when they came anxiously upon another rise, pistols drawn and rifle ready. Smith was looking back over his shoulder, locating the column far back in the distance, but as he came to the crest he looked back around, and immediately hauled on the reins.

"What the hell is that?" the Corporal asked sharply, pointing towards the subject of his exclamation with his rifle.

The Lieutenant's horse was more skittish than the other two, so it took the young man a moment to calm his mount enough to look. He then glanced at Smith, "A circle of ruins... wagons?"

Smith nodded, "Must be."

What had once been a wagon train was sitting on the crest of the next hill.

"This place feels like death," the Corporal wasn't in a mood to edit his thoughts for the officer present.

"It does," Smith nodded, then kicked his mare into a canter. He could tell his trusty Appaloosa didn't like the feel of this place any more than the Corporal did, but she trusted Smith, and took the first few hesitant steps forward.

The Lieutenant and the Corporal looked at each other, then followed.

Nearly fifty wagons had been circled on the top of this hill, and the circle was a tight one. Crates had been used to fill in most of its gaps, so Smith rode round the outside for a minute, looking in through the openings, before deciding he'd have to dismount to investigate further.

"Lieutenant, I'm going in. Look after my horse," Smith called as he dismounted. He climbed over the barricade with his gun drawn, dropping into the inside of the ring and searching the open area with his eyes before taking a step.

Most of the wagons had clearly been covered, because the frames for the canvas were still standing. The canvas itself was long gone, blown away years ago... if not torn away by savages before that. Smith decided that was a good thing — no easy hiding places for the savages. He could see just about everything in this large open area, at least 100 yards across.

And ten feet from him was a spring that ran down the hill heading west.

Smith walked slowly up to that spring, knelt, put a cupped hand into the water, and tasted a little. Tasted fine.

Standing up again, he walked out into the center of the circled wagons, looking all around him as he did. These wagons were all bleached to grey and had partly rotted, many of them having fallen twisted or collapsed... but they were still a circle, still a defensible position on top of a hill with water.

Someone had picked this place to camp, and it had been the last camp they'd ever made.

"Sir, over here!"

Smith looked to his left as the Corporal stopped his horse next to a wagon and pointed with his rifle at something inside. He walked to this wagon, still looking in every direction in case something came for him.

Carefully climbing up onto the half-rotted structure, Smith found a satchel with letters and documents inside it. It was old paper that had been sitting in the open for a long time, so the first pieces he grabbed started to crumble. Fishing deeper in the bag, he found one that didn't. A letter dated 1896.

Smith read a couple of lines but they were just personal correspondence. He didn't mean to spend all the time it would take to read the whole thing. What was important right then was that the letter was from 1896. So was the next letter, and the next. He began to quickly scan them, and they told a tale.

This circle of wagons had been sitting here in the grass for twenty-three years.

One letter spoke of a sure-thing gold mine 100 miles from Long Prairie, that'd make every man in this wagon train rich. Smith didn't have to read that whole letter to figure just what had happened here, it was a story he saw play out many times south of the border.

These folk had been sold a lie by some dude who'd rode into town, promising he alone had seen a gold mine 100 miles from civilization. He sold them a worthless map for 1,000 dollars... or pounds, because these were British... and they'd decided to make themselves rich.

But these folk had been smart, or had thought they were. They'd gotten a huge train together, probably armed to the teeth. Figured any savages that came at them, they could handle. The evidence Smith was standing in suggested they'd failed.

"There are no bones?" Lieutenant Kennedy called the question across the perimeter of the circle, and Smith shook his head.

"Savages don't leave anything behind. And these have been here more than twenty years... anything edible is gone."

Kennedy looked both disgusted and afraid, and Smith couldn't blame the man. These people had a fifty-wagon circle and they'd been overrun. Wasn't a good sign for the Newfoundlanders.

"We should water here," Smith called back to Kennedy. "We have a spring in the circle... might be a good place to camp tonight, too."

"Feels like a circle of death," the Corporal, still sitting on his horse near Smith, observed quietly.

"It does," Smith nodded. "But no settlers could have had your kind of firepower. And you're better off behind fifty wagons than six."

The Corporal nodded grudgingly, "That's true enough, sir."

"Let's get back to the column," Smith called that out so Kennedy could hear it.

Taking a couple of the letters, Smith crossed the large circle back to the way he'd come in, climbed out, and remounted. Stuffing the letters into a saddlebag, he pulled on the reins and turned his mare around.

Kennedy followed, his eyes locked on the haunted circle of death, and the Corporal joined them as they rode down the side of the hill and up the slope of the ridge. They weren't riding as carefully now, because they'd already cleared the hollows and sections of dead ground on the way back to the column.

But as Smith came to the top of the rise he hauled on his reins, "Stop!" He saw savages. Thousands of savages.

Kennedy stopped harshly, then asked nervously, "What is it, Mister Smith?"

Smith sat still on his horse for a second, then nodded in the direction of the column.

Kennedy looked, and he saw the column marching. Then he looked south, and he saw a horde of thousands of savages racing across the plain, right at the Newfoundlanders.

"Christ, come on!" Kennedy kicked his horse into a run, and the Corporal did the same.

For a moment Smith sat atop that ridge and watched. Was he going to do what he'd seen Captain Donahue do? Was he going to ride and die this time?

He decided he'd have to, and he kicked his mare forward.

CHAPTER XXIV

Waller and Devlin were walking together near the wagons again when the first shot was fired into the air. The second shot followed almost instantly, and the Major and the Lieutenant looked at each other. In a grim way, they were both almost relieved.

Here came the savages.

Looking south, the direction of the shots, Waller saw what had drawn the warning. The column was walking across the spine of a relatively high ridge that dipped down before a lower one rose about a mile away. Coming over the flatlands from the south towards the second ridge was a horde — a horde of thousands.

The flankers to the south had been walking their horses along the spine of the second ridge, and they were the ones who'd fired the warning shots. Now all those men were riding hard back to the column.

Looking to his right Waller checked the northern approaches in a flash, but the men flanking on that side waved the all clear. For now the attack was coming from the south only, which was a good thing.

"One way again," Devlin observed quickly, and Waller nodded.

"They look to be about three miles out. That gives us time. Get the wagons squared and the mules and horses behind them as best you can. I want the Colt machine gun central with a good line of fire. It'll engage when they get to the top of that ridge. Halloran to guard the ladies."

Devlin nodded and left Waller's side, while Waller walked away from the column onto the grassy down-slope to the left of it. Captains Tucker and Kearsey quickly stepped across to his side, and as Devlin halted the wagons and unlimbered the Colt behind him, Waller turned to face the column.

"Jimmy has the machine gun in the center. I want both companies in a line flanking on either side. Anchor your open flanks with Lewis guns. All men to the front, no reserve. Keep your platoons on the flanks ready to wheel backward if the bastards try to encircle us."

Waller's words were cool and calculated, and despite nervous dry mouths, both Captains replied with sharp acknowledgments.

Waller walked quickly back to the wagons as the men were pulled out of the column and marched around to form a line of two ranks on either side of the Colt which one of Devlin's sections was now manhandling into position.

He could have formed a square, as the British had done so many times against warriors in Africa, but he was determined to put every rifle to the savages. Forming square would leave half his men unable to engage the enemy... and he had a feeling that a square would not stop these beasts. They could probably leap over the hedge of bayonets and ravage everything inside.

Men from each section were coming to the wagon train now to collect an ammunition-bearing mule. There would be no interruption to the ammunition flow when the musketry started, and once the savages crested that second ridge and ran their last mile, probably in only three minutes, they would absorb every piece of lead this column was carrying.

Waller didn't allow himself to think of just what might happen *after* the thousands of savages traversed that mile. He doubted that even his men could knock them all down.

The riding flankers arrived at the column a moment later, "They're coming, sir! At least 5,000, maybe more. Jesus!"

Accepting this report, Waller directed the mounted men to the flanks of the position, "If they try to get around our flanks or come from behind, stop them. If this column is overrun, any man on a horse is to escape to Long Prairie to report what's happened. If anyone questions your courage, tell Captain Quinn and Lieutenant Gallway that it was my express order, and thank them for the Colt."

Waller didn't have time to write orders for the men, so there would be no written proof that he'd sent them away if it came to that. He'd have to trust that Quinn and Gallway would protect their honor in that case.

As the riders headed off, Waller turned to face south again, then looked left and right. Tucker's 150 men (fifty of his men were Devlin's, and thus with the wagons) were on the right, and were in a line of two ranks with the front rank kneeling. To the left, Kearsey's 200 men were similarly arranged. Waller stood in the middle, and just to his left the Colt machine gun was being settled in place. Boxes of ammunition were being stacked behind it, and the loading strips were being positioned for easy access.

Waller stepped closer to Sergeant Whealan, who was commanding the gun, "When they get to the top of that ridge, open fire. And don't stop."

The Sergeant nodded, "Yes sir."

A strained, artificially-generated calm spread over the men. They'd seen many types of death coming for them in their careers thus far, and were still alive. This was the worst of all, though — they'd seen savages before, but at Treeline City they'd had a solid barricade. Now their only shelter was going to be built of .303 rounds, and corpses.

"What is going on... let me out... Tom!" Emma appeared outside her wagon for the first time that day, fighting her way past a Private who'd tried to stop her. "Tom what is..."

She stopped as she looked south, then as Waller turned to her she shook her head, "It wasn't me. I promise it wasn't."

"We'll talk more if we're alive in half an hour. Unless you want to tell me right now what's going on."

Emma opened her mouth to speak but then stopped herself. Her eyes locked on Waller's, and she shook her head, "We *will* be alive in half an hour. Your men will do the hard work."

With that assured statement, she turned and climbed back into her wagon. Waller took a step closer and summoned Sergeant Halloran to his side with a jerk of the head.

"Sir?"

"Your section must look after them, Halloran. And if they're giving orders to the savages, don't give any quarter. Fix bayonets, don't kill them if you can avoid it. If they're giving orders I'll want to interrogate them later."

Halloran nodded slowly, "I understand, sir."

"Thank you, Sergeant," Waller said, then turned back to face south. The savages were now being eclipsed by the second ridge — meaning they had to be running up its reverse slope. The time was near.

"Alright men, when they reach the top of that slope I want every man with a rifle to start firing. We're not going to run short of ammunition, and I want every shot we have the chance to take. When they get to the bottom of the slope of that ridge, fix your bayonets, and get ready to receive. Stand fast and we'll show these savage bastards how Newfoundlanders fight!"

Waller yelled those orders to the whole company, which was a highly irregular way for him to deliver them, but was effective nonetheless. There was no time to bring all the officers together, no time to carefully explain what was going on in his head. The officers and the men would simply have to fight together, as they always did.

The savages would eat them alive if they failed.

Sergeants and Lieutenants began their musketry mantras again.

"Pick your targets."

"Watch your range, that's a mile to the ridge. Check your sights."

"Steady b'ys."

"Pick your targets."

"Look to your front."

Words Waller was certain had been repeated many, many times to men from across the British Empire, fighting in battles across the British Empire, against the many foes of the British Empire. Some of those men had died at the hands of their oppositions, and some had survived.

In just a few minutes, the Newfoundlanders would know which camp they fell into.

CHAPTER XXV

"Company... at the mile... rapid... *fire!*"

The savages erupted onto the crest of the hill and were met by an incredibly well-aimed volley of .303 rounds, which even at a mile's range had the power to knock a beast down. The Colt machine gun started its roar next to Waller, the weapon's crew unaccustomed to its kick and so taking a moment to direct its fire down into the horde.

Waller stood fast while his officers paced up and down the lines behind the firing men, and as the savages began to topple, the Major took a breath.

At this range, volley fire was all the men could do — there was no chance of aiming at one savage and hitting that body, so instead the Newfoundlanders were firing at a range, trying to send walls of lead into the horde as British soldiers had been doing since Wellington's time on the peninsula.

The effect was not devastating, but it was better than letting the creatures run up on the column unharrassed. Fire from the Colt gun swept up and down the line of savages as the Corporal manipulating the weapon tried to spread its destructive force.

The savages kept running — and running fast.

"Watch that range, it's down to 1,200 yards, change your sights!" one of the Sergeants nearer Waller roared, and the call was repeated up and down the line.

The sight on a rifle had to change to reflect the distance to target, otherwise the rounds would fly over the savages' heads.

The volleys slackened for a moment as men quickly switched their sights, but the hot, loud thunder of the Lee-Enfields regained its power in just a few seconds. As the range came down, more savages began to collapse, punched to pieces by .303 caliber lead.

Waller allowed himself to believe that as many as 1,000 had been knocked down at that long range, though he feared he was deluding himself. The real killing would come in the last 300 yards, when every man could pick a savage to shoot and be reasonably certain of hitting him.

His men were crack shots.

Smith crested the hill that the column's ridge led into, slowing his horse as he did. The savages were running fast for the column's south side. Waller had the men drawn up and the sound of rifle fire was intense. Smith could see a wide and thickening trail of savage bodies on the grass on that ridge and slope.

But they weren't thinning as fast as they needed to be.

Lieutenant Kennedy and the Corporal were already nearly at the flank of the Newfoundlanders' line, ready to join the defense.

The savages raced forward, though, and were just 500 yards from the lines... and there were still thousands of them.

Smith kicked his mare into a gallop. He'd aim for the wagons, where the ladies and Waller would be. If the savages were coming for those women, and if those women were up to no good, that'd be the right place for him.

"That's 400 yards. Come on b'ys, make the bastards feel it!"

The Short, Magazine, Lee-Enfield rifle was a fine weapon, and in these experienced hands it was able to snap fire as many as thirty rounds in a minute. Waller had heard tell of a musketry instructor who'd once used an SMLE to fire thirty-eight rounds through a twelve inch target at 300 yards in a minute.

His men were just about that good, and if one was counting — as Waller was in that moment — that meant that during the last minute of the charge, as many as 12,000 rounds would fire into the horde from just the men in line. The Colt gun would add another 400 or 500 beyond that, and hopefully all the savages would collapse under the weight of the lead.

But Waller wasn't certain. Men could miss, and an expected rate of fire wasn't necessarily a certain one.

A hand landed on his shoulder, and Waller turned quickly to see Smith had appeared behind him.

"Major," the drifter nodded, greeting Waller loudly over the din.

"Mister Smith. We may just hold these bastards yet," Waller called back. "That's 300 yards. Fix bayonets!"

As Waller looked back at the horde, now drawing closer, he started to feel a strange calm. Drawing the sword which he really had no idea how to use in one hand, and lifting his pistol in the other, he took a couple of steps forward.

Smith had his Winchester, and without another word to Waller he brought it to his shoulder and started firing fast, the action on his rifle allowing an even smoother fire than the SMLEs.

The savages were close now, and with bayonets locked onto the fronts of their rifles, the men fired faster, more doggedly.

Then the machine gun jammed.

Waller turned quickly, watched the men hit it in frustration — and desperation — and then shook his head, "Rifles men, no time to fix it!"

The crew left their weapon quickly, collecting their rifles and adding to the vicious fire that was blasting down the slope of the hill. The savages kept coming.

Lewis guns were firing short bursts out on the flank, but the savages weren't stopping. In a great stampede they raced forward, and as Waller turned back to the horde, he couldn't tell how much of it was left. He couldn't see through it — he couldn't see how thick the carpet of bodies behind it was. He couldn't see how deep the formation could be.

It was as broad as it had been when it started its charge, but how deep was it?

"That's 100 yards. Make every round count!"

The men were firing with desperation, now, as the savages continued to come, seemingly without end, and certainly without fear.

With blinding speed, the range continued to fall. The bastards moved like charging cavalry, but charging cavalry didn't eat you. What could the Newfoundlanders do? If the savages hit this line, they'd flank and overrun it in seconds. Standing still they'd simply have to absorb the charge and try desperately to keep the beasts away from the wagons...

And the women.

Waller looked over his shoulder and saw Halloran standing next to the covered wagon with his men, rifles ready. There was nothing more that could be offered in the defense of the ladies.

"Charge bayonets!" Waller roared as the savages came into fifty yards range. No one heard him, and there was no bugler with this unit. He grabbed the men near him — the former machine gun crew — and barked at them. "Follow me, charge bayonets!"

They paled, but they were being given an order by the Wall. The man who stood when others fell. They'd go with him.

Waller twirled his saber in the air the way he'd seen it done in pictures, and then raced out of the line, the six men he'd gathered following.

If the rest of the men couldn't hear him, they'd see him.

Up and down the line, officers began barking the orders, "Charge bayonets!"

The Newfoundlanders followed their Major down the last thirty yards to crash into the savage horde.

Waller changed the angle of his torso so he could lead with his Webley revolver, and as the savages drew near with their snarling human-like faces, he fired once, twice, and a third time. Three fell and then the rest were around him and the men he had with him.

He swung his saber clumsily and caught one leaping beast in the stomach, then shot another, and another. One of the men bayoneted a savage coming behind him, and then the Newfoundlanders huddled together, bayonets facing outwards as they lunged and recovered, trying to keep the savages from taking the initiative.

Waller fired his last bullet into a savage and then flipped his revolver in his hand, holding it by the barrel so he might club some of the beasts with the butt. He saw a savage coming and threw a thrust at the creature with his saber, impaling it viciously before recovering his blade and swinging again.

The savages who raced past him weren't turning around, though — he and his small party weren't being encircled.

The rest of the Newfoundlanders were slamming hard into the front of the savage horde, and were meeting them with a desperate ferocity that the creatures could not have been expecting.

Smith was standing back and emptying his Winchester for the last time. He didn't have a bayonet, just a bowie, and he didn't reckon charging a horde made sense to him, but the Newfoundlanders had the guts to do it.

At least 1,000 of the savages were still standing — it was two-to-one. Smith didn't know if the men could survive that, but he did know that savages were breaking past them, and coming right for the wagons.

Behind him, Devlin raced to the machine gun with a fresh party of men, "Try to clear it, while they're holding them back. Number three section, number four section, form a line, quick now!"

The men hurriedly formed a new line.

"Rapid fire at will! Watch your targets!" Devlin barked, and then as the men opened fire, the Lieutenant drew his sword and revolver and reached Smith's side.

The fire from the two sections of Devlin's platoon wasn't as fast, as the men were careful not to shoot their own. Those savages who broke past the Newfoundlanders were greeted by fresh fire, but the distance wasn't great — they couldn't all be stopped, because dozens upon dozens were coming forward.

"They're not stopping to fight your men," Smith observed, lowering his rifle and shifting it to his left hand as he drew his Colt pistol with his right.

"Leave the machine gun, fix your bayonets! Defend the wagon!" Devlin barked, then stretched out his arm, looked down the barrel of his revolver, and began shooting.

Smith fired almost from the hip, and at this range the drifter's bullets were flying true. But he only had six, so as he holstered his pistol and dropped back to lean his Winchester against one of the wagons, it was the Newfoundlanders of Devlin's platoon who raced forward with their bayonets leveled.

One near Devlin didn't get out of the way of a savage's swinging fist, and like a cannonball it smashed through his nose and collapsed his face, mercifully breaking his neck in the process. The Newfoundlanders fought hard, though, their bayonets keeping most of them alive.

But only because the savages weren't stopping to surround them. They were coming straight for the wagons, leaving surprised and sometimes unscathed soldiers in their wake.

Smith quickly reloaded his Colt as dozens more of the beasts came rushing past Devlin's men.

Waller was either very lucky, or the savages didn't care about him. None of the men who'd raced bravely down the slope with him were dead, though two were limping. The savages didn't seem to care about any of them. They were racing up the hill as if the Newfoundlanders weren't there.

Turning and looking back up the hill, Waller watched a dozen of his men get knocked flat by the attackers, and a few sections managed to force the savage charge to stall, leaving them in a bayonet fight for their lives. Remembering their drill, the Newfoundlanders kept the savages away, sometimes shooting them to finish them off.

But Waller realized what he'd done: he'd abandoned the wagons, and there were simply too many savages left for his men to stop from reaching them.

He raced back up the hill and the men who'd charged with him followed after.

The Lewis guns hadn't charged, and now their two-man teams got them into action from atop the ammunition wagons, shooting short bursts to try to keep larger clusters of savages back. The men who'd been mounted scouts defied their orders and leapt from their horses with their rifles. Surprisingly, none of the horses bolted, and the men, who didn't know how to fight on horseback, fixed their bayonets and charged.

There were only ten of them, but they'd do everything they could.

It wasn't enough, though. Dozens of savages kept coming, and soon they were too well mixed in with bayonet-wielding Newfoundlanders for the Lewis guns to be able to shoot. The crews came forward with bayonets, but it was still not enough.

All the savages went for the covered wagon. Smith stood with Sergeant Halloran at the back of that wagon, and he emptied his pistol in six straight kill shots, but still the beasts kept coming. Halloran's men lunged forward with desperate discipline, stabbed some of the savages back, but they were all converging at this point. One of Halloran's men had his back broken and his head simply crushed.

Halloran leapt forward one time too many, and a blow that he deflected away from his chest with his rifle glanced off his ribs and cracked them.

With practiced smoothness, Smith managed one more reload of his Colt, and used those six shots for cover while he pulled Halloran back to the wheel of the wagon. The rest of the men from Halloran's section tried to fight, but they were forced back, a few falling as they clustered around the back of the wagon with Smith.

The drifter pulled out his bowie knife, and reckoned his number was up.

As one of the savages leapt towards him, he stepped in to cut down the distance on it, and stabbed with the bowie as it swung with its arm. He ducked the arm, but the bowie went into the beast's throat.

He thought he had it, but he didn't. In its dying flail, the creature put its shoulder under him and pushed with explosive force. Like a rag doll he was tossed backwards, and he flew through the closed flaps of the wagon.

It was done now, surely.

CHAPTER XXVI

Most of the men were too busy keeping each other alive on the slope to notice that the wagon was being virtually crushed by savages, but Waller did. He saw Devlin leading a handful of men in a charge at one of the flanks of the savage concentration, and he raced to do the same, a few men staying with him.

There was a last, desperate hope here...

Smith was knocked out cold, and Kara Lynne put a hand on his forehead as he lay in the bottom of the wagon.

"Now?" Emma demanded impatiently. "We can't hide any longer, Kara. Come *on!*"

Nodding, Kara Lynne stood up and cast off her cloak. There was no point hiding Emma's abilities now, as much as she'd wanted to keep them secret, as much as she'd wanted to complete this mission without ever revealing to public eyes what the young Lady could do.

But at this point it was a question of survival.

Drawing the Colt M1911 magazine pistol from the holster on her hip, Kara Lynne stepped quickly to the back of the wagon, threw open the flap, and jumped out firing. The heavy pistol had a kick, but she'd been shooting heavy-caliber pistols since she'd been eleven, because, as her adopted father had said, you needed .45 caliber stopping power to survive a fight with savages.

The beasts surged at the men trying to keep them back by bayonet, but fearlessly Kara stepped forward and fired, and fired again. As the magazine emptied, she slapped in a fresh one. The men couldn't look back to see who was shooting, they had to use the falling savages as a chance to push back.

Behind Kara, Emma Lee descended from the back of the wagon in a short hop, holding her own Colt pistol out butt first to her elder protector, "Use mine. I won't need it."

Kara paused for a moment and then took the weapon without comment. Emma then knelt next to Sergeant Halloran and gently cupped his cheek in her hand, "I'm sorry about all this, Sergeant."

The man grunted and tried to struggle up, but she stopped him with a hand on his chest, then reached over him and simply pulled the locked bayonet off his rifle. She then recovered another bayonet, and with one in each hand she turned and walked to the line of six men — all that was left between her, Kara, and the savages.

Putting one hand on the shoulder of the nearest Private, she spoke sweetly, "Step back, please."

In utter shock, he looked, then stumbled backwards.

Seeing the object of their desire, the savages began to grunt. Emma's heart was racing, her limbs vibrating with excitement. She raised her arms and shrugged off her cloak, and then with a sword bayonet in each hand, she leapt.

Waller had to stop in shock. He was near enough to see a figure wearing tan breeches and a white blouse launch upwards over the crowd of savages that had collected at the rear of the wagon. From the color of her hair, he knew it was Emma.

At first he thought she'd been thrown by the savages, but then she landed perfectly, on two feet, with the ease and elegance of a dancer.

As the first savage lunged for her with hungry abandon, she decapitated it. The next came, and she gutted it. The Lee-Enfield bayonets she held in her hands were both covered in blood, as she soon was.

Waller, Devlin, every man with a chance to stop without dying at a savage's hands did so. They watched, speechless.

The savages closed in around her, and then like one of them, she leapt straight up, out over them, and landed in open field. They chased her, so she turned and ran... as fast as they could. They flooded away from the wagon, heading east a ways until Emma stopped in open fields away from the column.

"Secure the wounded!" Waller barked. "We must help her!"

"Don't bother," Kara Lynne interrupted with a yell. Waller looked up at the wagons, and the woman, also in tan breeches and a white blouse, stood with two Colt magazine pistols in hand. "She'll handle them."

Waller ignored her, "Jimmy, ten men with me now!"

He wasn't about to trust Kara — fifty savages was too many to allow one girl to face.

Racing after the beasts, the men had to run a difficult sprint that had been effortless for Emma. Ten seconds — instead of two seconds — after they left the wagons, they reached the back of the horde, and savages were still mobbing her.

Without mercy or quarter, Waller started hacking, but the savages didn't seem to care. They were fixated, desperately determined to fall upon Emma.

As Waller attacked, Emma leapt overhead again, and landed near him.

Her beautiful face and white blouse were soaked with blood, and yet she smiled at him with such innocence. One of her bayonets was gone, but as a savage raced at her from behind, she simply swung her fist and collapsed its face.

She had the strength of a savage.

And the speed.

Before Waller realized it, she was driving into the horde again like a rugby player going for a tackle. The savages collapsed as she hit them with such force that it broke their legs, shattered their knees.

More came.

"Sir, I have two Lewis guns!" Devlin called from behind, and Waller waved them forward.

"Emma, get out of that horde, we'll finish it with the Lewis guns! Hurry!"

He backed away and turned, watching as the men who'd abandoned their machine guns now recovered them from the carts and dropped to the grass.

As Waller got past them, they looked up for permission to fire.

"Wait..."

Emma leapt out of the horde and landed right next to the Major.

"Now!" Waller barked, and the Lewis guns roared. The horde caved before the quick fire.

Some savages remained standing, but as the Newfoundlanders who'd bravely charged down the slope reorganized themselves, they were shot or stabbed.

None of the beasts seemed to care about the soldiers, though. All their eyes were fixated on Emma, the object of their hunger.

As Waller turned and looked at the young Lady, whose breath was coming in the regular, strong heaves of a man who'd just run a sprint, he could see why more than ever.

Her breeches and blouse revealed her slender figure... But it wasn't just that. Waller realized almost immediately that his eyes were traveling up and down her body with an ease that was alien to him. Something about Emma was irresistible, was fogging his reason. It was making the savages want her, and it was clouding his judgment.

Her white blouse was soaked through with blood, and her face and her soft hair were covered in it.

She smiled at him with the excitement of someone who'd just won a race. But as his eyes hardened and he wondered at her abilities, her smile faded.

"I knew it. As soon as anyone finds out, they all look at me that way," she said quietly. "Suddenly I'm a savage too..."

Her smile died, she dropped the one bayonet she'd still been carrying, and she walked back to her wagon, gaze toward the ground.

Waller — and every man in the regiment — watched her walk with an unusual level of appreciation for her form, and Waller began to realize why she'd been so cautious about hiding herself.

"See to the wounded, get the horsemen out on picket!" he barked, forcing his thoughts to shift to productive matters.

He had to shake the reaction he was having to her.

It wasn't natural…

And he got the sense, too, that it wasn't her fault.

The Newfoundlanders started to collect themselves.

CHAPTER XXVII

"We have eleven dead, eight who'll soon be dead, and about sixty other wounded," Lieutenant Conway was one of the officers in 'D' Company, but he came from a family of doctors in Newfoundland, and in the absence of a field hospital or a surgeon, he was considered the next best thing. Having done some training and studied under his father and elder brother for several years before electing to answer the call to arms in 1914, he did actually know what he was speaking of.

"Only nineteen lost," Captain Tucker shook his head slowly. "I'm not complaining, mind you, but I did expect more."

"What'd your nan tell you about gift horses?" Captain Kearsey said quietly. "We better get the wounded who can't walk onto the ammunition carts and find a camp. Can't be here, too many dead savages and my b'ys are too exhausted to bury them."

Waller nodded at both Tucker's point and Kearsey's. As much as he didn't want to force the men to march after this struggle, this was no place to camp. It was, as Tucker had said, incredible that so many of his men were left on their feet. That many thousands of savages, and a bayonet-to-fist encounter… hundreds should have been dead.

Hundreds *would* have been dead, if the beasts hadn't all been fixated on Emma.

"Thank God they weren't focusing on us, though," Tucker shook his head. "Jesus, Mary and Joseph. I've never seen anything like that."

Emma had returned to her wagon, and it was only the immediate business of seeing to the many wounded and clearing bodies from around the column that was keeping every man in the battalion from camping out around that wagon to wait to see if Lady Lee would show herself — and her incredible powers — again. The men who'd seen her were acting as though they were under a spell, and Waller wasn't immune to it himself.

"We have to remember she is a Lady and she is our charge. Now that we know what she was hiding, I think we can stop any worries that she's on their side. But now we have to make sure the men maintain their discipline."

"I don't know if I like her," Kearsey observed quietly. "And I know I don't like the effect she's having on the men. Seems to me she could make them do anything she wanted, and that could be dangerous."

"And if they didn't go along with it, it'd take a good many men to bring her down," Tucker added to that with a nod. "I don't know if she's safe to have around. And dammit, I can't stop thinking about her. Jeeze b'ys, it's like I'm a dog and she's on heat."

"Enough talk like that, gentlemen," Waller held up his hand. "There's something unusual about her, but she remains our obligation. And I don't think we should fear her just because we can't overpower her. She helped us, and I'm willing to put some of my prior suspicions aside at least until I can talk to her... find out how the hell she learned to do that. Now, in the meantime, I am *not* camping the men out in this field. We need a site."

"Sir," Lieutenant Kennedy had his right arm in a sling, "Mister Smith and Corporal Wallace and I found an old circle of wagons about two miles up from here. Still intact, and it's enclosing a fresh spring."

Waller frowned, "People?"

Kennedy shook his head, "No sir, the letters Mister Smith found were from 1896, I think. All dead, long ago. The wagons are still there, though... a bit rotten, but they could provide us with a solid perimeter."

"Good, get the wounded onto the carts and let's get moving. Where is Mister Smith?"

Jimmy Devlin nodded towards the covered wagon, "Last I saw, some savage had thrown him in with the ladies."

Waller nodded, "I'll find him. Get the men moving. I don't want to be in the open for another attack."

***

Smith woke up feeling like he'd been trampled, so he sat up gingerly and rubbed his head.

"Oh Mister Smith, lie down please, you have a cut on your head from landing on the tea kettle... I'm just dabbing it... doesn't seem to be very deep..." Annie the maid was talking to him, and wincing at the sharp pain in his head, he glanced back at her.

"Nothing feels broke..." he realized he was sitting on fluffy cushions, "...think the pillows made the fall less painful."

"They did," Kara Lynne's voice came from the other direction, and with some difficulty Smith looked around, then hastily looked away as he realized Miss Emma was buttoning up a white blouse. A bloody red one sat next to her on the bench, and Kara was very gently wiping the younger girl's face with a damp cloth.

Emma looked crestfallen.

"Miss Emma, you're very pretty," Smith said, surprised at his own directness. "Miss Kara, you're very beautiful too. Better without the cloaks."

Smith stopped himself talking for a minute, not sure why he'd said something so direct to the two ladies. Plain speaking was something he was fond of, but not usually that plain.

Kara smiled, but didn't stop looking at Emma, "See, you're no monster. Come now, Emily, they're not going to hate you."

"Everyone always comes to it in their own time," she said softly, dejectedly. "Can't trust themselves around me. I make them do things. I can't be controlled. I'm dangerous. I'm a witch."

Smith was confused, and he was starting to think he'd done more than just cut his head on the landing. Kara gently stroked Emma's cheek, "That's not true. These men will have to respect you because you saved them."

Emma shook her head, "You know that's not true. I'll be a toy again. Or an experiment. They'll all want me to do something for them. One way or another."

"I'm sorry, Miss Emma, I'm possibly not recovered from my fall, but I have a hard time believing any good man wouldn't treat you right. And there are a lot of good men in this column."

Emma smiled sadly and shook her head, "You didn't see me drenched in blood, Mister Smith. Didn't see what I could do."

Annie was trying to be helpful, "I watched through the flap of the wagon... she moves like the savages do, she can jump over them, she's stronger and faster than them. She's a champion — she killed so many of them herself!"

Smith frowned and blinked a couple of times, "You've been hiding that?"

It surprised him, but in a pleasant sort of way. He'd been fearful that she was a mistress commanding the savages.

Emma nodded slowly, "Maybe you'll be different, Mister Smith, but I bet you won't be. Look at me, right now. My hair is matted with sweat and blood, my skin is dirty, and my clothes are plain. What are you thinking?"

Smith looked at her, and then he looked at Kara, and he found himself thinking things he wasn't generally prone to thinking.

"See?" Emma shook her head. "There is something about me... something that must have come with all these abilities. It's a curse. I cannot keep any company. Men either lust after me or hate me for having that effect on them, and women hate my effect on men and my strength."

Rubbing his head, Smith didn't argue, "So that's the reason for the cloak. Hide the temptation?"

Kara nodded, "My idea. We both did it but she's the one who needs it. I'm just an ordinary woman with some guns, she's the gifted one."

Emma protested, "Kara!"

"Well, I regret I missed seeing you shoot, but if you handle that thing as well as you look like you can, I'll have to be sure never to cross you," Smith nodded at the Colt magazine pistol on her hip.

"She's always looked after me," Emma said, just a tad more brightly. "She's a great shot. Our father... the man who adopted us... he taught us both. But she's the best."

Kara started to shake her head, but there was a knock on the wagon's side, "Emma, it's Tom. Is Mister Smith in with you, and is he alright?"

"Here, Major, and fine. Head's felt better."

"May I look in?" Waller asked, and Kara and Emma looked at each other for a second.

"Yes," Kara said finally.

Waller opened the flap and looking into the wagon, nodding to everyone within, "Pardon my interruption, we're going to march the column to that wagon circle you found, Mister Smith. Should be there in a half hour. Now... Miss Emma, could we talk, please?"

Emma let out a long sigh, "Here we go. Yes of course, Tom, I'll come and walk with you. And your section of men guarding me. And your sharpshooters covering me from afar."

Waller's expression became quite serious, "I've come to deserve that. At your pleasure."

He closed the flap and Emma pointed at the cape lying in a pile next to Kara. As it was handed to her, she hopped out of the cart, and left Kara and Smith to talk.

Waller had descended the northern slope of the ridge to get away from the sight of dead savages. As he reached the bottom of that ridge, almost 100 yards from the column, he turned to find Emma was already standing behind him.

"Ah good," he said, his tone not sharp, just fatigued. "You could have told us, you know."

"Let me guess, half your officers are imagining what a night with me would be like, the other half are telling you that I'm a dangerous temptress and that because of my strength, I can't be trusted."

Waller's eyebrows went up, "You've obviously had plenty of experience with this."

"Thirteen years, since... since I started to become a woman, if you understand. It started when the sixty-year-old man who'd raised me for ten years started lusting after me, so he sent me away to live with his sister in England. I don't control it. I don't want it," Emma's tone was strong and bitter now, and with a sigh, Waller took off his hat and shook his head.

"I can't imagine. And your abilities?"

Emma looked away from the Major, "The same time. One came with the other."

Waller nodded, "And let me guess, His Majesty's Government found out, some scientists poked and prodded you, trying to figure out what made you this way."

"Exactly that," Emma nodded. "They decided something I was exposed to out here, when Caralynne found me, made me change when puberty came. They want whatever it was. They want to be able to use it to build armies, and to make peers and Kings stronger..."

Waller's eyes narrowed, "There must be a better reason than that, if you're here."

Turning back to him, Emma's eyes were sad, "If they find the source of my change, they say they might isolate the part of it that causes everyone to lust after me. They might be able to find an antidote."

"Ah," Waller said quietly. He was too tired and too curious to feel at all embarrassed by the line of conversation now. "And your appeal... well it explains the savages' fixation."

She nodded, "The beasts look like us. They must respond to similar scents. Another lovely aspect of this."

Waller swallowed and nodded again, not entirely sure what he could say. He looked at her eyes — focused on her eyes — and tried to force his mind to burn away the fog that was closing around much of his brain.

"Well."

He failed on the first try to sound coherent, but Emma listened to his word, probably remembering similar comments from men with different perspectives.

"It's not that... I mean. I do enjoy the company of men, Tom. I really do.

But I can't have it, I can't be around men without intimidating them... or..."

"Yes, I understand."

"You seem different. You seem to be able to think when I'm around. And I really like that."

Waller swallowed again, "I can't profess an immunity. I don't possess it. But I was raised by good parents."

Emma smiled sadly, "I really appreciate that you try. But you're suspicious of me still, aren't you? Right now you know you're being influenced, and you're afraid of me."

That challenge almost sounded like a plea — a hope that maybe Waller wasn't like the rest.

"You know, Emma, if you want to harm me or my men, I'm willing to bet that you can do it, no matter how many rifles try to stop you. I'm going to trust you, because I have no choice. And because I believe you."

Emma looked hopeful for a moment, but then her expression darkened, "But your men."

"I'll tell them exactly what you told me. I'll tell them very soon. They're good men. They'll accept it."

Waller wasn't sure if that was a lie. He trusted his men — he considered them his family... but this was a very unusual situation. They might believe he'd been taken under the thrall of the temptress. He might well have been... so he'd tell them, and see what they said.

"I... alright," Emma began her protest but changed her mind. "Alright, tell them. I trust you."

Beginning to smile she flipped her cape up on her shoulder, revealing her attire again. Waller blinked and held up a hand, his expression changing sharply.

Emma's smile remained, and she flipped the cape back down, "I'll keep the cape on for now."

He nodded, "One step at a time."

With a charming laugh, Emma turned to walk back up the slope.

CHAPTER XXVIII

Waller couldn't delay the column's march to speak to the men about Emma's story — there was no time to waste in getting the Newfoundlanders into shelter, since shelter had been found. Emma returned to her wagon for the journey and the seriously wounded men rode in the ammunition carts. The walking wounded hovered around the carts too, near Lieutenant Conway in case one of them proved more badly injured than first thought.

It took nearly an hour for the column to cover the two miles to the circle of wagons, but as they neared it Waller paced up to the front of the marching men, studying the location through narrowed eyes. From simple appearances, it seemed to be an ideal position — the wagons were circled on the top of a shallow hill, and there was supposed to be fresh water inside.

The people who'd camped here had done so with good tactical awareness. They must have simply been overrun by a horde, perhaps after expending their ammunition, or perhaps lacking sufficient rifles to see off an attack.

As the column marched straight up to the ring of wagons, Waller found his Captains, "Send a platoon to check it before we get in. Fall the men out by platoon once it's cleared. I want a trench all the way around the outside of the circle."

No more instructions were required; the men, exhausted by the battle though they were, took their spades and set about digging a perimeter around the wagons. They needed no convincing — after the close call out in the open, every one of them was determined to build up as much protection as possible against another encounter.

With a trench line running around the outside perimeter of the circled wagons, the men would have additional separation, and more positions from which to defend. A layered defense was best, particularly against these beasts.

As the men began digging, Waller entered the circle of wagons, and was immediately gripped by a feeling of grim desperation. He could almost see the settlers, probably a mix of Canadians and Britons, who'd come out here in these wagons. Some of them had probably been ex-servicemen and officers — men who knew how to defend such positions against masses of determined attackers. They'd circled these wagons... they'd probably told the people in the train they were safe here.

And perhaps they would have been, against 100, or 1,000... but if thousands had come, as must have been the case...

Waller had read stories of the Alamo. He'd read stories of Rorke's Drift and of countless other posts being held desperately and sometimes in futility against massed forces outside. The concept had always sat bitterly with him — he preferred to fight while moving, and not to get bogged down.

Scenes like the one playing in his mind now horrified him. He could see the horses and oxen of the wagon train tied up inside the perimeter... the women and children hiding behind the thin canvas walls of tents that had been pitched in the middle of the circle. He could see the men — too few of them — running from wagon to wagon and screaming desperately to each other to close gaps, to stop incursions.

He could imagine the screams of the young girls and boys when the flaps of their tents were torn open and the savages pulled them out of their mothers' arms, and then killed their mothers. The last men racing from the wall, trying to get to the tents in a bitter, hopeless effort to save their families, being hauled down in the grass and pleading to God to save the lives of their children.

Waller could just see it. All of it.

It was as sickening an image as he'd ever imagined, and the desperation of it hung over this circle of wagons. The memory of those who'd died terrible deaths haunted this place.

But it was the most secure place for his men at the moment.

"I've opened the circle to the east so we can bring in the gun. Some of the more rotten wagons I think we should manhandle out of the way, replace them with some of ours, " Jimmy Devlin was suddenly beside Waller, and despite the images in his mind, the Major nodded.

"Very good, Jimmy. Pick firing positions all around the circle for the Colt gun. They could come from any side, and we need that thing to be able to face them. Is it unjammed yet?"

"Working on it, shouldn't be too difficult. We still have two thirds of the ammo left, too."

Waller nodded, "Good."

"Place feels like death," Devlin said, a bad taste in his mouth.

"It certainly does."

The two men silently looked over the circle for a few moments, then Waller turned back, watching as some of Halloran's men — now working without their Sergeant, who was among the walking wounded — led the ladies' wagon into the circle and parked it up near the east side of the perimeter.

"What about the women? Emma answer you, finally?" Devlin asked, looking at the covered wagon.

Waller nodded, "I think I trust her, now. I'll explain everything to the men as soon as we're secure here. Suffice it to say, whatever gave her those savage powers when she was a girl out here also made her... very appealing. So men either are wanton or suspicious, or both, and women hate her. I... I think I trust her."

Devlin frowned, "I'll need the long version of that story before I decide."

Waller nodded, "Good. I may be under her influence, that's why I'm going to put it to the men. I think what she's told me makes sense... but how can I be certain at this stage? You saw her, she's incredible."

"Could be a temptress," Devlin nodded. "We'll see. I hope we can trust her... because..."

Devlin couldn't finish that sentence without proving that her beauty was having a very overt effect on him, so he decided not to try. Waller simply nodded.

As both men watched the wagon for a moment, the flap opened, and Kara Lynne stuck her head out of it, "Where are we…"

She stopped speaking, and her expression changed somehow inexplicably. Her eyes swept over the circle of wagons, her mouth dropped open, and she gasped. Even from twenty yards away, both Waller and Devlin could see it.

What could…

Of course.

"Holy jumpin' Moses, you don't think…" Devlin asked the question almost breathlessly.

"That'd be our luck today," Waller nodded, and instantly the two officers set off for the wagon.

Inside the wagon, Kara Lynne pressed the palms of her hands into her forehead and started breathing heavily. Her heart raced, things she hadn't thought of in years started flooding back into her mind, and there was no stopping them.

Emma, who'd been much more herself since returning from her talk with Waller, frowned and quickly moved to her side, putting an arm around her elder friend's shoulder, "What is it?"

Kara Lynne's head dipped forward as she bent at the middle, breathing in sharp, rapid breaths.

Smith, who'd been obliged to ride up here in the wagon, slid up the bench to be opposite Kara, "She's panicking…"

Smith was not a slow sort of man, and immediately he put together the significance of the circle of wagons with the experiences of Kara's childhood. This was the circle of wagons she'd escaped from when she'd found Emma.

This was where her family had died.

"What is it?" Emma could see from the look on Smith's face that he had an insight she lacked.

The drifter nodded at the hunched woman, "This isn't the first time she's been inside this circle of wagons."

Emma's face drew tight and she nodded, rubbing Kara's back, "It's alright Caralynne, it's alright. We're safe this time... it's alright."

Smith did not quite know what to do. He wasn't skilled with women. Didn't have experience with panic, either. Not beyond the sort that ended with the panicking man killed or running. He hadn't expected Kara Lynne... Caralynne, apparently... to be vulnerable to panic, but then he couldn't say how he'd react if he was confronted with memories like the ones this circle must have left with her. This was only his second time in here, and it felt like a nightmare to him.

"Have her drink a little water," Devlin was climbing in the back of the wagon uninvited, but at his arrival, Annie, who'd been sitting wide-eyed in shock near the flaps, pointed at Kara.

"Jimmy, she's panicking!"

Devlin nodded, "We figured this wasn't her first time here."

"Looks like," Smith agreed, and then Waller climbed uninvited into the now-cramped wagon as well.

"We should probably give her some air," the Major said quickly, realizing his presence wasn't going to help matters.

"Emma, when she's ready, bring her out. We need to find out what happened here, in case we have to stop it happening again."

Emma looked up at Waller and nodded, "Alright. And Tom, call me Emily. Call me Emily."

It was a strange request to make at such a moment, but Waller nodded, "Whenever you're ready, Emily."

She nodded, and then Waller motioned to Devlin and Smith to exit with him.

The men jumped down from the back of the wagon in silence, Smith wincing as another pain lanced through his head. He wasn't the sort to be slowed by a bump on the head, though.

"Emma Lee and Kara Lynne... Emily and Caralynne," Devlin said quietly as Annie closed the flaps behind them. "Orphans with first names only? Didn't share their last names?"

Waller nodded, "That would be my guess. I'd have expected the man who adopted them to give him his name, but he mustn't have cared to."

The men stood silently and awkwardly for a moment, not sure how to react to what they were seeing. Their grim feelings about this circle of wagons had been confirmed, so now they had to hope that they'd already broken the back of the savages in this region.

But why would thousands have attacked this circle? A three-year-old Emily certainly wouldn't have drawn them with her scent — she'd said that problem had begun at puberty. So was it a simple matter of bad luck?

"Major Waller, sir!" Sergeant Whealan was coming over to their party, three men with him and all of them with a few rifles cradled in their arms. As they came to a stop they held up their guns. "Emilys, sir, dozens of them. And some of the carts over to the west have unopened and half-full cases of .303 ammo. Must be pretty old..."

Emilys?

Waller was confused for a moment as his mind shifted to the new subject, but he wasn't making the connection quickly enough, "Emily, Whealan?"

The Sergeant held up the guns in his arms again, "Yes sir. And they're still finding some. Looks like the men holding this ring were well armed."

"Not as well armed as we are, though," Devlin interceded. "Emily. M-L-E, Magazine, Lee-Enfield. The predecessor rifle to our own Short, Magazine, Lee-Enfield *S-M-L-E*, isn't that right, Whealan?"

The Sergeant nodded, "Heard the old soldiers in Afghanistan talking of them all the time. Same bolt as ours, longer barrel..."

"Old soldiers call them Emily," Waller said quietly. "I'm growing tired of coincidences right now."

That last comment was directed to Devlin and Smith, and the men nodded in agreement. There would need to be questions answered here, as soon as Kara… Caralynne could offer them.

"Whealan, stack all the MLEs you find, and check to see if any are serviceable. Any ammunition that's been open to the elements leave where it is, but add any closed cases to our stockpile."

The Sergeant nodded, then turned and barked at his men to go back the way they'd come.

"That'll be some old ammunition," Smith observed after a moment.

Waller nodded, "It's old, but even if it hangfires, it's better than being eaten by a savage if we run out of our own stuff."

That was true. The men continued to stand and wait for the ladies to emerge.

CHAPTER XXIX

The ladies did not emerge — at least, not in the next two hours.

Working with a determination born of receiving a savage attack in an open field, the Newfoundlanders dug a five-foot trench in the soft soil surrounding the circle of wagons, using the earth removed to shore up some of the more rotten wagons and to create a sturdy parapet. Devlin and his picked machine gun crew spotted the Colt to fire from multiple positions in a variety of directions, and succeeded in unjamming the old weapon.

As the sun began to set, pickets were posted, and the regiment set camp for supper. This, Waller decided, would be the best time to speak to his men.

Through his officers he called them all together, grouping them around the Colt machine gun to sit or stand as they pleased. This was something Waller had done in Afghanistan when the men survived some harrowing ordeals. It was a familiar routine: he called them together, spoke to them about what they'd done, and explained to them why it was significant (or at least why it seemed significant). Often, he didn't himself know why or *if* what they had done was truly important.

What mattered, though, was that they talked together. He shared his thoughts, they responded in kind. They discussed things, and that created a great cohesion that they might not have had otherwise.

"Well, b'ys, today we survived what I think many would have said was impossible to survive," Waller began. He was standing on top of the ammunition boxes for the machine gun, so that in the failing light he could see the 335 men collected around him. The wounded and the pickets would hear the gist of his speech from those who'd been present.

"Our survival, I have to say, is thanks to Lady Emily... the younger of the two robed women we're escorting. As you've noticed, she has... abilities. She was a girl out here over twenty years ago, and she was orphaned. Somehow, she survived. She tells me she roamed these plains, and must have come across something... ate or drank *something* that gave her the powers of a savage. We evidently have been sent out here to find whatever gave her those powers, because the Army figures it'd be pretty handy."

There was a murmur of comments, "I'll bet they do."

"Now, you've also probably noticed that Lady Emily is... well, she has an effect on men. Half of you are thinking things you better never let me hear about, half of you are thinking she's an evil witch trying to keep us from thinking straight. Well, I may be under her spell, but I think she's innocent. Whatever gave her speed and strength also made her... more appealing than is natural. She wishes it wasn't so, because it's complicated her life. But that's how it is, and until we find whatever caused her to be this way, she'll have no cure. For now we just have to control ourselves, and, I think, trust her."

Waller tried to gauge the men's reaction to that, but couldn't. Was he sounding like a victim of a sorceress' spell? He could well be. Or was it as he said? Would the men believe that Emily was both innocent and a victim — a victim of most men's fears of strong women, or of their lust?

"Well, b'ys, talk to me. I could be under some sort of spell, she could have manipulated me without me knowing. I bring it to you because I trust that you won't let me fall into a trap, if that's what you think this is."

The men began to look at each other, and somewhere from the crowd someone barked, "Well ye sound like yourself, b'y!"

"Takes more than a pretty girl to knock down the Wall!" someone else insisted, and Waller half-smiled.

"Even a fancy strong woman!" another pitched in.

These were the sounds of approval.

The seal came with Sergeant Halloran, who was using a rusted-out MLE as a cane to stay upright, "So sir, if I'm hearing you right, you're saying if we find whatever she fed herself with out there, we'll all be strong like the savages and irresistible to women?"

"Shit, Sarge, dunno about you but I'm both already!" someone called back.

A ripple of laughter crossed the men, and Waller felt a great wash of relief sweep over him. The men were in good spirits despite their clash, or perhaps because they'd survived the clash with the savages. And they evidently found Emily's story to be acceptable. Certainly, they hadn't spent as much time with her as Waller had, but that made them all the better judges. They'd come out here, felt the feeling of death, and been suspicious of the women from afar. Now they'd had an explanation offered, and to them it made sense enough.

That satisfied Waller, "Good, glad I'm not a puppet!"

"Well, if you're a puppet so are we! But what else is new, the Army loves pullin' our strings!" someone else called, and there was another laugh.

Newfoundlanders knew how to find the humor in everything. It was a necessity of surviving in Newfoundland — and anywhere else — with a measure of good spirits.

"Alright, so you all go back to your food, and keep your eyes off the women."

"Hear that b'ys, now that he knows they ain't evil he's taking dibs!"

"Typical officer!"

"Behave yourselves," Waller grinned. "We think this circle we're in might be tied to Miss Kara's past, so we may be here for a while."

The men started to break up and head back to their tents to start the fires going, and Waller hopped down from the boxes and let go a relieved sigh. Devlin and the Captains approached him, the Lieutenant leading the way, "Good talk, sir."

Waller waved a hand at the men, "They make it easy. God help me if I was ever stuck with a different unit."

The officers made agreeing sounds, but it was evident they too were getting hungry.

"We'll brief on our plans after supper, I think. Get some food," Waller nodded to them.

With smiles, the Newfoundlanders went to supper. Waller decided to check on the ladies, as they might be hungry as well.

Annie was perched on a crate that had been moved over to the back of the covered wagon for her benefit, and she sat quietly staring at the ground as Waller approached.

"Any word, Miss Annie?" the Major asked quietly as he stopped near her, and the young maid looked up in surprise.

"What? No... no, sir, nothing. But I was imposing, so I stepped out, as a good maid does."

Waller smiled, "Well that was prudent, I think. Not been with them long?"

She shook her head, "I was hired for Lady Lee just before she left to come here, by her aunt."

"Ah, so they're not used to you yet," Waller nodded. "Well, I'm sure Jimmy and the men would be delighted of your company at that fire, just over there. Not too far, you'll hear if Lady Lee calls."

Annie looked up and then followed Waller's pointed finger to the fire.

"I think I'll go there," Annie said, a little more brightly. She stood, "Thank you, Major."

Waller frowned, "I haven't done anything."

Annie smiled, "You mightn't realize."

She then walked away and Waller watched her go — and watched Jimmy receive her with flourish a moment later, sitting her on a crate next to him and a couple of the officers he was sharing his fire with.

Pleased, Waller remained distracted for a moment, then remembered himself and knocked on the side of the wagon, "Pardon me, ladies, I don't mean to rush you, but I have news."

For a moment there was no response, but then one of the flaps on the rear of the wagon swung open, "Come in."

Waller climbed in and found the canvas compartment bathed in lamp light. As he seated himself next to the exit, his eyes went from Emily to Caralynne, and he realized expressions had changed — Caralynne was appearing strained, and Emily somewhat... angry.

"I just wanted to tell you, the men have approved of what you told me... they'll be alright with you now," Waller began somewhat hesitantly. "Now, I'm sorry to ask this Miss Kara... Miss Caralynne... but we need to know what happened here, so we can make sure we've defended against all contingencies."

Neither of the ladies was looking at Waller as he spoke, which struck him as quite unusual. Instead, their gazes were fixed on each other, and the tension was evident.

What *now*?

"First thing in the morning. They won't come in strength at night," Caralynne said shortly. "Thank you for the news, Major. We have more to discuss... if you wouldn't mind."

Waller frowned and looked from Caralynne to Emily, saw no different message coming from the younger woman, and decided that he was perhaps in the most deadly situation of his soldiering career. If these two virtual sisters were warring, he was getting the hell out of the way.

"Good night, ladies," Waller nodded immediately, then opened the canvas flap and evacuated the area.

In the morning, he hoped, there would still be two ladies and a camp left to defend.

CHAPTER XXX

At dawn, Waller approached the covered wagon, a tin mug of coffee in his hand. There had been no more word from the ladies overnight, but there had also been an all-clear from the pickets. Hopefully the Newfoundlanders had destroyed the local population of savages in the field action yesterday, leaving them nothing to strike with until they concentrated further...

But there was absolutely no way to be sure of such a thing, so the men remained on alert.

"Morning, Major," Smith approached and started walking beside Waller, and the Newfoundlander nodded to the drifter.

"Good morning, Mister Smith. How're you feeling this morning?"

Smith sipped coffee, "Headache, but I've had worse now and then. You, sir?"

Waller waved his coffee cup dismissively, "I'm as fine as I could expect to be. Based on what I saw last night, though, Emily and Caralynne were in the middle of a quarrel over something... just what we don't need at the moment."

Smith frowned, "Bad timing."

"You've got that right, my friend. I need to know what happened here... I get the sense that something occurred that Emily didn't know about. That's the only reason I could imagine for the change in their demeanor last night."

"Makes sense," Smith agreed. "Going to wake them?"

Waller let out a short breath and came to a stop, "I'll wait a moment. Finish my coffee at least. Seems dangerous to go into a fight with a scalding liquid so near your face."

Smith gave an uncommon smile, "Wise words. I was impressed by your talk yesterday. You and your men have good relations."

Eyebrows climbing, Waller half-shook his head, "I suppose. Probably not the conventional way to lead a unit, but it's served us through some very dark days. I trust them."

"Wise," Smith nodded, repeating that word. "A man gets respect when he gives it. Many officers I've seen haven't understood that."

"Ah," Waller nodded, then drank the last of his coffee. "Yes, those who demand respect irritate me."

"They get other men killed, too," Smith finished his own drink.

"I'm well off then," Waller smiled, then stopped a passing Private and prevailed upon him to return his coffee cup to his tent, and Smith's to his.

With scalding liquids safely consumed, Smith and Waller crossed the last short distance to the covered wagon, and Waller knocked on the side. There was no immediate response, and Waller paused to wonder why Annie didn't answer — surely she'd be up at daybreak.

Smith caught his eye and indicated the direction towards Devlin's tent with a nod of the head, and Waller followed the nod to see Annie and Devlin walking this way, arms linked.

"Man doesn't waste time," Smith observed dryly.

"The threat of being eaten must motivate them both," Waller contained a smile. Jimmy wasn't a bad sort; his affections for Annie were deeper than most soldiers' might be... but Waller would have a word with the young Lieutenant later anyway. Nothing would be served by jilting the maid — and it would be entirely improper.

Just as Devlin and Annie came close enough to speak to, both Emily and Caralynne hopped from the back of the wagon, wrapped in their cloaks. Neither looked particularly pleasant, and neither stopped to explain the origins of their moods.

"They attacked from the southwest," Caralynne's tone was flat and direct, and was obviously masking painful memories. "My daddy said at least 5,000 of the beasts."

She started walking across the circle to the southwest, and Smith and

Waller frowned at each other — minds catching up to the start of the story — and then followed, Emily silently bringing up the rear. Devlin and Annie detected the harsh tone and elected to stay behind.

"Don't worry, if they're angry about you being gone, I'll take full responsibility," Devlin said dashingly, and Annie smiled.

Caralynne reached the southwest side of the circle after a fast walk, drawing the notice of most of the men. Many of them, bearing their coffee mugs and curious to eavesdrop, left their morning fires and followed, so behind Emily a crowd of about thirty men trailed quietly, including a couple of Sergeants and officers.

"My father was a Sergeant in the British Army. He'd been in Zululand and in the first Boer War... he knew how to fight. He was called Barnes. I'm Caralynne Barnes, but I don't use that name," that recollection sounded pained to Waller, and rightly so. "He brought many of his old men from the regiment with him out here. He'd been promised wealth from a gold mine, and he'd brought along his most loyal old soldiers, promised them the same. With thirty good riflemen, daddy used to say, the savages would be damned. No unthinking savages could be more dangerous than a brave Zulu *Impi*, he used to say. And his men had stood against the Zulu and survived. So we all thought we were safe."

As Waller had expected, then. He let out a short sigh, recognizing the confidence of this Sergeant Barnes — any soldier who'd survived hot action would be predisposed to assume that a horde of unintelligent beasts would be no match for well-executed volley fire, particularly back in the 1890s, before the savages' powers had been fully recognized.

"They bought new guns, many new guns and called them all 'Emily'. They had ammunition and they trained the non-soldier men on the wagon train to use them too. Daddy told me that any of these savages that attacked the wagons would die," Caralynne hopped up on one of the lower rotting wagons with ease, facing southwest as she spoke loudly enough to be heard.

"Daddy said the reason the Americans kept dying at the hands of the savages was because they were a bunch of cowboys who didn't know the proper way to fight..." her voice shivered very slightly, and then she turned back to Waller, noticing that the thirty followers was now sixty. She ignored them, perhaps too angry to care if they heard, or perhaps deciding it futile to hide anything, since Waller would tell them anyway.

"Then, one day, we camped here. We'd seen no savages, but my daddy and some of his men went out on horses to scout around. When they came back they had a little girl with them."

Waller digested that quickly, and then he looked back at Emily, who's face was grim. She was looking at Caralynne, but as she sensed the Major's eyes on her she locked stares with him, "Not how I thought it happened."

That, Waller reasoned, could be the source of the fight.

"Daddy told me this little girl had been found crying on the back of a savage man in a crowd of a dozen, and was obviously their midday snack. So daddy and the men killed the savages and saved the little girl. When they rode in with her, my mummy and I cleaned her up. She wouldn't talk, and some of the men said she was a savage, because the savages look like us. But mummy and I convinced them, because when you cleaned her up it was clear she wasn't savage. She was just too terrified to talk. We figured she was American, probably taken off a wagon train to the south, her family dead."

"She didn't just find me roaming in a field as she made her escape," Emily cut in, her tone bitter. "But I didn't know that. Didn't hear that until now."

"It would have done no good — I didn't want you to remember what had happened to you!" Caralynne shot back, and Smith shot into the air, literally.

The sound of the Colt's .45 caliber bullet firing surprised everyone present, and likely startled the pickets, but it quieted the ladies' argument before it escalated, "I think that's not important right now, please, ladies."

Emily and Caralynne both looked at him and quieted.

"My daddy named her Emily, since we didn't know her name. He and the men thought it'd be right and amusing to name her after their wonderful new guns that had saved her life. It was a pretty name, so mummy and I agreed. And then the next day, 5,000 savages came. My daddy saw them and got me and mummy on a horse with Emily when they got too close. Said there was no stopping that many. Daddy did that secretly, and all the other families were left to die... as far as I know. And then we were riding away, and the savages started following us, so mummy said the horse would go faster with only two, and jumped off before I could stop her..."

Caralynne's typically strong voice was beginning to quake. The horrifying images were already playing through Waller's mind... he could imagine what must have been going on in Barnes' head, the veteran soldiers of Zululand and he standing on the wagons and firing volleys into a horde far too large for them to survive, and then Barnes slipping away, secreting his wife and daughter onto a horse, knowing he had to do it quietly because if the other families tried to ride with them there'd be no chance of them slipping away unnoticed.

And then Caralynne's mother, trying to be brave as she probably wept in terror — as any man or woman would — when she leapt from the horse and prayed that her daughter somehow escaped the death following her.

By some minor miracle, Caralynne had.

"We got into a gulch miles from here and followed it for a while... I ran the horse into the ground without realizing it, and it died and we ran... I don't know how we got away..."

Caralynne's voice trailed off, and a tear slid down her cheek. Around Waller, the men were mesmerized by the story — the tragedy of the words was gripping.

"So we assume that whatever made me the way I am is close to here. Or that's the place to start looking," Emily spoke up after a moment's silence.

"Where Sergeant Barnes' patrol found you," Waller turned to her, and she nodded.

Smith looked at Waller, and Waller returned the gaze, "Suppose I'll be riding out."

"With me," Caralynne said pointedly. "I know the direction my daddy went. I know how he described the ground."

"And me," Emily insisted instantly. "Though I'll run, since I can."

Her tone revealed the deep wound Caralynne had inflicted. Waller didn't know the full story behind the relationship between these two, but it seemed likely that Emily had long wondered about her past, and that Caralynne, in hiding the truth of it from her — even if for her own good — had betrayed her trust. That would be for them to sort out, though.

"And me, Jimmy, and nine men," the Major took command of the discussion after that thought. "We'll hold camp here in case any of the savages return to make trouble. This sortie will be by horse alone."

They'd go to the place where Emily had been found, and hopefully near there would be a clue to whatever had given her special powers.

CHAPTER XXXI

"George has command while I'm gone," Waller said evenly, looking between his two Captains. Behind the Major, the horses were saddled and the men were ready to ride, but before he rode out Waller wanted specific orders to be left, in case he didn't return.

"Yes sir," Captain Tucker nodded in acknowledgment at his assignment, and Captain Kearsey nodded as well.

"Very good, sir."

"My orders are in a packet in my tent," Waller went on. He'd leave a written record of his commands to Tucker, so no man could blame George if things went wrong. "Simply put, if we don't come back, don't look for us. If we're not back in three days, break camp and march east for Long Prairie, report what we've seen so far. For the next three days keep all scouts to within sight of the camp, keep a picket of one section out there at all times, and have a platoon ready for quick action. The Colt needs to be ready at all hours as well, so rotate through crews."

The orders began to drift from strategic commands into operational tactics, and Waller realized he had begun telling Tucker and Kearsey things they already knew well to do.

"Alright, wish us luck," Waller stopped himself and nodded to his officers again.

Offering salutes, Tucker and Kearsey stood straight.

"Good luck, sir," Tucker said somberly.

"Bring us back some of the weeds that make for extraordinary powers, sir," Kearsey's tone was lighter.

Waller saluted in return, "We'll do our best. See you within three days."

With that, the Major turned and walked to the horse that had been saddled for him. Waller was not much of a rider, but he had watched enough riders in action to confidently be able to get one foot in the stirrup and pull himself up onto the great brown steed.

As he took the reins he looked over to Smith, the unquestioned leader of this expedition, and nodded. Tipping his hat in answer, Smith turned his Appaloosa mare around and eased her to a walk, heading for the 'gate' in the circle formed by the temporary removal of one of the older wagons. The column of riders followed slowly, with Waller and Devlin at their head, Caralynne just behind them, and Emily waiting until all the riders had cleared the circle to join them on foot.

They kept an easy pace all morning, but the slowness almost made the ride seem even more uneasy. Anxious soldiers on horseback had their Enfields close at hand, and their eyes scurried from horizon to horizon, looking for any sign of savages.

Caralynne's horse took lead position after a few hours, and at a canter she led the riders in the direction that seemed to best match the descriptions her father had made to her over twenty years before. Waller was not entirely confident she knew where to go, but the risk was worth taking.

Emily straggled behind, her face a thundercloud. Waller at one point dropped back to speak to her, "You know, Emily, I think she had your best interests at heart..."

"Do you know how much I've wanted to know where I came from?" was her cool reply. "Found lost in a field wasn't too satisfying. I've turned over every stone, tried to find out just a little more... and it turns out she's known more all along, and hasn't trusted me with it."

Waller could understand the wound that sort of revelation might cause. Being lied to by an intimate about something so important could cause great hurt. He decided not to attempt to intercede any further, so he left Emily alone for hours after that short exchange of words. This would be for Caralynne and Emily to work out.

They didn't stop for lunch, but rode on to the southwest into the afternoon, and the pace began to increase as Caralynne found a valley that she was certain had been described to her by her father.

"It's down here… this valley, see how it breaks out into four branches around the hills up ahead? The dip in the ground there? That's it… they found the savages down at the intersection of the branches."

The horses were kicked into a gallop as they descended the shallow side of the valley, and Emily jogged along beside the riders, a little sweat glistening on her forehead, but no fatigue slowing her at all. They eased up as they crossed the valley floor, and Smith raised his hand as they were about halfway along.

"I'll go ahead and have a look," the drifter said directly. "Get your rifles ready in case I need cover coming back."

Devlin directed the section of men on horseback to line their horses up and pull out their Lee-Enfields. They likely wouldn't be able to shoot well from horseback, but if Smith needed help they'd be in a better position to offer it with their rifles ready — even if they had to dismount to fire.

Smith galloped his mare forward as the anxious riders watched, and he drew his Colt revolver from its holster as a precaution as he neared the dip in the valley Caralynne had identified. He slowed his mare to a walk, then changed directions to skirt around the depression on its left edge.

He had a feeling something was in here.

Sitting on his horse, Waller abruptly realized that Emily was moving forward. He caught a glimpse of her face as she walked by, and a deep frown was creasing her brow.

"Emily…" he called quickly, "…Emily where are you going?"

She looked back at him without stopping, "There's something down there. He needs… help…"

There was an uncertain edge in her voice, and Waller started to ease his horse forward.

"No, stay," she looked away and kept walking without saying any more.

"Ready men," Devlin was frowning now as well.

"Don't go out there — come on, he'll call if he needs us…" Caralynne sounded quite certain of her order, but it drew only a cold stare from Emily as she continued to walk away.

Waller traded glances with Devlin and then started to ease his horse after Emily. The young Lady suddenly broke into a run, her cape flying back in heroic style as she raced over the plain at the pace of a racehorse.

Kicking his steed, Waller tried to follow, but he wasn't an experienced enough rider to keep his mount in check at those sorts of speeds. Caralynne was a better rider, so it was her horse who bolted after the younger girl, while behind, Devlin barked to the section to wait. Better to keep the nine rifles at range as a place of retreat.

Ahead, Smith hauled on his reins and kicked his mare into a hard run away from the depression. Waller watched that and didn't process its significance immediately, but as the first shots from the Colt New Service carried by the drifter cracked out and echoed through the valley, Waller eased up enough to draw his Webley revolver. Caralynne slowed too, and drew her Colt M1911 from its holster on her hip.

Emily surged forward, doggedly determined to kill any savages who came for her.

Then, as Smith raced past Emily in the other direction, yelling for her to turn around, Waller watched a silver automobile climb out of the depression.

No, it wasn't an automobile… it had an engine, but its wheels were wide and thick, and the body of the thing appeared wholly metallic — sturdy and angular, almost like the hull of a navy warship. It looked smooth, with the curves of a destroyer instead of a carriage. And it was moving faster than any lorry Waller had ever seen…

It seemed to have a closed front cockpit, and behind an open passenger compartment…

And standing in that compartment was… what?

Caralynne and Waller both hauled on their reins and stopped. As they watched, a loud 'zap' filled the air, and what appeared to be a burst of harnessed lightning erupted from the back of the vehicle. Smith pulled his mare to the left just in time to have the bolt miss them both, and looking back with his Colt he fired twice more.

Shock wore off quickly, and Waller gauged the range: it was about 200 yards away from him, and he was about 100 yards from Devlin. He wheeled his horse with some difficulty, then yelled, "Open fire on that thing!"

"At 300 yards, ten rounds rapid *fire!*" Devlin barked immediately, and though the surprised men each chose to either leap from their horses or to stay in the saddle, the fire began instantly.

Waller rode ahead again, being sure to stay out of the men's line of fire as he raced towards the silver vehicle with his revolver ready. Another 'zap', and Smith hauled the reins in the opposite direction this time. The bolt of electricity — or whatever it really was, perhaps a Martian heat ray as he had once read of in H. G. Wells — kicked up a plume of dust and dirt as it drove into the ground behind Smith's mare.

The .303 rounds were pounding into the metal sides of the vehicle, and Waller could hear the lead-on-metal clinks he'd only heard before when rifle shots had been directed at armored naval ships. Some holes, though, began to appear in the side of the silver vehicle, and it pulled sideways, revealing more of its open back, and a strange, small, blue-skinned creature in the rear.

"A Martian!" Waller called without thinking. Of course, this creature likely did not hail from Mars, as Wells' imaginary tentacled villains had, but it was certainly intelligent and obviously not from Earth. As he got within seventy-five yards, the creature's yellow eyes locked onto him, and it turned what appeared to be the heat ray rifle in his direction.

The weapon was slim and metallic, with no wooden stock... and if the delay between shots at Smith were any indication, then it took time to reload. Waller hauled on his reins and turned his horse on a different course, and the rifle fire abated for a moment as he cut across the field of fire.

Smith turned around now, and as he did he fired twice more, emptying his cylinder. He drew his Winchester from its sheath... and another vehicle, just like the first, drove up out of the depression, two more creatures in the back of that one shooting in his direction. The creatures were not skilled with their weapons, and the haphazard approach to their attack suggested to Waller that they were perhaps not professional fighters.

But who were they? *What* were they?

Close enough to chance a shot, Waller leveled his Webley at the nearer vehicle and fired off two rounds at the aiming creature. It ducked down and the shots missed, then it popped back up and fired wide.

Waller turned his horse away with some difficulty, trying to keep the nearer truck between himself and the further one, while Smith turned his mare again, took his hands off the reins, and cut loose with his Winchester. The second car swerved away under his fire, and just as it did Caralynne rode in front of Waller with her Colt magazine pistol in hand. Crossing in front of the first automobile, she fired four shots through the thing's windowed cabin, and one of the .45 caliber bullets must have clipped the driver. The silver car hauled hard to the left, and the creature wielding the lightning ray in the back was knocked off balance.

Riding past the surprised creature, Caralynne mercilessly emptied her clip into its chest, and it did not stand up.

"They can be killed!" she called as she turned back, kicking her horse into a gallop again. Waller turned his mount and followed her as best he could, while Smith rode the other way, firing after the second lorry until his Winchester was empty. He then sheathed it and drew his second one.

Then Emily dashed before all of them, running with impossible speed. She caught up to the big vehicle, and drawing her own Colt 1911 pistol, fired at the creatures. One fell, though Waller couldn't see how it had been hit. The other dropped its weapon and reached towards her, with blue, four-fingered hands.

For a moment Waller thought it was trying to surrender, and as the vehicle slammed to a halt, his assumption seemed confirmed.

Then Emily screamed.

Waller had never heard such a blood curdling scream in his life. It panicked his horse, the steed nearly throwing him as it sawed away. Before Caralynne or Waller could get near, Emily collapsed to her knees and dropped her pistol, clutching at her head as her scream continued unabated.

Smith rode hard to the left, trying to get a new angle to shoot at the creature, but the wounded blue Martian struggled upright and fired the lightning ray at the drifter, forcing him to turn away again.

"Go wide in the other direction!" Waller directed Caralynne to ride the other way, towards the second vehicle.

She nodded, but as she turned that way, savages appeared.

Waller hadn't seen them approach, but they must have erupted from the depression, and Smith was forced to ride away from them, firing as they charged. His mare was ready to run, and she out-legged the sprinting creatures by just a hair. Turning his horse again, Waller saw twenty were rushing for him and Caralynne, so he turned his revolver on them and fired, kicking his steed into flight.

Caralynne looked desperately from the savages to Emily and then charged for her young friend, who was still screaming and clawing at her scalp.

The first savage leapt high and knocked her off her horse, the second knocked down the horse itself. Caralynne yelled in surprise, then shot the beast that was lying on her. Turning with surprising agility, Waller shot the savage on her mount, and then Smith angled towards them, using his 1873 Winchester to shoot down four of the beasts in a row.

Lee-Enfield fire from the section behind cut down more, and as a gap opened, Waller rode into it, heading straight for Emily, shooting the first savage that got near enough to grab her.

"Emily, you must get up!" he yelled, but she didn't seem to hear him.

He turned his horse as he came to her, determined to get her up on his mount somehow. A savage came from the left and he shot it, and then he turned towards the vehicle and leveled his revolver at the creature who was reaching out to Emily. The creature saw him, realized a threat was near, and that it was too late; Waller pulled the trigger of his Webley.

The hammer fell on an empty chamber.

Cursing his carelessness, Waller dropped the pistol, letting it dangle on its lanyard while he reached for the dragoon saber at his side — not that he really knew how to use it, especially from horseback...

Just as he got the weapon out of its sheath, a savage slammed into him, propelling him off his horse and into the grass next to Emily. The impact knocked him out.

Smith and Caralynne fired fast and accurate, but the savages weren't slowing down.

The drifter tried to get close to Waller, but couldn't, and the savages were only barely being held in check by the amazingly accurate rifle fire from Devlin's section 250 yards away.

Watching as savages picked up Waller's unconscious body, and lifted the screaming Emily as well, Smith shot two with the last of his Winchester bullets. Two more beasts appeared immediately in the place of the fallen ones to help carry the captives.

Caralynne had struggled back onto her horse and was slapping a fresh magazine into her pistol, still riding around to try to find a way in.

"Pull back, Miss Caralynne!" Smith ordered with a forcefulness that wasn't typical for him.

Caralynne wheeled her horse, "I *can't!*"

"You want to save her, we can't die out here when we run out of ammo. We'll follow them and get help," Smith wasn't accustomed to saying things like that. As a drifter he relied on himself, he didn't often go looking for people to do his hard work for him.

But this was different.

The savages lifted Waller and Emily up into the back of the silver vehicle and it accelerated away, the beasts following it like a pack of escorting dogs.

Waller and Emily were captives, and Smith and Caralynne — soon joined by Devlin and the men — could do nothing but watch.

As he arrived next to Smith, young Jimmy articulated his thoughts very well: "Alright, excuse me here. What the *bejesus* were those blue things... and where the *hell* did they come from?"

That was a very, very good question.

CHAPTER XXXII

"They're going northwest... that means if we follow them, we'll probably have a more direct route back to the camp," Devlin was thinking out loud in frustrated tones. He should have come up with the men... he should have done *something*. His Major was now a captive of the Martians... or whatever these creatures were.

H. G. Wells' *War of the Worlds* had been one of the first English books that had found its way into the regiment when they'd been in Egypt in 1914, and many of the officers had read it to fight boredom. Now it was Devlin's only reference for this... this incredible situation.

What the devil were creatures like that doing out here? For years, everyone had thought — had *known* — that the savages were the only man-like occupants of this world. Who were these blue creatures, and why was this the first time they'd turned up? Their existence, in itself, wasn't a complete surprise — the possibility of men from other planets that didn't look completely human had seemed likely enough to Devlin even before he'd read Wells' book. But after all these years on the new world, it was such a surprise...

What Devlin had said was right, though, as far as Smith could figure. They'd come out of the camp going southwest, now the creatures were heading northwest. That meant wherever they ended up might be parallel to the camp, and make for a shorter march for a rescue party.

"We need to keep on them. But we need to make sure the camp knows what's going on," Smith spoke slowly and thoughtfully.

Devlin nodded, "Sergeant Reilly, take the men back, hard as you can. We'll proceed on, find wherever they're taking the Major and Lady Emily, and return."

"Sir, don't know if it's wise for you to be out here, just the three of you..." the Sergeant protested immediately, and Devlin recognized a good deal of sense in that point, though not enough.

"Better than even chance, Reilly, that where we go, no nine men are going to make a bit of difference. If we don't come back, at least this way we're only losing three more. And someone needs to warn the camp. The savages might be looking for us to retreat, though, so keep alert on the ride."

Devlin's firm orders forbade any further complaint by the Sergeant, and reluctantly he turned his horse and ordered his section to follow. They rode northeast, up and out of the valley.

Caralynne was sitting in shocked silence on the back of her mount, gaze locked on the ground between the remaining three horses. Devlin could understand her sense of failure, as it was one he shared.

"We'll get them both back," the young Newfoundlander insisted immediately. "And those creatures... blue things, men from another planet? Little bastards weren't very good shots. Next time we'll see how they like a real volley from 100 rifles..."

Devlin turned his horse to the northwest, and without commenting, Caralynne did the same.

Smith watched them walk for a moment, trying to remember all he could about the strange creatures' actions. They did not seem to Smith to have the skill of soldiers... their behavior had almost reminded him of ranchers protecting their herds. Of course, they were beings that no living human had ever seen — he reckoned at least — so there was no way for him to be able to rightly assess their behavior.

But Devlin could be right. These creatures might be unprepared for the Newfoundlanders.

Though the savages were still a hell of a problem.

Easing his mare forward, Smith left his worries behind him for a while. They had to successfully track these creatures first. Only after that would it matter how well the soldiers could handle the blue men from another world.

***

Moving fast as they were, the vehicles and savages had left quite an easy trail to follow, and Smith led the way as the three scouts kept their horses moving at a trot. Zig-zagging and slowing to avoid ambushes in suspicious areas, they covered six miles in the first hour of the chase, then another five in the second. That brought them to a broad, shallow valley with a stream running through it. They rode up onto the eastern slope, hiding themselves in a stand of trees, and dismounted quickly to look.

"It's like something out of a world's fair..." Devlin made the first observation about the large building sitting on the nearer side of the stream. It seemed to be metal-framed, to have glass panel walls between the frames, and to have electric lights.

"Savages in a pen at the back," Smith pointed, and following his finger Devlin nodded.

"What the hell are they... I mean... have they domesticated savages to work for them, the way we could domesticate dogs?" surprisingly few questions had been asked on the ride here, but now Devlin couldn't resist the suggestion.

Smith pulled off his hat and wiped his brow, "I guess that'd be the way of it. Never seen savages not eat somebody before, and they seemed awful helpful to those vehicles."

It seemed unlikely, but then again, so did a lightning ray and silver automobiles that were sturdy and fast, driven by Martians.

"I see the lorries," Caralynne was only half listening to her male companions, and Smith shifted places to be nearer the woman.

Squinting, he saw what she was referring to: the two vehicles were on the north side of the building, gleaming in the late-day sun.

"Our two companies can take this building," Devlin said firmly, and Smith looked back at him.

"Take it?"

Devlin nodded, "I've been thinking, Mister Smith. These things seem to control at least some savages, and the first chance they get to come for us they take Lady Emily, as if that was their plan the whole time. Why the interest in her? Well looking at the blue fellows, I very much doubt it's because they want to bed her. No, I think they somehow knew that she was one of us with the powers of the savages. They want her, either to find out how she got those powers... or because maybe they gave them to her."

Smith frowned and Caralynne looked up, "You think that's where she got them?"

"Well, I haven't seen any unusual plants nearby. This seems the likeliest place to get super-powers to me. They probably found one of our children orphaned, decided to experiment on her, try to make her into a new kind of savage for them."

Smith held up a hand, "Hang on there, Jimmy. We don't know how long these things have been here for. If they've been here that long, we haven't seen them before, and that's—"

"Haven't seen them before that we know of. They could have taken people before, but left no witnesses. But that doesn't matter, Smith. That building looks solid, it's near water, and if we take it, we'll rescue the Major and Lady Emily, and we'll have more answers than just my guesses."

Having been shot at with the lightning ray, Smith wasn't quick to underestimate the small blue creatures, "They had some pretty fancy firepower."

"Yes, but they still don't take well to bullets," Caralynne said coolly. "I'm with you, Jimmy."

Smith didn't like this, but he had to admit that getting Waller back was important. He approved of that man, and leaving him to the hands — if you could call them hands — of those creatures wasn't right.

"Let's ride back... see how far we'll have to march to get out here," Devlin instructed, and with agreeing nods, all three backed out of the trees and mounted up, riding east at a gallop.

CHAPTER XXXIII

Waller awoke on a table and realized immediately that his hands and legs were in restraints. He struggled for a moment but gave up quickly — there was no point wasting strength against those sorts of bonds, he'd wait for a different opportunity. Turning his head, he looked around as best he could. He was in a brightly lit room, filled with many shining silver surfaces, some with flashing lights. There was also a hum of electricity in the air.

This was the den of the blue creatures, and it seemed their control of machinery and electricity was far in advance of humanity's own.

"Emily, are you near?" Waller asked the question in a loud voice, but no answer came from the young Lady.

Then he heard her scream... the sound seemed to be coming from another room, probably nearby. His teeth gritted and he jerked against the restraints, but they were too strong to break.

His mind started making quick judgments based on what he'd seen. The savages had helped these creatures... perhaps the creatures had domesticated them, had some sort of control over the beasts. Savages would make for powerful dogs; with their strength and their human-shaped bodies they could be used for many different purposes.

So the table Waller was on had probably been designed for a savage. And if that was indeed the case, the bonds would be much too strong for him to break.

As Waller was thinking, a royal blue-colored creature appeared next to him, and he stilled in surprise. The creature seemed to have the skin of a whale, very thick and like rubber. Its yellow eyes were slits without pupils, and it had a tiny mouth at the bottom of its long, narrow head.

"I am Major Thomas Waller of the Royal Newfoundland Regiment. I insist you release me and the Lady you've taken prisoner, or you will be treated as an enemy of the Empire by my comrades," the direct approach seemed the best to take, though Waller was almost certain the creature would have no idea what his words meant.

The blue being studied him for a moment, and then Waller's mind started to race. Something was happening ... a picture was forming in his mind's eye, placed there from the outside.

The blue creature appeared, standing over a horde of savages who were behaving in a disciplined fashion — standing in ranks.

It was as if to say that the creature was lord over the savages. Was that a counter to Waller's statement? Had the blue Martian understood the words... was he now communicating with pictures flowing into Waller's mind?

The Major realized with a start that, one way or the other, this creature was in his head — but perhaps this would be a communication medium. Waller focused his mind, and pictured tens of thousands of Imperial troops on a parade ground in India. The blue creature hesitated, then pushed back.

Without him seeming to have any control over what was happening, a string of Waller's memories flashed through his mind — a Royal Navy squadron he'd seen on maneuvers in the Mediterranean, pictures and newsreels of the French and German armies marching into their great war, the Afghan campaign...

The blue creature took a step back in what Waller assumed was surprise. Then it drove into his mind, inserting again the picture of itself standing over ranks of savages, then replacing those savages with men in British Imperial uniforms.

Waller didn't understand for a moment... then the message became clear. The savages were the servants of this creature, but they weren't smart. They roamed this planet in hordes like packs of wild dogs. And this blue creature could seize them when it needed them, to use as an army. So it needed troops... but why...

Another image: the savages rushing forward... on a different world. A world where the sky was green, and the ground yellow. Waller saw a whole battlescape as though he was flying overhead in a plane... in the rear, great silver vehicles like those the creatures had used to capture himself and Emily, but larger, and with fixed lightning rays. But there were few of these... and between them raced savages... and forward raced savages.

They... what?

Waller focused on the image being placed in his mind. He concentrated on it as best he could and watched as the savages raced across the yellow ground... and slammed into different creatures. Creatures that appeared like dragon men... lizard creatures, who were fighting with great strength and power...

Suddenly, it all made sense to Waller. They... the blue creatures were at war with the lizard men, and being fragile themselves, needed attack dogs. Warriors. So they bred savages here on the new world, let them roam free, but then took control of them and used them as berserkers when they were needed to fight...

But how? Waller pictured a savage in his mind — an uncontrolled savage, roaming and eating at its leisure.

The blue creature's face appeared in Waller's mind, staring at him. In his mind. It was *in* his mind. This was... Waller had heard of this. It was... *telepathy*. It was a manner of communicating from mind to mind — though up until now, only a theoretical one. The stuff of parlor tricks at home... and the tool of commanding the savages here.

In his mind, the blue creature found an image that seemed to convey the right message to Waller. A savage appeared in his mind, and then faded into a blood hound. One of the soldiers from Waller's memory came next... and faded into a handsome german shepherd dog. The creature wanted to upgrade its army?

A new picture formed: the same battlefield, but with Canadian troops bounding forward at savage speeds, firing lightning guns and then falling on the lizard men with no mercy.

Waller resisted that; he pictured the savages knocking him from his horse, his relative weakness evident enough.

As an immediate counterpoint, though, the creature produced Emily's smiling face, and then reviewed the images of her assault on the savages. Then it created a new image, a savage on the left, Waller on the right, and the two moving together, merging in a bright light that cooled to reveal Emily.

So the creature wanted to make him more like Emily. The Army had sent Waller out here to find the secret that had given Emily her powers, and found it he had... now he didn't know what he could possibly do with the knowledge.

Instead of wondering, he again engaged with the creature, forming a picture of something being fed to him, making him stronger. The creature stepped back again, and Waller thought he detected surprise.

Perhaps it wasn't a food that made the strength...

The creature fished through Waller's mind and produced a new image: Waller standing at the front of a schoolroom, with naked young toddlers sitting at the desks. That made no sense... so the creature changed the image. Savages sat at the desks, but then they grew younger and younger until they were toddlers.

And then they grew older, and each became Emily.

Waller countered bitterly, picturing what he imagined Emily looked like as a baby with her family. She was human, she was not a savage. The savages couldn't simply learn to be good soldiers.

But the Martian answered him instantly. It faded the picture of Emily with British parents... it replaced it with Emily as a young toddler running with a pack of toddlers... with savage women herding them.

It then aged Emily, and put her amongst savages, as *one* of them. A savage who had learned.

Emily was a savage?

"No..." Waller said it out loud. "Not possible."

His disbelief must have been evident in his thoughts, because the creature placed in a new image: a savage standing next to one of his soldiers. It then merged them... and a white man remained.

What was this now?

The creature's thoughts started to feel frustrated, or at least that was all Waller could detect from them. It pictured what looked like the grasslands... but then at night... and it had one moon. It pictured Earth. It showed tribesmen... people who looked like the Indians Waller had seen in Canada... those people walked towards the mountains... the Selkirks.

They went through the tunnels, and were welcomed by the creatures... who then began to...

Breed them. Like dogs.

To make better warriors for their wars. The way dog breeders created breeds that were better suited to different jobs on Earth.

A terrier and another german shepherd appeared in his mind. This was the message... the savage and the soldier, different breeds of the same species?

No. No not possible.

The creature forced more pictures into Waller's mind. A silver disc was in the sky over Egypt. It was watching the pyramids being built... not building them, but watching the men building them. It was silently observing... then the disc... a ship in the sky... went over the ocean to Canada and made the tunnels, and then started beckoning Indians to come through...

And then the breeding. Buildings like this one, forced breeding, the way a man breeds a dog for its skills... and the children being taken control of by the blue creatures, never learning to think for themselves...

Then being shipped off to war... and the wars being won... and the savages being moved to breed on other planets... and many of the breeding buildings here being taken away... except for some, like the one Waller was in now. This for the caretakers... for the ranchers of the free-range herd.

This was not the only place. Savages were bred elsewhere.

But now this blue being had discovered and captured one of the savages that had learned to think. Perhaps the blue creatures had known about the Selkirk Mandate before this — had known about humans and their skills — but Emily was a thinking woman who also had savage strength.

This discovery... like finding a dog who could play cards — or shoot a rifle — would make the career of this blue being.

Waller wasn't certain whether the pictures he was seeing in his mind now were his own or were being planted, or if they were a mix of both.

But the answers were there, even if the images being provided to Waller were disjointed.

The savages were humans, taken from Earth thousands of years before, and bred to serve these weak blue beings in their wars. And this new world, which had been the first breeding ground, was now only one of many, probably in a rear area, and thus sparsely garrisoned by the creatures.

When Emily had returned, they might have detected her with their telepathy... or perhaps the savages themselves caught her scent... had the hordes been sent to get her, or had they stampeded on their own?

And there were more questions. Why hadn't they come after Emily while she'd been living in the Selkirk Mandate as a child? Did they actually believe they could control the minds of regular humans? Could they?

Waller tried to put these questions into pictures in his thoughts, but the Martian seemed to slam a door, blocking further communication. It left the side of the table, and Waller couldn't see it anymore. He yelled at it, but it was gone.

He became more aware of the screaming from the other room. Screaming and pleading.

It was Emily... and she was a savage.

But savages were human...

The enormity of what had been sent into Waller's mind finally began to sink in, and his heart raced. What could be done?

CHAPTER XXXIV

"I'd make it about ten miles from here."

Captains Tucker and Kearsey had just heard the full report on what had taken place in the valley that day, and now Smith offered his guess as to the distance between their camp and the creatures' building.

The trip from the building back to the camp had taken surprisingly little time — had the column continued marching west unassailed for another day, they would probably have sighted it on their own... which perhaps explained why the wagon train led by Sergeant Barnes had been attacked here, just short of it. The creatures had wanted to make sure they remained undiscovered.

"Amazing that they've been here and no one's known," Kearsey observed, shaking his head. "Always thought they should send an aero plane out this way."

"Yeah, find one with a pilot willing to chance an emergency landing out here, b'y," Tucker shook his head. "Wonder if this planet belongs to those Martians... taken their damned time mentioning it if they do own it. And they're running the savages like dogs? Those hordes haven't look too controlled to me."

Devlin shrugged in reply to both Captains' words, "Maybe they only control them when they need them. Leave them to roam free for the rest of the time. But the savages were definitely acting as escort for those motor cars, looked like they were trained and under control somehow."

Kearsey looked at Tucker and the two Captains shook their heads. Tucker looked back at Devlin, "If these Martian bastards found out about Emily somehow, they could have stampeded the savages to go after her... they might want to experiment on her or something such."

"Seems possible," Smith agreed. "So if we're going to move, it has to be fast."

Tucker nodded. Having been appointed to command the unit in Waller's absence, this was his decision to make — and he'd be damned if he'd leave the Major to be dissected by a bunch of Martians. None of the Wall's orders had covered him being captured by little blue men, so it wouldn't actually be a violation to go after him.

"So it's like the book by Mister Wells, with the heat rays and things?" Kearsey asked next, his mind moving over to a tactical assessment of the scenario.

"They didn't have tentacles or walking machines. What they had were... I'll call lightning rays," Devlin replied quietly, "but they weren't too accurate and they were slow to reload. And Miss Caralynne and Mister Smith will attest to the fact that they're vulnerable to bullets."

"How many do you think were in the building?" Tucker scratched his chin thoughtfully and Devlin glanced at Smith and then Caralynne.

"Building that size... could be a hundred, could be ten... depends. I get the sense that these things are like ranchers, keeping an eye on free-range savages out here. Didn't seem like military types to me. So it could be a fancy Martian homestead," Smith observed with a frown.

"But they won't be expecting an attack," Caralynne said firmly, her eyes continually drifting westward despite her efforts not to fixate.

The officers and the drifter frowned at her comment, and Devlin asked the question, "Pardoning me, Miss Caralynne, but why wouldn't they be expecting us?"

She looked back with a frown, paused, then shook her head, "Well, maybe they're waiting for us, I don't know. But we must leave soon."

Her preoccupation was evident and understandable. She wanted to ride in with guns blazing... the officers just wanted to make sure it was with plenty of guns.

"Alright, we'll leave the wounded and a platoon here... that's about eighty men. And we'll leave them with the Colt machine gun. If they get attacked, that should be enough to see the bastards off..." Tucker began after a moment. "And if we do our job, any savages who'd be coming here will get called to defend that building."

"We'll have the b'ys leave most of their kit... canteens, a day's rations and rifle and ammo only. Move fast on foot... we'll be there in under two hours," Kearsey thought out loud now.

"Good, pick the men to stay behind, Fred, and get them up. Make sure we take all the Lewis guns. We'll go right now. See if we can be in position to attack by moonlight."

Kearsey left immediately, and began barking orders. The rest of the officers assembled around him and he started explaining what was to happen, and then they scattered and started calling up the men.

"We could run into a horde out there," Smith pointed out cautiously, still not convinced that this approach would be the best. Then again, he had no better option at the moment.

"If we do we'll fight them off," Devlin said simply, pulling out his Webley and double checking it was loaded.

"And if we catch the bastards napping, we'll show them what for," Tucker got to his feet. "Excuse me now, I'll go arm up."

The Captain left and Devlin slid his revolver back into his holster, "You both should replenish your ammunition. I'll move on foot with my men, but you both should continue to ride — take command of Sergeant Reilly's section."

Smith looked at Caralynne, and the distracted woman nodded abruptly, and got to her feet. As she left in a hurry, Smith frowned, "You want me to look after her?"

Devlin nodded, "I think that's what the Major would want. She was in a fight with Lady Emily back there and then she let her get captured... if that were me and my sister I'd be beyond livid."

"I'll keep an eye on her," Smith agreed, and then left Devlin alone.

With a sigh, the Lieutenant turned and headed for his tent.

***

Caralynne was in her wagon, opening her suitcase and Emily's to withdraw a box of .45 caliber automatic pistol ammunition from each. There was precious little left — Emily's weapon and ammunition had been taken with her, and Caralynne had shot most of hers during the attack on the column. But she'd have to make do.

Annie sat in the back of wagon looking pale, "So... they have the Major and Lady Lee? And Jimmy and you are going after them? And they're Martians?"

Caralynne was barely paying attention to the nervous girl, "Yes."

Annie shrunk down against the side of the wagon and let out a long sigh, "Didn't realize how... exciting... this adventure would be..."

Just then there was a knock on the side of the wagon. Looking to Caralynne but getting no guidance, Annie swung open the flap, and Smith tipped his hat to her, "Miss Annie. I have to see Miss Caralynne. Have a gun for her."

The latter bit got Caralynne's attention, and taking the last box of ammunition she turned and moved to the back of the wagon, "A gun?"

"I wasn't sure how much ammo you were carrying, but if you're low I can offer you a Colt single action revolver. I have plenty of rounds for it. Never had much use for the second gun, just stays in my saddle bag. And if you can shoot that magazine pistol, you can handle this," Smith lifted a gun belt up and laid it inside the back of the wagon.

Caralynne nodded her head once, "Good of you. I'll see you later, Annie."

With that, the lady leapt from the back of the wagon, leaving the frightened maid on her own.

"Miss Caralynne, I should tell you that I'm going to be watching you closely," Smith said plainly as they walked away from the wagon. "If you think you're going to ride in there by yourself to rescue Miss Emily, you're not. I know you're good with that gun, but I'll find a way to stop you."

Caralynne didn't look at him as she walked towards her horse, "I'm sure you'll try."

"I don't try without succeeding very often, Miss. And this won't be an exception. I'm not letting you throw away your life on some foolish charge."

Stopping abruptly, Caralynne turned on her heel, "What would you know, Smith? You didn't let her down, that was me. I'm going to get her."

"We're going to get her, Miss Caralynne. That simple. Don't test my abilities and I won't test yours."

Caralynne glared at Smith, "We'll see."

Devlin was on his way back from his tent when he saw Smith and Caralynne's exchange, and then he realized he had one more stop to make. Quietly moving over to the back of the covered wagon, he knocked softly on the side, and when Annie opened the flap he climbed in.

"Jimmy, you're going to fight Martians?" Annie asked in a small voice, and the Lieutenant flashed a smile.

"Yes, I am. Would marrying a Martian fighter suit you?"

Devlin was carried away in the moment, to be sure, but in his mind there was no good reason not to be. He was young and certain of his love for Annie, and that was enough to warrant a marriage, as far as he was concerned.

Annie's expression bubbled over with surprise followed by joy, "Of course!"

With the romantic flourish of a soldier going off to fight in a battle from which he wasn't sure he'd return, he took Annie in his arms and kissed her.

"How many of you have read the book about the *War of the Worlds* that Mister H. G. Wells wrote? We had it with us in Egypt for a while." Tucker had the men assembled and ready to run.

There was dead silence, and then aside from the officers, only one man put up his hand, "I have, sir."

Tucker looked around for more raised hands, but there were none.

"Well shit. Alright b'ys, the Major and Lady Emily have been taken by a bunch of little blue Martian men. They're not human, they're strange creatures, and they have guns that shoot lightning bolts. But they aren't good shots, and their guns take time to reload. It looks to us like they use savages as their attack dogs. Now Lieutenant Devlin and Mister Smith and Miss Caralynne found the building where they took the Major. We're going to go take that building, and whatever's in it. Might well hold the key to Lady Emily's powers, because it's too much of a coincidence for it to be out there and not, eh?"

The men were staring at Tucker, perhaps wondering if he was drunk. Didn't matter if they thought it, though — he was in charge, and he was telling them to go rescue the Wall. They wouldn't take much convincing to go out after the Major, even in these savage grasslands.

"It's ten miles west of here, and we're doing it at a forced march. I want to be storming that building in two-and-a-half hours."

There was a murmur of grumbling — it was ten miles, after all — but then someone cried out, "Bastards got the Wall? I don't give a shit what planet in God's heaven they're from, they're fuckin' dead!"

Tucker grinned at the enthusiasm, then barked out the order, "Alright, b'ys, let's move out!"

Some 300 Newfoundlanders marched out of the wagon circle moments later, on a fast march to meet the Martians, or whatever the blue creatures were.

CHAPTER XXXV

Waller was taken from his table by savages after the blue creature left. He struggled a little, but not too much. He had to save his strength, wait for an opportunity. Being manhandled by four savages was not the time to make a move — they'd tear him to pieces if he tried to fight them all.

The beasts... the *men*... dragged him out of the room he'd been in, and into a corridor outside. He got his first good look at the large building he was being held in: it was magnificent, with glass walls showing off the moonlit valley outside, and many electric-type machines on the wall... all at the height of his stomach, probably because they were intended to be used by the shorter blue creatures, not savages. The ceilings and doors were tall enough to accommodate the beasts, though.

Emily's screaming had stopped before they unstrapped Waller from the table, so he had an outside hope that they would be made captives together. At least then he could check on her...

It struck him again that she was a savage. How was that possible, and would that change how he reacted when he saw her next? He was surviving this experience with a surprising level of detachment, or perhaps he was just so shocked that he had yet to react properly.

As the savages dragged him around the next corner, he looked down the long hallway and there she was, being dragged, struggling, towards him. The savages dragging her were also groping her, and their arousal was evident due to their unclothed state. One forcibly ripped her blouse half-open, and she managed to free one arm just long enough to collapse that savage's face with her fist.

"*Off!*" she yelled desperately. "*Stop!*"

Waller began to struggle instinctively, and the savages holding him actually let their attention move to Emily... they wanted her too. Using the distraction to his advantage, Waller jerked an arm free and took a swing at one. The punch connected, but the savage didn't even react — all the creatures started moving forward, away from Waller.

He'd be free in a minute, but even Emily couldn't fight off that many. Luckily, she wouldn't have to.

Two blue creatures stepped out of a room between Waller and Emily and reached out with their hands, locking the savages in place as surely as if they'd been tied in steel cable. One of the creatures then approached Emily with what appeared to be a gun.

Waller, now unfettered, burst forward, but the blue creature nearer him telepathically directed one of the frozen savages to take hold of him. As it moved to obey, Waller plunged to the floor, just managing to break his fall with his hands, "Emily, run!"

Emily was still in view, and her eyes found Waller's, but it became evident that she couldn't move any more than the savages. Whatever control the blue creatures had over the savage breed of man, Emily had inherited.

She couldn't speak, but panic filled her eyes as the creature walked forward, pulled aside the torn blouse, put the gun to her heart, and squeezed the trigger.

There was a soft thud, but no shot. Frantic, Waller tried to struggle forward, but as Emily's eyes found his he realized she wasn't harmed. It hadn't been a gun...

The blue creature with the device returned to the other, and then they released their savages. Waller and Emily were picked up and hauled forward again, but the savages' interest in Emily seemed to have dwindled. Emily struggled as she was dragged past the creature with the gun, and as she managed to lock eyes with it, she froze in telepathic union with the Martian. Waller tried to watch, but the savages came to an open door and tossed him through it.

It was a cell, for which he was actually grateful, with four blank silver walls and a soft, cushioned floor. He heard Emily start to laugh, and then she was unceremoniously, and literally, tossed in on top of him.

Her blouse open, her bare collarbone ended up pressed into Waller's face, and that was simply awkward, so he gently pushed her off. Laughing happily, she rolled onto her back beside him.

Waller shook his head, "May I ask?"

She turned her head and looked at him, "I just landed on you, Tom."

"And that's funny?"

She rolled up onto her side, her blouse falling open again and showing off her undergarments, "I'm nearly half naked here."

Waller sat up slowly, shaking his head, "Still not following, I'm sorry."

"How irresistible am I right now? I'm not irresistible, am I? Not two days ago your eyes would glaze over if you saw me without my cape. Now look," she pulled the collar of her blouse open, "collarbones! And you're confused instead of amorous!"

She sounded giddy — despite being locked in a silver box — and Waller started to slowly come around as to why. He looked at her collarbones. Certainly, Emily was lovely, but there was no fog creeping over his mind...

"That gun against my heart, it turned off whatever was making me irresistible, because I was too much of a nuisance. The savages were too hard to control with me around!" she nearly hopped off the floor in her excitement. "I got it from that blue thing's head... it's done, I'm switched off. No more irresistibility. I'm a normal woman!"

Waller found himself smiling, "Well thank God for that."

Emily launched herself toward him with a beaming smile, wrapping her arms around him in a great hug that revealed she'd retained her strength.

"Back... breaking..." he rasped, and she pulled back, turning red.

"Sorry, sorry! Just got carried away!" she beamed. "I'm a normal... normal girl..."

Her smile started to fade as the elation passed. This immediate little personal victory had bought her a moment of unmitigated happiness, but then the memories of the images that had been driven into her mind started to reassert themselves.

She slid back from Waller, pulled her knees up to her chest and wrapped her arms around them, her chin sinking forward a little, "Mostly normal."

"You were born a savage, you mean?" Waller couldn't believe he stated it so plainly, but perhaps he'd taken his cue from Smith's style of direct honesty.

Emily paled, and he realized immediately he'd been too forthright.

"I... they told you that?" she asked quietly.

"Put pictures in my mind to that effect, yes. You're from a different breed of human, is what I gathered. Likened it to breeding dogs with specific skills... which I think was rather unkind of them. Dogs are far more civilized than the savages that we've had the displeasure of meeting."

The elation was gone, and Emily's eyes fell to the floor, "I didn't want to believe it. I mean... you know how the Darwinists are. They'll think I'm inevitably a lower race... even though I look like a white Briton. They'll... I mean... I'm from savage blood..."

"I've never abided by Darwinists," Waller said, his tone much less casual now. "Seems to me you can't judge any race as better or worse than another. It's foolish to do so. I make a point never to underestimate anyone, because then you can be rudely surprised."

Emily let out a long sigh, "Yes, well, you're not typical."

Waller frowned, then lifted himself up off the padded floor and moved around to sit quite close to Emily, "Maybe, but I also happen to be the only other person to know your background. And I can promise I'll tell no one, if you don't want them to know."

Emily looked sideways at him, "You still trust me, don't you?"

"Apparently, yes. So if we get away from here, we can tell everyone that you just had an inexplicable experience as a toddler..."

"It won't work," Emily shook her head. "Someone else will find the creatures, and the creatures will tell. And if I could be saved from being a savage, then other children can be too. And we must..."

"Saved?" Waller asked, narrowing his eyes as he thought back to the pictures that had been placed in his mind. The children of the savages were never allowed to think for themselves.

"It's the way they can control me, and the way they control the savages," Emily said quietly, looking back at the floor. "It must be something to do with the way we're bred, we're susceptible to their telepathies. I think that if you grow up with them always in your mind, you never learn to speak, or to think for yourself. Like any unused muscle that weakens, your brain probably degenerates. And then they probably train you to be aggressive and savage, and they let you loose to live on the grasslands on your own... to feed yourself and stay strong until they come for you, and harness you with their minds to fight in their wars..."

"Ah, but take the child away from the blue fellows at a young enough age, and it learns to think," Waller was beginning to understand. "And if you're to be held as evidence, taking a child into a civilized house for upbringing and feeding can produce a body that looks healthy by any standard, not hunched or feral like a savage..."

Waller paused as he realized how that might have sounded, but Emily looked at him and smiled, scrunching up her face, "I don't look feral to you, Tom?"

"Oh dear," Major Waller replied.

CHAPTER XXXVI

The Newfoundlanders moved with speed and determination. They were going to face an unknown enemy, but for them that was nothing new — in Afghanistan, any manner of enemy could appear from behind rocks or out of caves, and here in the new world they'd learned to face the savages. Now there were Martians, or whatever these creatures were to be called, with guns that shot lightning and lorries that were large and impressive.

Well that was dandy, let them have their lorries and lightning: the men had Short, Magazine, Lee-Enfield rifles, Lewis guns, and plenty of ammunition.

Devlin was moving at the front of the fast-moving column of men, his platoon in the lead because he was the only regular officer who knew the way. Smith and Caralynne were riding just a little ways ahead. After an hour of very quick marching, the men had already covered nearly six miles — a rapid pace indeed, considering they were carrying almost twenty pounds of kit, between rifle, ammunition, canteen and ration tin. They'd be at the building in no time, and under the ghostly light of two moons, they'd attack.

Keeping his feet moving quickly, Devlin followed the course that Smith and Caralynne were setting.

"No sign of savages so far," Caralynne said quietly, looking at Smith as the two riders crested the hill Devlin and the rest of the Newfoundlanders were still climbing.

The drifter nodded, looking around again to make sure saying the thing hadn't jinxed it, "Not so far. I hope you were right about them not expecting us."

Caralynne nodded, "So do I."

Smith watched her carefully as she said it, noting the way she was tensing — getting set to kick her horse into a gallop. He had seen enough men try to ride away from him to know the signs, and though he'd left his mare back at the circle of wagons to rest, and had taken a foreign horse for this mission, he knew he could ride her down if she tried to go.

Caralynne had clearly grown up with horses and guns, but she'd been away from the frontier for many years, and her skills at the reins were rusty.

"So who taught you to shoot?" Smith asked, for once deciding not to say exactly what he was thinking.

Frowning, Caralynne looked back at him, "The man who adopted Emily and me, he'd been a Captain in the British Army. He was a kind man, and he told me and Emily over and over that the savages gave no quarter, so we should know how to shoot them down."

"Good man," Smith said approvingly. "You have a talent for it."

Perhaps he'd been around the Newfoundlanders too long now, but Smith was finding this sideways approach to a comment to be a useful one.

"I enjoy practicing, and this new gun is very handy," she tapped the Colt 1911 pistol on her hip.

"I've never taken an interest in the magazine pistols, but with your recommendation I might well," Smith said thoughtfully.

Caralynne nodded, "Good, yes, they're very good. I'm very glad I have mine with me. And yours too, I certainly appreciate the backup."

"Yes," Smith agreed, "but your gun only has seven shots, and the one I gave you only has six. So if you ride away right now like you're planning, it'll only take fourteen savages to kill you. And there are more of them than that."

There came the usual direct statement, and Caralynne opened her mouth to protest.

"I know you feel responsible for Emily. We'll get her back, don't fret about that. Just don't ride alone. Because then I'll have to ride with you, and we'll both get et. And I don't want to get et. Just wait another hour, we'll all be there together."

Again, Caralynne's protest failed to emerge from her open mouth. Instead she looked away and relaxed enough to reassure Smith that she wasn't going to bolt. He let out a relieved breath and the two riders eased their horses on.

Captain Tucker came up alongside Devlin after they crested the hill, the older Newfoundlander huffing more than he'd have liked, "Getting a bit too old to move like this, Jimmy."

"Old or round, sir?" Devlin asked with a smile, and Tucker laughed sharply.

"Same thing aren't they? You wait 'til you're a married man, you'll be right sawed off and hammered down once you get to my age. A good wife's cooking stays with you… even after you've been in the field this long!"

Devlin stopped abruptly in place, and Tucker passed him, but when he realized he'd done so, he turned around in surprise, "Jimmy?"

Shaking his head to restore his thoughts, Devlin jogged forward and then fell into step next to his Captain, "Sorry, just realized I proposed to a girl before I left."

Tucker frowned first, then laughed again, "Jesus, Mary and Joseph, you and that maid sure do move fast."

Devlin smiled and wiped his forehead with the back of his hand, "Well, sort of. Caught up in the moment, I guess. Not that I regret it."

"No reason you should. Just make sure you get back there so you don't disappoint her," Tucker patted him on the shoulder with a smile, then dropped back.

For a moment, Devlin didn't fully understand what George Tucker had meant. Then it occurred to him that he might die out here, attacking these Martians. That really hadn't sunk in for him yet. He'd feared for his life when the savages attacked, but not the blue men… he'd come out all this way hell bent on driving the blue men into the ground and freeing the Major...

And he'd proposed to poor Annie just before he left.

"Oh Christ," he muttered to himself, and Corporal Walsh — who'd taken over Sergeant Halloran's section while Halloran stayed back with the wounded — looked at his Lieutenant with a frown.

"There something up, sir?"

Devlin shook his head, "I'm just an idiot is all, Walsh. Propose to a girl before going into battle? It's as good as painting a bullseye on your chest. Jesus."

Corporal Walsh nodded somberly, then looked at the next man in the section, "Devlin proposed to the maid, tell the b'ys she's off the market. Pass it on."

"Oh Jesus!" Devlin protested, but it was too late. The regimental rumor mill was already churning. By the time they attacked the building, every man in the regiment — probably even the b'ys back in St. John's — would know he'd asked Annie to marry him.

So like Tucker said, now he had to make it back.

CHAPTER XXXVII

"So what do you think our fate will be?" Waller was exploring the smooth walls of the cell, trying to see if there were any seams or openings that might yield an escape.

Emily was lying on the floor, hands behind her head and legs crossed at the ankle as she stared at the ceiling of the room, wondering where the light was coming from, "Oh I don't know, if they're breeders, then they're probably going to breed us. Possibly with each other."

Waller paused and looked back at her, "You really should stop with the teasing."

Smiling, she looked up at him, "Come on, you know it wouldn't be the worst fate in the world, you and me."

"Yes, but you're awfully liberal in talking about it," Waller went back to studying the wall, and Emily laughed.

"Come on, I'm a born savage, I love to roll naked in the grass and take advantage of strapping Majors, what can I say?"

Waller shook his head, "Something else. My mother would be appalled if I was so forward with a woman…"

"Oh relax, Tom, it's just talk. I mean, that's not to say I won't have a go if you're willing…"

"Would you please stop?" Waller turned around, and Emily laughed.

"It's so easy to distract you," she smiled as his eyes met hers. "Come sit down, there's not going to be any way to get out of here until they open the door."

Waller shook his head, "I'm not so sure. They probably use this cell for savages, and aside from you, can you think of any savage who'd know how to work a door handle? There may be something exposed in here that we can use to escape, because we can think."

Emily's smile switched over to a frown, and she sat up, "Alright, so that's why you're the Major and I'm the silly girl."

She hopped to her feet and joined Waller near the door, running her hands over the smooth silver paneling in search of anything that might work to their advantage.

"I'll take my b'ys down from the north, deal with the vehicles so they can't use 'em," Tucker pointed down the slope towards the building, and his officers nodded in the moonlight. "Fred, work your way around from the west, use one of your Lewis guns to kill every damned savage in that pen back there. Then surround the far side of the building. Damned if we know what sort of reinforcements they might have."

Kearsey nodded and left the huddle of officers, quietly calling his Lieutenants together and then waving his men to move down the slope to the right.

Smith and Caralynne were standing near Devlin as Tucker gave his company orders; Devlin's platoon would lead the way down, while the other three platoons — each understrength — would fan out behind in a long skirmish line that would hopefully be immune to the inaccurate fire from the lightning rays.

"Jimmy, you take care of those motor cars and make sure the bastards can't get away. We'll take prisoners if we can, but if it comes to it, kill all of them. We'll figure a way to pickle them so our doctors can dissect them later if need be," Tucker said unceremoniously. "Let's go."

The attack plan had been hastily prepared, and no time had been taken to assimilate the curious oddity of the structure they were attacking. There would be time for that when the blue men were either dead or prisoners, and when any savages they summoned were seen off.

"Mister Smith, Miss Caralynne, would you care to come with me?" Devlin asked as he drew his revolver, and Caralynne drew her pistol instantly. Smith nodded once in his own reply, and Devlin called to his men to follow him down the slope.

There was no attempt to be quiet, and that was perhaps careless, but Devlin didn't care if the bastards knew he was coming. It was only 400 yards down the slope of the valley to those motor cars, and they wouldn't have time to do anything to save themselves.

Waller and Emily sat defeated on the padded floor, leaning against each other shoulder-to-shoulder.

"So, I suppose you should be the Major then," Waller said, shaking his head.

Emily smiled, "Yes, I was right after all."

They continued to sit there, both thinking different things, neither particularly inclined to move.

"I wonder what Jimmy is doing now. I bet he and Tucker are probably cooking up a plan to come after us," Emily said lightly, somewhat hopefully.

Waller shook his head, "Attack Martians who we know nothing about, just for the sake of two people... I'm afraid not, Emily. We're on our own."

The distinct report of an Enfield rifle sounded outside, followed by the barking of a Lewis gun.

Emily smiled very brightly, and Waller looked up at the ceiling of the room in disbelief. He'd been unconscious for the ride out here... it couldn't have been so short as to allow the men to get here this quickly. How had they... well... well he'd find out, either when they rescued him, or when prisoners from a failed attack were thrown in here with them.

"So, no rescue?" Emily looked at him, and he sighed.

"I surrender," he returned her gaze.

As he did, she leaned over and kissed him, which was a terrible distraction from the sound of gunfire outside.

Devlin slid to a halt and ducked for cover behind the nearer of the silver cars. The electric hiss of a lightning ray cracked out and the car rocked, presumably having been hit. Over to the right, one of his men stopped and aimed his SMLE, then fired.

"Got one! Got one!" the Private yelled with glee, then dove for cover as another lightning bolt ripped over him.

"How many?" Devlin demanded loudly as he crouched and then rose up over the back of the car.

"Three out here!" someone yelled back. "One's down, the other two are trying to get to the pen to let out the savages!"

One of Kearsey's Lewis guns began firing sharply over on the right, and there were wails as the savages in the pen, trapped in their cage, were systematically murdered. Devlin had no sympathy, and seeing his chance, he worked his way around the back of the car, leading with his Webley revolver.

"Down, Jimmy!" Caralynne was right behind him, and she unceremoniously grabbed him by the upper arm and dragged him down as a lightning bolt crossed over his head. It had come from inside the building, right through the glass.

Well that was a neat trick, shooting through glass without breaking it. Smith, who'd been third in line, saw a blue creature with a lightning ray inside the glass building, so he aimed at the Martian with his Colt New Service revolver and fired twice.

Both bullets bounced off the glass as if it were armor.

"Whatever the building's made of is tougher than the car windows," the drifter reported, ducking.

"I thought glass was supposed to insulate against electricity," Devlin complained, crawling forward. "There has to be a door on this side, to let them use the vehicles. We have to find it!"

Crawling forward, he saw at least three more Martians inside, and realized that any one of them could probably shoot him. The third blue creature that had been outside fell under rifle fire, and Devlin's section moved forward, still shooting in vain at the Martians shielded by the building's special glass.

"They can fire through that wall, take cover!" the Lieutenant barked, and then one of the Lewis guns from his company got into position and began hammering away at one of the panels of glass.

Devlin cursed as the ricocheting rounds started to pelt the ground near him, and backed up, getting Smith and Caralynne to move backward behind him. Returning to the shelter of the lorry, he prepared to yell a cease fire order when one of the Privates preempted him.

"It's starting to crack!"

Frowning, Devlin crept up enough to look over the motor car again, and sure enough, the panel had chipped and the lines of a fracture had begun to spread.

"At that panel, ten rounds rapid *fire!*" he barked, hauling his Webley up over the car and firing quickly. Smith and Caralynne came up beside him and as his platoon began a vicious fusillade against the same point the Lewis gun was targeting, the cracks began to spread faster and further.

"Wish we had our bloody mountain guns now," Devlin grunted as he pulled his empty pistol down and cracked it open, reloading its six bullets.

The men stopped to reload, and Devlin looked back up to see the Martians had backed away from this side of the building, perhaps fearing the imminent penetration...

"Hold your fire!" Devlin roared, and as the Lewis gun stopped he leapt up onto the motor car, then jumped off it and rushed right for the panel. Dropping his shoulder as if he was readying to tackle a man in rugby, he launched himself at it. He didn't see the lightning ray gun until it fired, and he went shoulder first into the glass.

On the far side of the building, Captain Kearsey's men caught a blue creature as it was going inside, and managed to grab the thick glass door as it started to swing shut. Leading the way in was Lieutenant Boyett, revolver drawn, and his platoon followed him into the building with bayonets fixed.

"Try to take prisoners, but take no risks," he reminded his men, and then a lightning bolt blasted him off his feet and killed him instantly.

The Sergeant nearest the fallen young man roared and shot in the same instant, the bullet from his rifle passing through the long head of the blue creature who'd fired. The Martian fell to the ground and twitched, so three of the men shot it again for good measure.

Captain Kearsey pushed his way in behind the men, "Keep moving! Flush out the bastards!"

Kneeling next to his dead Lieutenant, Kearsey shook his head with a sigh, "Brave b'y. Brave."

He then went forward with his men, and shot a Martian with his revolver.

Smith and Caralynne rushed through the opening where the panel of glass had shattered, and as two Martians emerged from opposite sides to attack them, they each shot one. The shots were fired almost simultaneously, and both .45 caliber bullets passed through the heads of the creatures.

Newfoundlanders hurried in behind them shouting as they advanced, while Smith grabbed Devlin by the back of his collar and hauled him out of the way. The Lieutenant was face down, so Caralynne helped turn him over, and as this was accomplished, it became clear the lightning ray had missed him.

"Jimmy," Caralynne slapped his cheek. "Jimmy wake up now. You're supposed to marry my maid. Come on now."

His eyes flew open, "How did *you* know that? You were riding ahead!"

The cheers of the Newfoundlanders were audible through the walls of the cell, and Waller knew that meant they'd soon find this room. He thought about protesting the kiss he was receiving just then, but he wasn't insane.

After a moment, there were voices outside the door, "Must be in here!"

The door slid open a second later, and leading with her Colt pistol, Caralynne leapt in, followed by Smith.

Emily stopped kissing Waller and smiled, looking at her rescuers mischievously, "Would you mind closing the door?"

Smith was a man not easily surprised, but that one caught him wrong footed and he fumbled for words.

Devlin stumbled in next, looking as though he'd run through a wall, "Sir, you alri..."

He stopped mid word, eyes darting from Emily, with her blouse torn open to Waller, sitting right next to her and looking guilty.

"Oh. You're *fine*," the Lieutenant concluded, somehow managing not to grin.

The Major quickly got to his feet, "It's not what it looks like, Jimmy."

"Yes it is," Emily protested. "Now Jimmy, you're marrying our maid?"

The poor Lieutenant just about fainted.

CHAPTER XXXVIII

By the time day broke over the valley, the dead savages had been hauled out of the pen and burned, and the men had manhandled the two motor cars into a position where they could defend the panel Devlin had gone through. The material this building was made of was incredible — it was transparent but nearly bulletproof, and when it shattered it wasn't sharp. Devlin wasn't too badly off.

Waller had personally led one of the sections of men that had swept through the building, checking each room for a blue creature and finding no more than had been killed in the battle. The bodies of those dead creatures were lined up in the cell that Emily and Waller had shared, and the men had collected and piled the lightning ray guns so that someone could attempt to figure out how they operated. If savages came back, the lightning power would probably be quite useful.

It was a few hours after dawn when Waller, Smith, Devlin and Captains Tucker and Kearsey walked slowly up the northern slope of the valley and then turned to look east.

"We'll need to bring the rest of the unit here. Between the building and the pen, we have enough room for all of the b'ys inside, and it's crucially important to hold," Waller said evenly, and the men nodded.

"It's ten miles — it was a quiet ten miles last night," George Tucker observed, then looked back down at the building. "If savages come here, that can be held by fifty men. I could leave Jimmy's section and the rest could march back, collect the wounded and the wagons… if any hordes come, we'll have the best chance, then."

Waller nodded, "That's a very good idea. I'll stay here, with this building. Can you have the b'ys here by the end of the day, George?"

Tucker glanced at Kearsey and the two men agreed with a nod, "Shouldn't be a problem."

Waller kept looking east, "We're probably about seventy miles from Long Prairie... perhaps a little less."

Smith took a step eastward and nodded, "I'd say so. Travel light and that's a hard day's ride. Maybe a day and a half."

Waller smiled at the drifter's intuition, "Well, Mister Smith, would you mind going back to the wagon circle, then taking a section on horseback for that ride? I need reinforcements, and even if they were in Long Prairie today, it'd be three days before infantry could get here."

Smith turned around and looked at Waller, opening his mouth to say he'd rather stay, but catching himself. For a quick second he questioned his own reaction — why would he want to stay here, in an inhuman homestead? He'd seen the Newfoundlanders to safety, they'd be in as secure a position as he could dream of now.

He had another reason that was compelling him to stay. But despite her early signs of interest, which had been strangely appealing to Smith, there was no sign that Caralynne had any real regard for him, or at least that's how he saw it.

"I'll take them that way. Might ride on after that, since you don't need me out here now."

The smile on Waller's face faded at that prospect, and he and Devlin exchanged quick looks before he answered, "Well, I don't know how popular that would be... with the men and particularly with Miss Caralynne. But it's your decision of course. I'll draw up a chit you can give to the paymaster at Long Prairie for your compensation."

Smith wasn't sure it was what he was going to do, yet, but he nodded in thanks at the Major's words, "Well I'll see, I suppose."

An hour later, Devlin's platoon was left holding the building while Tucker and Kearsey led the expedition to evacuate the wagon circle. The Lieutenant watched them go from the roof of one of the silver motor cars, then hopped down and went inside the Martian building.

Within he found Waller and Emily searching through one of the rooms near the cell they'd been kept in. Emily had charmed the tunic off one of the smaller men in the regiment, so until her suitcase came up with Tucker's column, she'd be dressed as a private soldier.

"The drab green suits you, Lady Emily," Devlin said with a smile as he entered the lab, and Emily looked up.

"I really do like it, I'm thinking I'll have my own tailored when we get back. Now that I can show off, I think I should do it in His Majesty's uniform!"

Devlin nodded slowly, finding that to be the perfect opportunity to ask his next question, "So you're... you're no longer... irresistible? I mean, no more than your natural loveliness makes you... I mean..."

"Good thing Annie took a liking to him," Emily looked across to Waller. "He'd never charm another girl with that."

Waller smiled, his tone amused as he opened drawers on the other side of the room, "Jimmy's smooth most of the time, he's just worried I'll shoot him with a lightning ray if he comes out and says how truly lovely you are."

Emily smiled, "I think you can speak freely, Jimmy. Tom hasn't said one way or the other what he wants to do with me. Though don't betray Annie, I wouldn't like that."

Poor Devlin just shook his head, "You're no longer stuck in your cape."

She nodded, "They used some sort of device to change me. I was proving too much of a handful... the savages they had restraining me were all male, and they had more of an interest in... well, I don't need to explain more."

Devlin nodded, "Indeed not."

Waller stopped rifling through a drawer and stood up, a frown on his face, "Jimmy, in that pen... any female savages? Or children?"

It had occurred to the Major that, if this was a breeding facility, it would be necessary to have both sexes present. Devlin shook his head, "No, all males. Don't think we've ever seen a female savage, sir. Or a baby one, for that matter."

Emily's smile collapsed, and she looked at Waller, who anxiously rubbed his chin, "Close the door, Jimmy."

Devlin took his turn to frown, and as he closed the door he turned around, "What's so secret?"

"You told Caralynne yet?" Waller put the question to Emily, and the young Lady shook her head.

"Not in a rush to tell anyone."

"Well, Jimmy must know," Waller crossed the room to stand next to Emily, and then he locked eyes with his trusted Lieutenant. "Jimmy, the savages are humans. The blue men brought them out here from our Earth through those tunnels thousands of years ago, and started breeding them like dogs. Made them stronger and faster, and trained them to be vicious so they could use them as troops in a war they were fighting on some distant world. They let them run free until they need them, but when they do need them, they control them with their minds."

"Minds, is it?" Devlin asked with narrowing eyes. "Did they send them to Treeline to get Emily, then? Or did the savages just smell her?"

Looking from Devlin to Waller, Emily could only shake her head and shrug. She had no answer.

"Don't know, Jimmy. But when I was in here, one of the blue men was in my head. Showed me things…"

Devlin frowned slightly, "Well… nice of him. So they mess with human bodies. Stronger, faster. And then train them to be vicious?"

Waller shrugged, "The blue creatures invade their minds at a young age, take over all thought so they never learn to think for themselves. But living out here, free range… and probably taught from a young age to be vicious warriors… they're savage after all that."

"Ah," Devlin nodded. "So we've killed a lot of *men* over the past few days."

There was no note of guilt in that statement: it was difficult for someone who'd been nearly eaten by the savages to feel anything but relief at having killed them.

"And you've seen a female savage," Emily said quietly, and as she said it Waller's hand slid around her back and gently pulled her shoulder against his. She looked down, away from Devlin, and the Lieutenant's sharp mind quickly figured out what she meant.

Devlin's eyes travelled up and down Emily, and then looked to Waller's somber face. His heart started to race slightly, and different thoughts flooded his mind. He didn't think her dangerous... no she was an ally, that had been proven. She was a savage? Did that mean she had urges... well yes, to roll naked in grass, but that really wasn't sinister. Was she... well... could she be... was... dammit... could...

Stopping his mental questions, he forced himself to use reason. She was a savage child, plucked from her horde at the age of three, and raised as a human for the rest of the time, and she'd turned out quite alright. Yes, quite alright.

"So you're saying..." Devlin began, and Emily looked up at him, biting her lip and hoping that her new-found liberty wasn't about to be taken away. If the men didn't trust her all over again, she'd be crushed. "So you're saying, the reason the savage men are so savage is because their women look like you, but they don't get to spend any time with them?"

Emily's relieved sigh was so loud it was intrusive, and Waller let out a short breath of his own, "Smooth, Jimmy."

"I'm shocked, best I could do. So... so we're not going to share this with many people," Devlin said with a nod. "We're going to stick with the story about you being taken at a young age, and getting these powers some other way. Right?"

Emily bit her lip again before replying, "Well... if I come forward, that means the government might have reason to save other savage children... they must exist, if I was one. So we must find them and help them. And the only way for that to happen... well, I must admit it."

Devlin stood still for a moment, then nodded, "Alright, the men won't have a problem with it. And… and we'll worry about the rest of the world when we get back to it. Do you want to tell them or should I?"

He addressed that last question to Waller, and the Major frowned, then looked at Emily, "I think Emily should. When the men get back from the circle."

Devlin nodded, "Good. Good."

Smith was about to ride out after Tucker's column when Caralynne found him.

"Were you going to leave and ride south without saying goodbye?" she asked as she walked up to his horse, and Smith looked down and touched the brim of his hat.

"Miss Caralynne, I don't know what I was going to do."

She nodded slowly, "Well… well, if you don't feel a great urge to drift on to Pacifica immediately, why not come back? I think I'd like to get to know more about you."

Smith stared at Caralynne for a moment and then nodded once, "I'll do that."

Caralynne smiled, and Smith set off. She watched him go, surprised to a certain degree at her own interest in the man. She'd thought she'd long ago gotten past this sort of thing — she'd always felt too obliged to protect Emily to think about a life for herself.

Perhaps things had changed.

CHAPTER XXXIX

Caralynne took the news of Emily's origins in stride.

"I'm a savage," Emily said softly. The two were walking along the slope of the valley, far away from the ears of the men. "The Martians showed me that. I was born one of them."

Caralynne stopped walking, looked Emily up and down, and then smiled, "Well, I guess I've done a great job civilizing you."

Emily threw a great hug around her elder friend — her elder sister for all practical purposes, she realized — and the hug was returned.

"So," Caralynne said as they hugged, "you're not going to tell too many people. I imagine you told Waller..."

Emily pulled back, shaking her head, "No... I mean yes, I told Tom. But I can't keep it secret. I know it might make me an outcast again, but think of it... if we find more savage children we can free them and civilize them. We can save them. I have to admit to what I am for their sakes."

"It could make you a pariah all over again," Caralynne protested. "And what about their irresistibility? The creatures took yours away, but how do we take theirs? Every girl will face the same problem you did."

Emily shook her head, "No, there's a device in there that can fix it. Tom and I will find it... and if it needs to be refilled, our scientists will find a way to do so, I'm sure. But I can't stand the thought of letting children who could be like me grow up into *that*..."

Pointing to the burnt circle of savage carcasses, Emily added emphasis to her point.

"You don't have to protect me, though, Caralynne. You can have your life now, with Mister Smith or whoever you like. I don't want to hold you back any more."

Caralynne was at a loss for words, but it didn't matter because Emily didn't give her the chance. After closing the distance between them and giving Caralynne another hug, Emily turned and walked away. Caralynne didn't know what to say.

Her own life... what a scary thought.

The rest of the men returned from the wagon circle without incident that evening, the wounded being ushered inside the building where they could lie on padded tables and Lieutenant Conway could look after them. Running water had been discovered in the building, so the place was quite comfortable.

What wagons had been brought along were used to increase the size of the *laager* around the broken panel; they formed a semi-circle jutting out from that side of the building, with the two Martian motor cars integrated as well. That was perhaps the weakest point in the building against savage attack, so increasing its defensibility was a high priority.

Outposts were established on the heights leading down into the valley, so pickets could watch for a savage counterattack from all sides. The building was made secure, and the Newfoundlanders set up their tents in the savage pen, after it had been thoroughly washed out by hose.

It was in that pen that Waller assembled the men, and as they came together from their cooking fires, Emily hopped up onto a pile of .303 ammunition cases, gaining some friendly cheers as she did.

Her smile was very small as she accepted those cheers, and she held up her hand, "I have to tell you all something. I know I've only just earned your trust, and I've only had the opportunity to be cloakless around you for one day... but I owe it to you all to be honest. I... I..."

For a moment her voice abandoned her, and the men, faces now mostly serious, stared up at her.

She took a centering breath, "I was born out here. A savage."

To quote Waller's nan, you could have heard a pin drop.

"I just found out when they captured me last night. I didn't come across something that gave me special powers like I thought... I... I was bred to have them. Like you breed a hound with a good sense of smell, I was bred to be stronger and faster."

More silence.

Unsure of how the news was being received, Waller stepped up onto the pile of boxes as well, "From what I got out of the blue creatures, they took some humans from Earth thousands of years ago, brought them here and bred them as we would breed dogs. Made them stronger so they could use them in a war against some lizard men. They control savages by telepathy... that's one mind directly controlling another. And when they start that at a young age, a human loses the ability to think for itself, and is trained to violence. It becomes a savage, and it's left to live on the grasslands until the Martians harness it for their own purposes."

The men looked from Waller to Emily and back. This was a very strange revelation — they'd thought they'd finally pinned down just what Emily was, but now they were being told something new.

Well, she'd proven her loyalty to them, and Newfoundlanders weren't the sort to discriminate simply because someone was born savage. She'd already saved their lives and proved herself.

"So you're saying we can't make ourselves into supermen, but that there are more women like her Ladyship out there roaming naked in the fields, sir?" one of the men asked the question, almost seriously.

A ripple of laughter — some of it nervous and rather forced — passed through the crowd, but the overriding message seemed to be that, at least for now, the men would accept Emily. And Waller hoped that as she continued to be herself around them, they'd realize she was not to be feared or mistrusted.

Emily hoped the same.

Over the next four days, the Newfoundlanders waited anxiously, watched for an attack, and wondered what reinforcements would come. On the second day of the wait, Waller authorized the men to start trying to figure out one of the lightning rays, and those efforts proved to be quite entertaining.

An old Sergeant who'd at one point taught musketry was the man selected to handle the strange silver weapon, and though enough witnesses to the weapon's operation existed to tell him which was the business end, no one had any idea how to trigger a lightning bolt from it.

At first there was a concern that perhaps the weapon was fired by telepathic power — that it took the blue creatures' minds to pull the trigger — but that didn't make much sense to Waller. If the blue creature was to focus on controlling its savages, then the distraction of thinking 'fire' might interrupt that control. As it happened, Waller's assumption was correct, and as the Sergeant discovered, two points on the rifle had to be squeezed simultaneously, and then the lightning bolt cut out. The range was at least as long as an SMLE, but obviously, lightning was more terrific to watch than a .303 bullet, which was invisible to a man's eye.

The weapon did not require reloading, either. After each shot, it recharged itself, and then shot again. There was no way to know how many times it could recharge before running out of ammunition, but that would be for the scientists to determine. The distraction was not allowed to take up too much of the men's time — Waller was not keen on allowing them to play with too much Martian technology.

On the third day of waiting, Emily at last found the gun that had cured her of her reliance on the cape, and it was put in a safe place for the scientists to examine as well. When this place was properly occupied and fortified, the best minds in the Empire would presumably spend much of their time here, and there would likely be further expeditions into the west, to find more facilities, and perhaps to find the breeding sites for the savages.

On the fourth day of waiting, Devlin found Waller standing outside the semi-circle of wagons in the morning.

"Jimmy," Waller nodded at the Lieutenant's approach, and Devlin touched the brim of his hat.

"Good morning, sir."

"Pleasant night?" the Major asked the question with a smile, and Devlin reddened slightly.

"As pleasant as can be in a tent in a pen built for savages," the Lieutenant replied, and Waller chuckled. Annie was no longer sleeping in the wagon with Emily and Caralynne, and Devlin's tent was close enough to Waller's for him to have heard Devlin referred to as Annie's 'heroic Martian fighter'.

"We'll be married as soon as we get to a chapel somewhere, I figure. Can't wait to introduce her to mom, I think they'll get on great," Devlin continued, smiling.

"I'll give you credit, you certainly accomplished your mission out here," Waller chuckled. "As I recall, first day on this planet you were trying to decide how to convince a woman to marry you."

Devlin snorted a laugh, "Getting her to move home with me when we're done will be the real trick."

"One step at a time, my friend," Waller nodded. "So aside from talking of your fiancée, anything interesting this morning?"

His expression sobering, Devlin stepped closer to Waller, "I was thinking, sir... well, we wounded at least two or three of those creatures back in the valley, right? When they attacked us in the lorries. So... where'd they go? Either they healed up quickly, died and were buried... or they were sent somewhere for treatment."

Waller's brow creased. To his shame, that question hadn't even occurred to him. And it was a very good question.

"A hospital... maybe even a settlement," Waller nodded slowly. "I think there are probably more of these blue men out here than we could ever have believed, Jimmy."

Devlin nodded, "Aye. Hope the reinforcements come today, eh sir?"

"Yes. Yes indeed," Waller agreed.

They waited for the rest of the day.

CHAPTER XL

Cheers filled the valley on the fifth morning when General Sir Julian Byng rode into the valley at the head of 500 Royal Canadian Dragoons and 1,000 Royal Canadian Voltigeurs. Waller had been drinking coffee with Emily and Caralynne, and he emerged from the wagon *laager* just as Byng came down from his horse, staring at the building in some wonderment.

"Bloody impressive thing," the General said quietly, and Waller had just enough time to hand his coffee mug to Emily so that he could salute the man.

Smiling and shaking his head, Byng looked from the building to Waller and quickly saluted back, "Damned good work here, Major. And Lady Lee, I'm pleased to see that your... problems have been solved."

Emily smiled charmingly and dipped her head forward in a mock bow, "Thank you General, it's a pleasure to be able to be seen."

Byng smiled at Emily, then looked back at Waller, "As soon as the cable came in, we rushed every man we could onto a train and got them down here. It's been forced marches all the way, but we have food to top off your rations, and ammunition if you need it. I'll be relieving you and sending you back to New World City for now. You'll become the new reserve."

Again, Byng impressed Waller with his forthright approach to giving orders, and the Major nodded, "Thank you, sir."

Smiling, Byng shook his head, "I think it's thanks to you, Major. We may have found exactly what we were looking for — and more."

Waller frowned and glanced at Emily. They had some explaining to do.

"Sir, perhaps if you'd come inside... there are a few points you need to be made aware of that weren't in the report I sent."

Smile fading at the tone of that warning, Byng tweaked his mustache with his finger and nodded, walking towards the building while the dragoons began to dismount, and the French Canadians fell out to be greeted by the Newfoundlanders.

Emily and Waller followed the General inside, and Caralynne moved towards the soldiers, looking for Mister Smith.

"I'm sorry, say that again," Byng was standing with his hat tucked under his arm, and Emily took a deep breath.

"I was born a savage. These blue creatures made that clear to both Major Waller and I separately."

Byng's face appeared neutral, and he began to nod slowly after a moment, "I see."

"The savages are human, sir. But bred over thousands of years to be stronger and faster, the same way we'd breed a terrier and a bloodhound with different strengths and skills," Waller had become accustomed to explaining this, as many confused soldiers had approached him over the past few days, politely trying to understand exactly what Emily was.

"I see," Byng repeated, "and they have been under the control of these blue men... Martians you said... the entire time? The hordes never seemed controlled to me..."

Waller shook his head, "I don't believe so, sir. It seems to me the savages might be allowed to roam on their own, and are only harnessed by the Martians when needed... but I can't say for certain. Those hordes that attacked us on the way out here might have been ordered to do so, or they might have been following Lady Lee's... er..."

"My scent," Emily kindly said the awkward words.

"Yes," Waller glanced to her in thanks. "There are still many unanswered questions, sir."

Byng nodded slowly, "Well, it's useful to know these blue men are here. Martians, you were calling them?"

Waller winced slightly, "Well sir, it was just the name that came into my head because of that book by Mister Wells. Made the rounds in the officers' mess in Egypt. I don't expect these blue men are from Mars, but I didn't know what else to call them. The scientists can choose a better name."

With a smile, Byng shook his head, "It's already in the papers, Waller... your name may have stuck. But Lady Lee, this business about where you were born... you may not want that in the papers. As you no doubt have predicted, that revelation might bring you some unwanted attention, and some unkind treatment. Not from me, I think you've proven sufficiently that I can trust you. But you may not wish to reveal this."

"Everyone's told me that," Emily said firmly. "But I will. Because this means that we can save the children of the savages... if they're taken away from those blue creatures at a young enough age, they can turn out as I did."

"Ah," Byng said simply, his mind clearly analyzing the possibilities of that sort of project. "We could have loyal armies of civilized people with savage strength... yes, I think the War Office will approve of that. But I don't imagine many will want to give these savages the chance to live their own lives, Lady Lee. They'll be inducted into the army, raised in it... nothing I say will change that."

It didn't sound like a promising life, but it was better than growing up a cannibal. That much was evident.

Emily thus nodded, "It's the best alternative. We can worry about their rights later, we should begin trying to save them *now*."

Byng nodded slowly, "Yes. Yes, we'll have to find their breeding areas and free them. I have to say, Waller, your men did well here. First thing I thought of when I heard of these Martians... or whatever they are... was of course that book you mentioned by Mister Wells. We didn't do so well in his imaginings."

"I had similar fears," Waller agreed. "But I would caution, sir... Mister Smith and I agree this place is likely a homestead, or an outpost. I think we were dealing with non-military creatures... based on their lack of ability, compared to those soldiers one of them showed me in my mind's eye. If we want to hold this place, I think we must fortify it."

Byng nodded immediately, "Any creatures with savages as their attack

dogs and lightning rays for rifles have my respect. This is just the first dose
of troops. The War Office was ready for a good report, and they've put the
screws to Ottawa. We'll have at least 15,000 fresh troops from the British
North American establishment here within a month. I've also used my pull
with some of the prospecting companies out here, and we're getting the rail
line extended from Long Prairie to this valley. That's our top priority. I've
been pledged trains in two months, and field telephones this week."

That sounded promising and Waller nodded.

"Now, the Voltigeurs will relieve your men, and we'll send you back to
Long Prairie. Train will take you up to New World City, and I want your
men to take over the barracks there, to serve as our reserve. I'll send more
orders when the time comes, but Colonel Currie has command there for the
time being."

Waller nodded, "Very good, sir."

"Alright, show me these blue Martians. I imagine they're ripe now, but
I still want to see them!"

Caralynne passed through the ranks of the dragoons and the Voltigeurs,
ignoring some of the interested glances she got from the officers and men
of the two regiments. Who knew what rumors they'd heard back in Long
Prairie — it didn't take long for stories to spread when soldiers were telling
tales of Martians and savages, so she was ready to be queried.

No query came, but there was no sign of Smith either. She came to the
end of the long column and realized he was nowhere to be found... had
he ridden south? It seemed possible — the man had no evident ties to this
place, and she'd be quite arrogant to assume that, just because she'd taken
a liking to him, he'd have felt obliged to come all this way out to danger
again.

She stopped at the end of the column and shook her head. She'd been
quite foolish.

Her hand dropped to her hip, and she ran her fingers over the handle of
the Colt revolver he'd loaned her. Her own ammunition had been exhausted

in the attack, so Smith's gun was now her sidearm. She wondered if he might come back to collect it from her. She wished he would.

Turning, her eyes grazed over the horizon... and stopped.

An Appaloosa mare was standing riderless next to the clump of trees she, Smith and Devlin had sheltered behind on the day they'd discovered this place. Caralynne's fingers slid around the grip of the pistol, and she prepared to call an alarm, but then a figure walked out of the stand of trees, raised its hat off its head, and waved.

It then walked back into the trees.

A smile formed on Caralynne's face, and she let go of her borrowed gun and started running up the slope towards the trees. The men of the dragoons and Voltigeurs simply shook their heads at each other, and cursed the drifter's luck.

EPILOGUE

Waller looked back at the Martian building as he walked with the column away from it. He had a feeling this wasn't the last time he'd see the great glass structure, but for the moment he was happy enough to be heading back to civilization.

It was a long walk to Long Prairie, but since the fall of that building, there had been no sightings of savages nearby. Either they'd all been killed, they'd fled in panic... or more blue creatures were not too far away, and were holding them back to avoid revealing their whereabouts.

For the moment, that didn't matter a great deal to Waller. His men would march as quickly as they could, probably taking three days to reach the town, and then it would be a train back up to the mountains, where there would be time for rest. The men had definitely earned their respite.

Cresting the slopes of the valley, Waller picked up his speed and caught up to the wagons, again making up the center section of the column. He smiled as he saw Devlin walking behind the covered wagon, talking to Annie, who was leaning out the back. The b'ys of Jimmy's platoon had apparently taken bets on how much time the Lieutenant would spend walking, and how much time he'd spend riding in the wagon with his fiancée.

Caralynne wasn't in the wagon; she and Smith were riding somewhere up ahead of the column, keeping an eye out for savages and getting to know each other better. It was quite evident that Caralynne liked the drifter very much, though as much as he'd come to know Smith over the course of this mission, Waller still couldn't decide what the American thought of Caralynne. It wasn't really his place to observe anyway — he had his regiment to be concerned with, and he already had enough distractions as it was.

Emily was suddenly beside him, panting in a surprisingly lady-like way, "Well, I just checked four miles ahead, and we're all clear."

Waller smiled at her, "You're enjoying this, aren't you?"

She smiled back, "I love to run the grasslands!"

"That was what I was implying, I think," Waller shot back playfully, and she laughed.

"I think I'll check to the right next. See you in half an hour!"

She burst away again, and Waller — along with many of the men — marveled at her as she bolted away with inhuman speed. She was a remarkable woman, Waller was very impressed by her.

As he looked ahead again, and kept marching, it occurred to him to wonder what bets the men were taking on him and Emily.

"Too many distractions," he muttered to himself and walked on.

Out far ahead of the column, Smith was feeling contented. That was unusual, because Smith rarely felt contented unless he was on his own, riding a trail to see where it went, and keeping his own peace.

It was a strange thing, he figured, to find the same contentment riding a trail with someone else. He looked to his right, and riding with equal contentment was Caralynne. They hadn't said a word since they'd left the column, but Smith reckoned they didn't need to. He liked her well enough, and she liked him.

But liking a person, on its own, didn't mean much to Smith. He liked plenty of people in one way or another, and didn't think it was too special.

Caralynne was different. He didn't just like her, he liked riding with her. When she was around, he was at peace, even on an open trail in silence.

As they rode, a crisp, cool breeze came across the grasslands, and Smith recognized it. It was a wind from the mountains, reminding them of where they were going, and he enjoyed the taste of it. Caralynne did too, in her own quiet way. She looked at him and offered a simple nod, and he nodded back. Then he smiled, which was not something Smith often did, and she smiled back.

Still without words, they rode on.

They were leaving the grasslands behind.

For now.

HISTORICAL NOTES

These notes contain spoilers — it is recommended that you do not read them until you have finished the book!

Writing alternate history has been a new adventure for me, and with it have come some serious responsibilities. I'm a student of history in the formal sense — I've studied it for both a Bachelors and a Masters degree. I've seen how movies, popular histories, and even some alternate history novels have twisted historical events beyond the point of plausibility, and I generally find that quite frustrating. As a result, when I sat down to write *Grasslands*, I did so with two objectives: to stay as faithful as possible to the period in which I was writing, and to make sure any real historical figures integrated into the story were treated with due respect. What follows are some notes on the real history of this period, and its relation to our alternate timeline.

The Royal Newfoundland Regiment

The Newfoundland Regiment is, of course, a real unit that long predates the First World War. The particular edition we deal with was raised (*without* purchased commissions, I believe) as the Newfoundland Regiment in 1914 to fight the First World War. Over the course of that war, 4,668 men volunteered to join its ranks, and they fought in some of the war's bloodiest battles. Newfoundlanders were on the disastrous Gallipoli campaign, and then they went over the top alongside British troops on the first day of the Somme in 1916. For those unfamiliar with the history of World War One, the Somme was a massive attack that left more than 60,000 Imperial troops dead or wounded on just its first day — the bloodiest day in British military history. Participating in this assault, the Newfoundlanders got further across no man's land than any of the regiments around them, and as such they earned their motto from their British commanders — they were said to be "Better than the Best". The motto came at heavy cost: 790 men went over the top, and 710 were killed or injured. Only 68 could answer roll the morning after. In 1917, after further gallant service at the Battle of Cambrai, the Newfoundlanders were granted the "Royal" prefix, and they went on to be remembered as one of the war's hardest-fighting units.

Growing up in Newfoundland, I learned about the Royal Newfoundland Regiment beginning in Grade 4. The memory of this unit remains strong in Newfoundland, and when it came to choosing men to march onto the new world, I could think of none better. Of course, the history in this alternate universe has gone quite differently — there was no Gallipoli, no Somme, and no Cambrai. As such, I've kept the "Royal" and the "Better than the Best" motto as a personal conceit; in this universe, the Newfoundlanders earned those honors in their fighting in the Third Afghan War. More on that in a moment.

None of the characters in the Royal Newfoundland Regiment on His Majesty's New World is intentionally based on a real member of the regiment — if any of these characters shares a name with a real man from the RNR, it's by pure coincidence. My goal has been, as much as I can, to capture the spirit of the regiment in this story, and to let the RNR prove that it is indeed "Better than the Best" on a whole new planet. I hope that the exploits of Major Waller and his men will encourage you to learn more about the real regiment, and the gallant men who joined it to serve their country and empire.

Altered World History

Being a history grad, I could write many pages of historical back story here, but I'm going to confine myself to a few details. If you're interested, look for expanded alternate historical essays at www.newworldempire.com. If you'd like a bigger background on the real period of the First World War, there's a wealth of resources both online and in print. Beware any books or sites that tell you that the Generals were wholly incompetent, though — for the past century, Generals like Douglas Haig have been scapegoated, and blamed by historians for military realities far beyond their control. Some Generals really weren't up to their jobs, but many — like Haig — were in fact very, very competent. They truly did their best to spare the lives of their men while having to win a war that was more brutal than any that had been fought before — or, in some respects, has been fought since.

First, regarding the Canadian Army in these books: it's rather big. In reality, the Canadian Army before the First World War was a very modest force, numbering just over 3,000 full-time fighting men. There were another 59,000 or so in the militia, but by and large, the country had a very small army. The opening of a new world in our alternate 1881 changes that. I've posited here that, with a new planet to look after on behalf of the British Empire, the Canadian Army would become much stronger, with a regular establishment of 40,000 men. The Royal Newfoundland Regiment joined these Canadian forces in forming the British North American establishment — so called because Newfoundland was not part of Canadian confederation in 1914.

Also in this alternate timeline, the First World War itself did not happen as we know it. With their new world to preoccupy them, the British took an interest in defending Belgian neutrality at the start of the war, but did not join France and Russia when hostilities began. Without the BEF's assistance, the French did not fare well, and the Russians fell before the Germans ever needed to send Lenin into the country to begin his Bolshevik revolution. As such, the Russian Empire collapsed not into communism but into chaos, and the British and the Japanese saw an opportunity — the former to secure India's borders, the latter to take resources in Siberia. Britain therefore launched an invasion of Russian territory through Afghanistan, sparking the Third Afghan War.

In reality, a Third Afghan War did happen in 1919, but it was launched by the Amir of Afghanistan against British India, and it was a three-month conflict with very few casualties on either side. The Third Afghan War in this alternate timeline was a much more bitter affair, and it was there, instead of at Gallipoli and on the Western Front, that our RNR learned to war.

Meanwhile, drifting briefly south to Smith's side of the line, the Wild West endures on the new world. My belief here, I think rightly, is that as the Wild West of the United States filled in, those who longed for the frontier life would go to Pacifica, and start anew. In reality, Alaska did have an influx of people who wanted this very opportunity in the early twentieth century; it seems only too likely to me that the new world would have preserved the old west mentality.

Real Figures

Two characters were introduced in this book who are in fact real historical figures: Arthur Currie and Julian Byng. To students of Canadian military history, these are familiar names from the First World War, so I'll just say a few words about each here.

Arthur Currie was an Ontario-born man who moved out to the Canadian west to make his fortune, becoming a land speculator. He also rose to be Colonel of one of Canada's militia regiments, thus positioning him to be one of the leading officers of the Canadian Expeditionary Force during the First World War. He went on to distinguish himself, and he eventually took over the Canadian Corps, Canada's first 'national' Army. In our altered universe, Currie's personal mission to make a good living carried him to the rich new world, and instead of being a Colonel of the militia, he took a full-time commission in the much larger Canadian Army. The new world greatly benefits from his fine soldiering, leadership, and expertise.

Sir Julian Byng was a soldier's soldier, and an innovative cavalryman. Though an aristocrat by birth, his officers and men always found him willing to get into the messiest parts of the job, and he was well respected by all who served with him. In the First World War, he led the Canadian Corps with Currie under his command (before Currie eventually took over) to great effect. He was so popular with Canadians that he was appointed Governor General of Canada after the war. In our alternate timeline, I've taken the conceit of moving Byng to the new world as military Governor, a post he receives after distinguishing himself during the Boer War.

In reality, the teaming of Currie and Byng proved very successful… the new world needs just that sort of partnership at its head.

On Rifles

Students of Canadian military history will know that the Canadian Army, under the *guidance* of Sam Hughes (a *unique* figure in Canada's military history) were equipped not with the Short, Magazine, Lee-Enfield rifle, but with the Ross Rifle. This weapon, a fine target rifle, proved to be too fragile for the battlefield, so the CEF switched to the SMLE while in France. People who know about the history of firearms will also know that the SMLE was almost replaced just before the First World War broke out. The British had been impressed by Mauser rifles in the hands of the Boers during the Boer War, and wanted their own weapons of that type. Only the coming of the First World War — and the need to mass-produce an existing weapon — saved the SMLE from being replaced.

In our altered timeline, the Canadian Army is too large a professional force for Sam Hughes to be able to manipulate it to suit his equipping whims. And the SMLE proves itself in the Third Afghan War and on the new world, so no one tries to replace it.

Yes, that last explanation was a little thin, but to be honest, the SMLE is so iconic (an only slightly modified version, the No. 4 Mk 1, is still the primary weapon of the Canadian Rangers today) that it simply had to stay in the alternate timeline. For battling savages, there really is no better rifle.

Final note on the subject of firearms: the Lewis gun was not adopted by the British Army until it had entered the First World War. It's another conceit of mine that, in the altered timeline, the British would see the utility of this American-designed weapon, even without taking part in the First World War. The Lewis gun is thus being added steadily to the arsenal of the Imperial Armies, albeit in smaller numbers than was the case in historical reality.

Savages

Perhaps the most important matters have been saved for last. First, I want to make it clear: the savages in this case are Caucasian — at least the ones we've seen so far. And it wouldn't matter what ethnicity they were, they'd still be called savages. I am not making any sort of sly attempt to suggest that a certain ethnic group is 'savage'.

To be quite clear: these savages are humans who, for centuries, have been genetically redesigned ('bred like dogs' in the parlance of the early twentieth century) by an alien race. What color they are matters no more than the color of a police dog. I'm forthright about this because, these days, it's all too easy for someone to assume too much — to suggest, for instance, than I'm using the savages as an outlet for some desire to attack a certain ethnic group.

Well, I'm not. They're not First Nations people, African peoples, Indian peoples or any other group fought by the British Empire or the United States. They're humans who happen to look Caucasian, but are very far removed from humanity as we understand it.

Blue 'Martians'

Finally, what about the 'Martians', and particularly, what about the Newfoundlanders' reaction to them? My personal opinion about this period in history is that people would have been far more ready to meet 'men from Mars' than we give them credit for. They wouldn't have understood interstellar relations in quite the way we do now — they haven't had decades of science fiction to explore the possibilities — but they were far more familiar with meeting culturally-alien peoples than we are.

In the twenty-first century, we tend to think we'd be ready to meet aliens. Obviously it wouldn't be easy, but we do often seem to think that our science would be able to comprehend at least some of theirs, and that we'd possibly be able to adapt their technology, or counter it with our own. Depending on how this idea is handled, it can seem ridiculously far-fetched, or quite possible... either way, we often assume we're close. This naturally might make us think that this current age is the only one in recent history that could cope with extra-terrestrials, but I disagree.

During the age of Empire, there were still blank spots on the map, and human cultures that were seemingly alien to each other were meeting frequently — and without the benefit of the internet for research ahead of time. These days, we can learn about the customs and traditions of any society by simply going to the web. In the days of empire, learning had to be done through awkward first contacts, long periods of cohabitation and sharing of traditions, and often through war. This is not to say that it was better to do things that way (I rather prefer to be able to research in advance) but I do think that the people who grew up in an era of unknowns would be ready to accept that there were 'men from Mars', and that those 'men' would be quite different.

By the same token, those people would fully understand the potentially vulnerable situation humanity would be in during such a meeting. When H. G. Wells wrote *War of the Worlds*, it wasn't just a fantastic feat of imagination: he put the British in the place of many of the peoples they'd conquered, facing an otherworldly foe with superior (though not invincible) technology. Then he felled the invaders with disease. This was a current story at the end of the nineteenth century — while Wells was writing it, the French were living it (yet again) during their assault on Morocco. Theirs was not the first, nor the last such experience.

What I'm getting at here is a simple point: it's easy to assume that we, now, are the only edition of human civilization so far equal to the task of meeting aliens on reasonably level footing. Technologically speaking, this might be true — we have a better chance (albeit not a good one) of understanding an alien's science than the Empires would have... but I think the people of the Empires would have been able to accept the possibility of life on another planet, and to understand that trying to meet and interact with it would be no easier than meeting and understanding any of the alien cultures they were routinely encountering on Earth.

The question now is what will come of this meeting. Things certainly didn't start well, and with the discovery about Emily's true identity, London and Washington will undoubtedly begin forming plans. What's next? The Royal Newfoundland Regiment will have a whole new mission south of the border in *The Frontier*, and partnering with some of the famous and elite Buffalo Soldiers of the American Army, they will uncover more of the blue creatures' secrets.

ABOUT THE AUTHOR

Born in 1984 in St. John's, Newfoundland, Kenneth Tam holds both a Bachelor's and Master's degree in history from Wilfrid Laurier University in Waterloo, Canada. His MA thesis examined the creation and operation of the Caribou Hut, a hostel for Allied servicemen in St. John's during the Second World War.

In 2006, Kenneth received a prestigious Canada Graduate Scholarship from the Social Sciences and Humanities Council of Canada. He was also awarded a Balsillie Fellowship at the Centre for International Governance Innovation during 2006-07. In that capacity, he worked for Mr. Paul Heinbecker, Canada's former ambassador and permanent representative to the United Nations. He presently serves as a Communications Consultant for Kitchener–Waterloo's federal Member of Parliament, Peter Braid.

Since releasing his first novel in 2003, Tam has promoted his books across Canada, speaking with junior and high school students, delivering writing workshops, and doing book signings at bookstores and Iceberg-organized events. He frequently appears as a guest author at science fiction events across the country.

Kenneth is a partner in Iceberg Publishing, the company he and his family started in 2002. He has authored many of the company's existing titles, and is also responsible for graphic design, including the company logo, website, banners, advertisements, and other marketing materials. He acts as a primary contact with printers and suppliers, and is also key in new author development and recruitment.

He remains very lazy about writing his author bios. When they told him to make this one longer, he mostly copied and pasted it together from the Iceberg website, www.icebergpublishing.com.

CPSIA information can be obtained
at www.ICGtesting.com
Printed in the USA
BVOW09s2312240417

482044BV00002B/212/P

9 781926 817026